D1020436

By the same author

Last of the Tasburai

Scream of the Tasburai

The Chronicles of Will Ryde and Awa Maryam al-Jameel

Book One

A Tudor Turk

Rehan Khan

HopeRoad Publishing
PO Box 55544
Exhibition Road
London SW7 2DB

www.hoperoadpublishing.com

First published in Great Britain by HopeRoad 2019
Copyright © 2019 Rehan Khan

The right of Rehan Khan to be identified as the author of this work has
been asserted by him in accordance with the Copyright, Designs and
Patents Act 1988.

All rights reserved. No part of this book may be reproduced,
stored in a retrieval system or transmitted in any form or by any means,
electronic, mechanical, photocopying, recording or otherwise,
without the prior permission of the publishers.
This book is sold subject to the condition that it shall not,
by way of trade or otherwise, be lent, re-sold, hired out or otherwise
circulated without the publisher's prior consent in any form of
binding or cover other than that in which it is published and
without a similar condition including this condition being imposed
on the subsequent purchaser.

A CIP catalogue record for this book is available from the British Library.

Supported using public funding by
ARTS COUNCIL
ENGLAND

ISBN 978-1-908446-97-8

eISBN 978-1-9164671-2-5

Printed and bound by Clays Ltd, Bungay, Suffolk, UK

For my mother, the first storyteller I met.

CONTENTS

CAST OF CHARACTERS

Anne Ryde	Will's mother
Anver Jacob	Metalsmith's apprentice
Awa Maryam al-Jameel	Songhai noblewoman enslaved at the Battle of Tondibi
Earl of Rothminster	Rising noble within the Elizabethan court
Gurkan	Turk, member of the Rüzgar unit within the Janissaries
Huja	Jester at the Ottoman court
Ismail	Turk, member of the Rüzgar unit within the Janissaries
Ja	Odo's accomplice
Kostas	Greek, member of the Rüzgar unit within the Janissaries
Mehmed Konjic	Bosnian, Commander of the Rüzgar unit within the Janissaries

Mikael	Albanian, member of the Rüzgar unit within the Janissaries
Odo	Slave trader
Sir Reginald Rathbone	Loyal to the Earl of Rothminster
Stukeley	Rathbone's bodyguard
Wassa	Songhai woman
Will Ryde	Englishman kidnapped and sold into slavery at the age of five

1

MEDITERRANEAN SUMMER

1591

THE GREY-HAIRED GALLEY SLAVE collapsed against Will's shoulder. The Mediterranean summer with its suffocating heat had certainly kept the Grim Reaper busy, Will thought. In the two years he had rowed below decks aboard the *Al-Qamar*, a Moroccan galleon whose name meant 'the moon', he'd seen many of the older slaves die from the heat, from exhaustion or in the cut and thrust of naval battle.

The oar-master, a hulking Portuguese, shouted at the Sudanese drummer to quicken the pace. 'Faster!' he screamed, cracking his whip on the deck.

At that moment, the old boy beside Will mumbled, 'Can't breathe . . .' So, he wasn't quite dead. Will wanted to help, then caught sight of the oar-master glowering at him. He put his head down and heaved on the oar, keeping pace with the other rowers. At sixteen, Will had a patchy beard dripping with sweat and his muscular bare back was soaked as though he had been in a rainstorm. As they pulled on the oars, Grey-hair slumped backwards, mouth open, eyes fixed. *Now* he was dead.

There was no time for sympathy or regret. The enemy vessel was close and they needed to pick up speed. The Moroccan sailors would be preparing the cannon above deck. The past

1

week had seen four skirmishes with Spanish ships, as two empires vied for supremacy in the Mediterranean. Every day Will expected to be his last, yet somehow, he survived.

Whack. Waves thumped the side of the hull. The helmsman was turning them hard to starboard, without the *Al-Qamar* slowing down. It was a risky manoeuvre and meant that the enemy vessel must be readying her cannons. Now they were in a race to see which ship fired first.

'Oars down to starboard!' bawled the Portuguese oar-master.

The *Al-Qamar* cut through the waves, shifting right.

'Oars up!'

Boom. Their cannon exploded. *Boom. Boom.* They waited for a response. None came. They fired again, and then again, each explosion shaking the hull.

Will winced, his head aching from the blast that reverberated around his insides.

Silence, but for the panting breaths of the oarsmen, gripping their oaken oars with sweaty hands, as though the wood itself contained magical properties to protect them from enemy cannon fire. Seawater trickled below Will's feet, his manacled ankles chained together with other galley slaves along his row. He glanced down at the dead man, whose eyes stared upwards. Perhaps he had seen his soul departing, onward to heaven or the other place. Will thought about death every day. Dying must be better than living like this. *No.* Not until he returned to London and found his mother. He had been separated from her for eleven years and had vowed that he would see her again before God took his soul.

Cannon fire erupted once more from the *Al-Qamar*, a ferocious volley of carnage. Yet there was still no response. They waited, moments feeling like clammy hours . . . and then there was a euphoric roar from above: the Moroccan sailors must have seen the Spanish ship sink or surrender.

'Oars down,' the Portuguese commanded.

Will and the galley slaves collapsed onto their benches. Exhausted but still alive. The oar-master strode down the aisle, to the centre where Will sat.

'You - English!' He spat on the floor beside Will, before pointing at the dead man. 'Get that body overboard.'

Grey-hair had been a Greek, that much Will did know. In fact, he had been in the *Al-Qamar* long enough to recognise where most of the men came from. There were Abyssinians, Balkans, Turks, Greeks, but mostly West Africans. He was the only Englishman - and the Catholic Portuguese hated the Protestant English even more than they did the Muslims. The chain around his manacle was slipped out, before it was also removed from the dead Greek. Will stretched to his full height, towering over the Portuguese by a good few inches. The man didn't like it, and he shoved Will back.

'Get on with it!' he barked.

Will lifted the Greek under his armpits and hauled him off his bench. He shuffled backwards, dragging the corpse along to the staircase leading up to the deck. The Sudanese drummer, also a galley slave, helped him to hoist the body up the wooden steps. Emerging on deck, the midday sunlight blinded them. The Moroccan sailors were smiling and chatting, pointing over at the enemy vessel. The Spanish galleon, flag still fluttering above the waterline, was going down fast, sailors jumping overboard. Some would be picked up by the *Al-Qamar* - the officers to be ransomed, the sailors to be used or sold as slaves. Others would try to swim away, fail and drown at sea.

They lugged the dead man to the stern of the *Al-Qamar*, where the shortest mast of the four was located. Will and the Sudanese readied themselves then together they threw the corpse off the back of the galleon, watching his body splash down into the blue waters.

3

'May God rest his soul,' whispered Will.

'From God we come and unto God we return,' said the Sudanese.

The seawater was inviting. Somewhere out there, the waters connected with the English Channel and then home.

'How far is it to land?' asked Will.

The Sudanese looked around nervously. 'You want to swim, with those?' he said, gesturing at the fetters round Will's ankles.

He had a point. Death waited with a certainty if Will jumped overboard now.

'English!' The Portuguese oar-master had ventured up on deck and was signalling for Will to return to his position.

'Another day maybe,' muttered Will to the Sudanese, as they trudged back towards the hatch.

The Portuguese grabbed Will by the arm as he walked past. 'I'm watching you, you English spawn of Satan.'

Will didn't respond. He simply gazed down at his feet. The Sudanese had gone ahead down the narrow stairs to the galley.

'The English Queen is a heretic, so says the Pope. So say I. What do *you* say, English?' The Portuguese shook him. Will kept his mouth shut.

'Her father, Henry VIII, so-called Defender of the Faith, burns in hellfire. What say *you*, English?'

Will knew that Henry had been excommunicated from the Catholic faith for divorcing his wife, Catherine of Aragon, to marry Anne Boleyn. Not only that, he'd set up the rival Church of England, which followed the Protestant version of Christianity. The Portuguese, staunch Catholics like the Spanish and the Hapsburgs, despised this.

'All the English will join him in hell,' sneered the Portuguese. 'Your mother will rot in a pit of vipers.'

At this, Will stood up straight, chest out, towering over the Portuguese.

'Yes, English, your mother, your father . . .'

Will took a step closer to the oar-master, eyes hard with menace.

'Christians!' It was the voice of the First Officer on board the *Al-Qamar*.

The Portuguese instantly let go of Will as the other man approached, Moroccan sailors close behind him.

The First Officer was a man in his middle years, dark-skinned for a Moroccan, his beard bearing flecks of grey. He smiled at Will and the Portuguese, saying, 'Why do you fight? You worship the same God, believe in Jesus Christ. You have more in common than the differences you have created.'

'First Officer Said,' the Portuguese replied, nodding respectfully.

Will remained silent. Slaves like himself had no right to speak to the crew, unless they asked him a direct question. Said seemed to take Will in for the first time, looking him up and down.

'You - where are you from?' he asked.

'I was born in England,' Will replied. 'Since the age of five I have lived in Morocco, serving Hakim Abdullah, a quartermaster in Marrakesh. For the past two years I have been a galley slave, on board various ships.'

'Hakim Abdullah, quartermaster of the Bayt Ben Yousef?' asked Said in Arabic.

'Yes,' Will replied in Arabic. 'He who has made the finest blades, even for the great Sultan al-Mansour himself.'

'And you were his apprentice?'

'Yes.'

'Why were you taken from him?'

'My master was visiting Aleppo, when a naval recruiting party passed through the quarter of town where my master's workshop was. I was running an errand for his family: they

5

mistook me for a runaway slave. I protested my innocence, showed them the insignia of my master, which I wore as an amulet around my neck, but the soldiers did not believe me, saying my word as a Christian could not be trusted. I was taken and have not seen my dear master since.'

'Hakim Abdullah is an honest man, and his skill is famed throughout the empire.' Said calmly removed his sword from its scabbard. The Portuguese took a step back. Will's instinct was to do the same, but he remained where he was. Said then drew his blade and rested the weapon horizontally across his open palms. 'Tell me about this sword,' he commanded.

Will felt the itch to hold the weapon, assess its weight and balance, but he would most likely be struck down if he moved towards its hilt. Instead he focused on the component parts which made up the sword.

'From the welded patterns in the blade, it is clear it is made of the finest Damascus and Wootz steel, forged by a master swordsmith. The blade is in the decorative form known as Muhammad's ladder. It is damascened with gold and there is a cartouche bearing the name of the swordsmith, Babak.' Will looked closer. 'The pommel is interesting, as it is adorned with an image of a *Simurgh*, a gigantic mythical winged creature, indicating it came from Persia. If I were to guess, I'd trace the sword's origins to Isfahan. Sir.'

Said raised his eyebrows. He turned to the oar-master. 'Portuguese. You have a talented apprentice quartermaster here, wasted as a galley slave. Which fool put him there?'

'I do not know, sir,' mumbled the oar-master.

'What is your name?' asked Said, turning to Will once more.

'Will Ryde, sir.'

'Will, how would you like to act as a runner for the cannons? We could use a man who knows his weapons.'

Will studied the oar-master.

'Never mind him, we have plenty of new galley slaves. Look, some of the Spanish are swimming towards the *Al-Qamar*. The Portuguese will have more in common with the Spanish than the English.'

'I would like that very much, sir,' said Will.

'Unlock his shackles,' ordered Said.

The Portuguese removed a key-chain from his belt and grudgingly knelt down to open the lock around Will's ankles. The skin was raw below the metal: it was the first time in two years his fetters had come off.

'You are dismissed,' said Said, waving the oar-master away. 'Jamal,' he called out to a short, wiry Moroccan sailor. 'Will Ryde was apprentice to Hakim Abdullah, quartermaster of the Bayt Ben Yousef. Use him for weapons duty.'

Will couldn't believe that his shackles had come off. He kept peering down at his ankles. 'Thank you, sir,' he gasped.

'You did well, controlling your temper with the Portuguese. How you react to a situation is an illustration of your character,' Said declared, before he turned and walked away along the deck.

As Will followed Jamal to the weapons store, he saw the Portuguese oar-master lurking beside the stairs. The man met his eyes, then raised a finger to his neck and made a slicing movement.

2

PLAINS OF TONDIBI

THE NIGER RIVER CUT THROUGH the vast expanse of desert creeping in at Tondibi. Fresh water, pure and lustrous, flowed down from the river's source in the Guinea highlands, quenching the thirst of the harsh West African terrain. To the north was the desolate Sahara Desert and to the south the lush jungles of the continent. Tondibi was a point between two extremes. It was also where the Songhai nation had decided to meet the Moroccans in battle.

Awa Maryam al-Jameel stood, straight-backed, bow loosely gripped, peering across the plains at the Moroccan army. With the other Songhai women archers, she formed a single row behind the infantry. Her hair was tied back and she wore a long white dress woven with green threads, loose enough to ride in, and with a hood to keep the sun out of her eyes. Twenty arrows were lodged in the leather pouch slung across her back and she carried a small hunting knife strapped to a brown leather belt round her waist.

'The Moroccans come out of the Sahara to die at Tondibi,' said an infantryman ahead of Awa.

'King Askia claims victory is certain,' agreed another.

But nothing was certain as far as Awa was concerned. Until a year ago, she had been brought up like other noblewomen of the Songhai, schooled in Arabic, logic, rhetoric, grammar, mathematics and the study of the *Qur'an*. As the Songhai empire fell into political plots and infighting, however, and it became apparent that the kingdom was disintegrating, many noble and learned families had seen fit to train their women in the skills of archery and swordplay.

Awa rubbed her fingers on the black leather pouch tied to her necklace. Inside was an amulet - a parting gift from her father. He disapproved of King Askia's call to arms, believing negotiation with the Moroccans would better serve the Songhai nation. He told his daughter she was a natural when it came to the martial arts; whereas he himself was more comfortable lifting books than swords. The amulet contained a prayer for her protection. After giving it to her, Awa's father had hugged her, kissed her on the forehead and then walked away. She could not see his face, but her forehead was wet from his tears. She had called out to him that she would return, but he had merely lifted his right hand to acknowledge her comment. It was the last time she had seen him.

As she remembered that moment, the young woman's eyes became moist. She put the amulet to her lips and kissed it.

Both armies were spread out on raised ground, with the plain dipping between them. The battle was to be fought in a natural basin, rocky and pockmarked with patches of uneven ground. Awa tightened her grip on her bow. They would stop the Moroccans, she vowed, and then she was going to return home. The Moroccans had already plundered the rich salt mines of Taghaza in the north and if they were not stopped at Tondibi, then the capital Gao was in danger of falling. The Songhai army vastly outnumbered the Moroccans, eighty thousand to their twenty thousand, and King Askia had even brought one thousand cattle to create confusion and stampede the invaders from Marrakesh. The result was a foregone conclusion - yet doubt gnawed at Awa.

9

She watched King Askia deliver a short address to his officers; she was too far away to hear but it ended with him raising his sword and the chant of *God is Great* confidently ringing through the army. Awa stared over at the Moroccans who also beseeched the same God for victory. Whose prayers would the Divine answer?

'It is wrong, my sister,' said Suha, standing beside her. Her fellow noblewoman was unusually tall and was often mistaken for a man from behind. 'They are Muslims, we are Muslims. We should not fight.'

'I agree - but raising the sword aloft is sometimes the only way to make the other side stand down,' Awa replied.

'If women sat on war councils there would be less fighting and more reconciliation,' said Suha.

Awa imagined women sitting on war councils: they would consider the safety of the children and how to protect them; they would bear in mind the harvest and how to nurture it; they would reflect on future generations, and what legacy they should leave to make life better for all. In fact, if there were to be an all-women war council, Awa could not imagine them *ever* going to war.

'You have a point, Suha,' she acknowledged, and tested her bowstring, flexing it back and forth. A year's rigorous training had built muscles in her arms: she still remembered how, the first time she lifted a bow, she could barely draw the string back a third of the way.

The religious scholars of the Songhai had issued a *fatwa*, which proclaimed that they were fighting a defensive war, so spilling the blood of a fellow believer in the field of battle was permissible. The scholars also made it clear that if the enemy showed remorse, then it was better to be clement, for God would only be merciful to those who exhibited mercy to others.

10

It was time to move. The infantry were lined up before her in two long blocks made up of thousands of men. The archers, predominantly women, stood behind, and the cavalry were arranged on either flank. Their battalion commander ordered them forward, keeping pace with the infantry. They strode, then jogged, before breaking into a run, crossing the ground towards the Moroccans, whose smaller infantry advanced with equal speed. The morning air was hot, with little wind. Awa felt a sense of exhilaration as she raced into the basin. The red flags of the Moroccans fluttered behind their lines and Awa noticed six great cannons, placed in the space before the enemy cavalry. She had heard of such weapons. Surely the Moroccans would not fire, when their own forces were deployed at the front?

'Halt!' Their battalion commander pulled them up. 'Ready position!'

Awa drew an arrow, nocked it to the string and kept the bow facing the ground. Ahead of her, the Songhai infantry tore into the enemy ranks, cutting through their smaller number. Swords and shields clashed, metal on metal. Each Moroccan soldier wore armour to protect most of his body; the Songhai men did not. It made the defenders far more mobile but also left them exposed to being caught by a blade or spear. Men fell on both sides, but it was clear the Moroccans were coming off worse from the initial engagement. The archers studied the melée, looking for any enemy troops who might break through. None did.

The Moroccan infantrymen suddenly rushed back towards their own ranks.

'Cowards,' snorted one of the archers beside Awa.

'I would rather die fighting than die of cowardice,' said another.

The Songhai infantry were chasing the retreating Moroccans when a whole row of gunmen emerged from behind the lines of Moroccan cavalry where they had been hiding. The Songhai infantry were running directly into the line of arquebus fire.

'Get back!' Awa urged them uselessly, the words catching in her throat.

In their wild charge forward, the Songhai infantrymen didn't see the arquebusiers' long guns. *Bang. Bang. Bang.* Puffs of smoke filled the horizon as the Songhai soldiers collapsed to the ground. Further rounds tore the infantry apart. Hundreds fell. What could they do, against such weapons?

'Retreat!' bawled Awa's battalion commander.

The archers turned and sprinted back, just as a new set of gunmen fired another volley, the smell of gunpowder drifting over the basin. Awa saw that the Songhai cavalry were now on the move, their camels and horses trotting. Ahead of them thundered the cattle. She retreated, pulling up at the base of the higher ground and watched as the cattle led the charge towards the Moroccans, kicking up an enormous screen of dust and sand, the accelerating Songhai cavalry beside them.

Across the basin she heard a fresh round of arquebus fire. Some of the cattle fell, but the majority kept charging. King Askia's plan to stampede the enemy lines was going to work. The herd picked up speed.

Then a terrifying sound echoed for miles around the flat plains. The Moroccans had fired three of their cannons. The impact shook the very ground Awa stood upon. Suha grabbed her by the arm.

'What devilry is this?' she said.

'Cannons,' said Awa, her voice trembling. Her father had instructed her about such weapons. He said the Moroccans employed a new form of warfare which the Songhai had not adopted. Perhaps this was how the Moroccans had defeated the Portuguese at the famous Battle of the Three Kings which she had learned about from her tutors.

12

Awa gazed down at her bow. What good would that be, against such monstrous weapons? As she peered across the basin, hundreds of cattle burst through the smokescreen, careering back. Spooked by the cannons, the beasts were ploughing into the retreating Songhai cavalry and knocking riders from their mounts. *Boom. Boom. Boom.* Further cannon fire added to the terror as the animals stampeded straight towards her.

'Oh no!' whispered Awa.

The battalion commander raised his arm, drawing the archers into a straight line. 'Hold your positions.'

The command was issued, up and down the line. Surely it was the wrong order, with the herd charging at them?

'Arrows ready!'

'I'm scared,' sobbed Suha.

Awa checked the arrow in her bowstring, drawing strength from the prayer her amulet contained: it would shield her. The cattle were close. A group of Songhai cavalrymen on camelback raced over the open ground ahead, trying to divert some of the cattle away from what remained of the infantry and the archers. Some cattle re-routed to the side, but others thundered on, bowling over the riders on their camels, heading for the archers.

The sound of terrified cattle filled the air, peppered by the cries of fallen Songhai soldiers. Awa ran, but got caught on the shoulder and pushed into the path of a bull, which knocked her flat on the ground. She rolled athletically to the right, rising as quickly as possible, only to find herself face to face with another bull, whose horns she grabbed, using them to swivel up and over its back to land on her feet.

As the flow of cattle slowed, Moroccan riders mounted on horses and camels burst through the dust, swords and lances swinging. Awa immediately went down on one knee, drew an arrow - hesitated. *They are believers, like me.* But on seeing a

13

rider cut down a Songhai soldier, she let loose her arrow and it caught the Moroccan in the eye. He fell from his horse. For the first time in her life, she had killed another human being. Her stomach felt heavy, her head light. She had to support herself by placing the palm of her hand on the ground.

Surveying the carnage unfolding around her, she saw that some of the women archers were being carried away on camels. Where was Suha? Awa reloaded her bow and fired, hitting the next Moroccan in the shoulder. His armour, however, deflected the arrow. Spotting her, he snarled, readied his sword - and charged. She pulled another arrow, nocked it, raised her bow . . . but he was upon her and she darted away from his horse. By the time he had swung his mount back towards her, she had already taken up position on one knee and fired, striking him flush in the neck. The Moroccan collapsed, sliding off his horse. Alert to the sound of hooves behind her, Awa flung herself across the ground. A tall Moroccan soldier sprang off his horse, making a grab for her. She twisted away, snatching the sword of her dead opponent. The advancing soldier paused, smiled evilly, then drew his weapon. *He is not showing remorse. I cannot be clement.*

Other riders streamed past, dust kicking up. Where were all the archers? Was she alone on the field of battle? Planting her feet, she prepared to fight for her life.

The Moroccan approached, still grinning. He was enjoying this: he underestimated her. Good. She pretended she was having difficulty holding the sword. Losing patience, he attacked. Awa dived under his strike, came up behind him and swung the sword straight across the nape of the soldier's neck. His sword clattered to the ground, then he hit the ground face first.

Awa spun around, but before she was able to take on the next assailant, she felt a *crack* against the back of her head. Everything went dark and she collapsed.

3

PRAYER OF JONAH

STARLIGHT WAS A WELCOME RELIEF. Exhausted, Will slumped down beside the cannon. His thighs and lower back ached, yet he had no complaints: being a slave on deck was a world away from being a galley slave in the hull. The Moroccans had just completed the night prayer, which asked for God's mercy and grace. He certainly needed some of it, Will thought, if he was to get back to London. Closing his eyes, and for the first time in months, Will too prayed. He begged God to guide him home, so he could be with his mother, hear her laugh, smell the lavender she always had about her person.

He vaguely remembered the moment when, as a small boy of five, he was taken from her.

She had left him on the street corner, so she could duck into one of the wealthy houses for whose inhabitants she stitched clothes. She had told him to stay where he was. He did. But then a hulking great fellow marched up, lifted him up off his feet, clamped a cold hand across Will's mouth, and strode away with him down cobbled lanes, heading for the docks. Will didn't remember much else, having blanked a lot of it out, until he met the kind Hakim Abdullah, who took him under his wing years later in Marrakesh.

Violence was all Will had experienced in the galleys. Yet often lying awake at night, chained to his oars, he wondered whether peace was just a matter of each individual making an effort to better understand another. Unfortunately, in this unruly world, a man of peace would be a pauper, for violence was the only currency that mattered . . .

'Will.' He opened fearful eyes to find Jamal standing over him, holding out a steaming bowl.

'Eat,' the Moroccan said kindly.

Will scrambled up, receiving the meal with grateful hands. It was a lamb stew, with chickpeas and vegetables.

Noticing his surprise, Jamal said, 'You are part of the crew.'

'Thank you,' said Will. He had grown up never expecting anything from anybody. That way, he would never be disappointed. Jamal strolled away and Will devoured the stew before it could be taken away. He realised he had eaten too fast when his stomach ached and he had to stand up again.

The night sky was clear, glittering with stars. He located the North star and then cast his gaze to the west of it. Somewhere in that direction was his homeland - and for the first time he felt a sense of hope. Maybe his luck was finally about to change.

His eyelids were drooping and he decided to lie down where he was, beside the cannon, snuggling himself inside a large piece of canvas used to cover the ropes. Something told him to pull the canvas fully over him, the image of the Portuguese cutting his throat whilst he slept having something to do with it. He yawned and before he knew it, he was asleep.

Will woke with a start. Cannon fire - as loud as he had ever heard it - and the cries of men all around him. Then he remembered where he had slept, and hurriedly yanked the material off, sitting up to take in his surroundings. The sky was still dark, but the first glimmers of dawn were overhead.

The deck of the Al-Qamar was filled with sailors running to their stations, slipping and sliding, knocking into one another, grabbing at ropes and rigging to stay on their feet.

When Will stared across at the starboard side, he caught sight of the largest Spanish galleon he had ever seen, emerging from the early morning fog. It dwarfed the Al-Qamar. His mouth fell open as he saw the Spanish cannons take aim at the Al-Qamar and instinctively flung himself to the deck as the artillery-shot ripped into the hull. The Al-Qamar lurched to starboard. The next volley hit home and the vessel toppled to port, before momentarily righting itself. Then Will heard the most awful splitting sound. The hull was coming apart.

Where was First Officer Said? Where was Jamal? The Al-Qamar juddered violently. Around them was nothing other than miles and miles of deep water. Will wasn't prepared to try his chances with the Spanish, who had recently failed to invade England with a great armada. They would most likely torture him as a heretic. He imagined the Portuguese administering the punishment with relish.

As the ship settled in the water, men were leaping overboard, crying out in their terror. The vessel tilted and Will toppled back. Under the canvas were some blocks of wood, which had been used to adjust the height of the cannon. Will stared at the canvas, then at the blocks of wood - then at the rope which was used to tie the rigging. It might work!

Scrambling to his knees, he slammed four blocks of wood together, each one the length of his arm and the thickness of his chest. He found a small piece of the canvas, tightly wrapped it around the wood blocks and then used the rope to tie a reef-knot. The deck of the Al-Qamar angled further, the wood splintering, permitting Will to glimpse down into the hull. The galley slaves were still chained to their benches. In the darkness below he saw the Sudanese drummer, trapped. What could he do?

17

Nothing. He could do nothing to save them. He should have been one of them, he should have drowned. He still might.

Lifting his home-made float, he jumped off the back of the vessel into the waves. Salty sea-water immediately filled his mouth. He went under for a few moments, then resurfaced and found the blocks of wood in the canvas still floating and the rope holding. He seized the float, bobbing up and down as the waves swished around him. As he stared back towards the sinking vessel, he felt the ship's weight dragging him down. Will clung to his blocks of wood and tried to kick away from the ship, but he was being sucked downwards. He felt his fingers loosening. Then he went under.

He shot down, straight as an arrow, murk enveloping him on all sides, following the trajectory of the Al-Qamar as it sank like a stone. Other bodies were floating, men dying in the water. The drag on him finally lessened and he was able to swim towards the surface, where he emerged, choking, weeping, gasping for air.

The Spanish vessel had dropped anchor, and was now picking up Moroccan sailors who swam towards it. Will gazed around for his blocks of wood and through sheer good fortune located them about fifteen yards away. He swam towards the float, clutching at the rope, before heading away from the Spanish ship. He would rather take his chances with the sea than the vengeful Spanish.

The next few hours passed quickly. The summer sun reflected its heat off the Mediterranean, and it wasn't long before Will felt his skin burning. He had spent two years below deck, with barely any exposure to sunlight, and now he was getting it in full measure. Thanks to the previous night's meal, it wasn't till afternoon that he felt his stomach grumble loudly. He had not seen any other vessels, nor any sight of land. He knew England was to the north-west and he optimistically oriented himself in that direction. It was impossible to know how close he was to land. He kept swimming, then resting on his canvas blocks, swimming, then resting. The waters were relatively calm and the current took him in the right direction. He was still alive. How? It was a miracle. Maybe God was sending him home to his mother.

By sunset, Will's eyes were closing and he knew he was in danger of falling asleep and drowning. He had to stay afloat, but he also had to get some sleep. Unfortunately, the wooden blocks weren't large enough for him to actually lie down on or even sit on. They were just enough for him to hold onto, for which he was grateful.

Starlight danced around him, as the moon showed a little more of itself than the night before. The wind had been strengthening steadily; now he felt a powerful gust strike his face, followed by a wave curling around him, lifting him higher and then lowering him. There was going to be a gale, so it was even more imperative that he hold on. Will undid one of the ropes, then tied a knot around his left wrist, before securing it back round the wooden float.

The sea swelled, elevating him enough to see large waves approaching from the north, before he plunged down once more. Maybe he was destined to die alone, after all, out at sea. Will remembered Hakim Abdullah telling him the story of the prophet Jonah who, when he was distraught within the belly of the whale, cried out to God for help. Will wished he could remember the words of the prayer Jonah had uttered, but he couldn't.

The water slapped his face, stinging his skin with its force before the next wave lifted him then plummeted him into darkness once more. Will squinted upwards. The blocks of wood flailed around, sometimes over him, other times below him.

19

Dear God. Please, I need Your mercy. The wind increased. If the sea could speak, he thought blindly, it would be screaming at him. He was flung sideways, then forced deep underwater, further and further into the gloom, till there was no light, there was no hope.

Only silence.

4

DESERT CARAVAN

T HE SUN WAS A FIERY furnace of gold, but finally it set in the west and the cosmos glittered like a million burning embers, briefly reminding Awa of poetry readings under starry skies in Timbuktu. With dusk came mosquitoes, tormenting the travellers in the caravan as it snaked its way north across the Sahara Desert.

In her home town of Timbuktu, Awa's family had devised a system using vinegar and peppermint to deter the parasites. The whole mosquito season could pass with only a couple of bites. She feared she would not see those days again. Awa was now part of the Moroccan caravan, being transported as a slave. In the last eight weeks, she had been bitten more times than she could remember, so much so that her once-soft skin had become lumpy and rough. Awa hadn't bathed for weeks - but that didn't seem to bother the mosquitoes, which continued feasting on her. Not surprisingly, all fifteen women in the caged wagon smelled as awful as she did. All were Songhai. The Moroccans had separated the men from the women and then further split them by age.

One of the women in Awa's wagon had been coughing violently for the past two days and Awa was sure she had seen blood mixed with the woman's spittle. The sick woman was sweating, as were they all, but she was also shivering from a fever. At one point, a soldier mounted on a camel drew close to their wagon, giving the invalid a hard stare before riding on.

Daytime was too hot for travelling across the Sahara, so the Moroccans transported their newly acquired Songhai slaves and plunder at night. The journey to Marrakesh was going to take several more weeks, and travelling as part of such a large caravan meant slow progress across this most inhospitable terrain. Awa sat, her back pressed against the uncomfortable metal bars of the cage. Her stomach rumbled. The daily provision of one piece of bread and a small cup of lentil soup was insufficient. Water was scarce. The Moroccans drank first, then their animals, and finally the Songhai. What had her people done to deserve such a punishment from God? Her cheek felt wet and she wiped away a precious tear, using it to remove some dirt from her forehead.

Outside, the caravan stretched for miles. Lit by oil lamps in the night, to a bird it must have appeared like a snake of fire coiling its way across the sand. During the day, it was easy to detect where the Songhai gold was kept, for those particular wagons had soldiers clustered round them. The slave wagons near the rear were sparsely guarded, one soldier defending four or five wagons, sometimes ten. Bandits were common in the desert and with high-value cargo so closely protected, brigands often picked off lesser scraps. Awa had already witnessed a group of well-organised bandits make off with an entire wagon of Songhai slaves. They would be easy to sell to buyers in port markets along the west coast as well as in towns to the north of the Sahara.

Movement beside the caravan trail caught her attention. Two bodies, both of Songhai men, lay sprawled on the track. One still moved, pitifully raising an arm, his eyes imploring her for help. Awa could not help, only say a prayer for him in her heart. Those poor souls, too sick to be considered worth saving, were left in the desert. By midday, they would be dead. Awa knew she had to keep her strength for returning to the dusty bookshelves of Timbuktu and its glorious university. Listening to erudite scholars, with their fine legal discourse and scientific treatises - that was all she desired.

She looked up. The soldier who had passed earlier was now back with a colleague. They ordered the wagon driver to stop and open the cage door.

'Out you get,' said the first soldier, pointing at the coughing woman.

The other women shuffled away from the accusing soldier, leaving the sick woman alone.

'*Out*, I said' he repeated.

The sick woman placed a hand against her chest and the other up towards the soldier, imploring him to show mercy. Ignoring her, he cursed, then tied a scarf over his mouth and nose before grabbing the woman by the ankle and hauling her out. She screamed, but this only served to bring on another coughing fit. The cage door was locked and with the help of the second soldier, she was dragged away. Awa peered through the iron bars. Were they going to throw her on the track with the men? Thankfully, they stopped beside another wagon much further back, opened the doors and shoved her inside. It must be where the other sick slaves were kept.

The wagon driver urged the dromedaries on, the wagon resuming its laborious tempo through the desert. Hours later, their cage door was opened once more, but this time a woman was told to get in. She did not appear unwell, but all the inhabitants shied away from her, for fear she might be carrying a sickness.

The young woman crawled in, spotted her and said, 'Awa?' She was a little older than Awa, and her intricate black braids

23

were clogged with sand. She felt her way along the wagon and sat down beside Awa.

'I don't know you,' said Awa, puzzled.

'My name is Wassa,' the stranger said, placing her hand on her chest. 'Salaam.'

'Salaam,' Awa responded, surprised at the other woman's interest in having a conversation. Weeks on the road had passed in silence, no one having the energy to talk to anyone else.

'They say you killed ten Moroccan cavalrymen by yourself,' Wassa whispered.

Awa regarded her quizzically. 'How do you know it was me?'

'Everyone in the wagon I came from witnessed what you did on the battlefield. When others ran, you stayed, you fought and you killed. You are a hero for the Songhai.'

Awa herself had no recollection of who else had been around her, or what they had witnessed. She just remembered being separated from her friend Suha, then being alone, surrounded by cattle and Moroccan cavalry, trying to avoid the stampede and having the good fortune to fell a few soldiers.

'I'm no hero, just a slave like everyone else,' she stated.

'But you fought and slew the aggressor.'

Awa couldn't help but smile. 'More like three soldiers, not ten.'

'Three or ten, it doesn't matter, you are a symbol of hope,' said Wassa. 'You are a warrior.'

Awa shrugged. What good had it done? All the past year's training and she still ended up a slave. The Songhai had vastly outnumbered the Moroccans, they even had cattle, but the invaders had brought firearms and cannons. Each cannon was like a thousand soldiers. The Songhai possessed mountains of gold, why then did they not have weapons like the Moroccans? Why had King Askia not purchased these? Had they had an arsenal of weapons, she would still be safe with her family, for

24

the Moroccans would not have attempted invasion knowing that the Songhai owned weapons of equal power. The King and his court politics were to blame. Petty rivalry resulted in disunity, and the Moroccans had preyed on this weakness.

'Where are you from?' asked Awa.

'Gao,' said Wassa. 'My family has lived in the capital for generations. We are *Julia*, merchants who trade kola nuts, leather, and dates. You?'

'Timbuktu. My father teaches at the University,' said Awa.

'What does he teach?'

'Geometry and poetry.'

Wassa let out a short laugh. 'So, the warrior is the daughter of a poet! Will you recite some verses? Something hopeful,' she requested, placing a hand on Awa's arm.

Awa thought for a moment, then remembered a favourite poem of her father's.

'Though my chains be hefty, a weight too great to bear, I endure them.
Through earth cleft by fire, I crawl, my body dried to bones.
Banished from my own land, torn from my ancestors' plains, I submit.
For the lover seeks to return to his Beloved -
And so my journey takes me back into His arms.
Why would I not suffer, for as Jesus, son of Maryam, said:
'This world is a bridge: pass over it, but do not build a home upon it.'
I am crossing the bridge into the next realm
For a union with The One I love.'

Wassa was silent. She nodded, then said: 'Thank you. The Songhai are one another's shield; we are the hands which sow the seed and reap the harvest.'

Awa sorely missed her father. He was witty and studious, he was approachable yet reserved. Her eyes began to fill with tears as she remembered him. He had implored King Askia to consider a negotiated settlement with the Moroccans. It would have meant the Songhai had to pay an annual levy to Marrakesh, but at least it would have kept their culture alive.

Her father's voice had, however, been drowned out by those clamouring for war; assuming the superiority of numbers made victory a foregone conclusion. Awa too had been infected by this euphoria, as had many of the young warriors. Her father was despondent when she told him she was leaving Timbuktu to fight in the army. He asked her to reconsider, but when he realised her mind was made up, he said he would pray for her safe return and embraced her.

Once again, tears flowed down her cheeks. Would she ever get to see him again? He was a scholar - surely the Moroccans would not kill such men of learning? Maybe he would even be asked to travel to Marrakesh and join the Court of al-Mansur. She knew it was wishful thinking, but she had to have some hope, a belief she would meet him in this world before they were reunited with her mother in the hereafter.

5

CITY ON THE BOSPORUS

THE SOUND OF RATTLING CHAINS woke him. Will opened his eyes and blinked, taking in the surroundings: a wooden hull, so he was below deck on a ship, but it wasn't the *Al-Qamar*, for he had seen it sink. His hand moved down to his ankles and his worst fears were confirmed: he was shackled once more. But at least he hadn't drowned.

Around him, strewn across a filthy wooden floor, were about ten men, all manacled, either sitting or lying. Some were Africans, others lighter-skinned Europeans. There was a lot of noise from above - sailors moving around deck, ropes being pulled, sails tied back. They must be approaching land. Would the galley slaves be allowed on shore? After two years, Will longed for the stability of firm ground. If he never saw a ship again, it wouldn't be too soon.

To his right sat an African, a big man, with powerful arms and shoulders, a clean-shaven head and penetrating dark eyes.

'Where am I?' asked Will.

The African turned towards him. 'You are on the *Al-Shams*.'

That meant 'the sun' in Arabic. It was a good omen. 'Moroccan?' asked Will.

The African snorted. 'Turkish.'

'Turks!' mumbled Will. He had heard all sorts of terrible rumours about the Turks. They drank the blood of their enemies. They ate human flesh. They were filthy and barbarous, preferring to live in caves and deep underground, where they would drag their unsuspecting victims. Their capital, Istanbul, had once been the great Christian city of Constantinople, seat of the Holy Roman Empire. Since the Turks had taken it, they had burned it to the ground, and defaced its monuments. Now all that remained were hovels barely fit for human habitation. In Marrakesh, the Turks were hated, though he did sense that the Moroccans were envious of them, which seemed odd, if the Turks were such a backward nation.

Will straightened up, so he didn't feel quite so dwarfed beside the African. 'Where are we going?'

The man shrugged his shoulders. 'I am not the Captain. But,' he added, 'it looks like we are coming into port.'

'Will they let us off the ship?'

The African raised an eyebrow, replying, 'Yes, of course. This is a ship belonging to the Janissaries.'

In Marrakesh, Will had heard about the formidable elite army corps of the Turkish Sultan, called the Janissaries. They were fearsome warriors. Split into many brigades and at all times loyal to the Sultan and his family, not only were they powerful militarily, they were also reputed to be very rich.

'So, we aren't going to be galley slaves?' asked Will.

The African shook his head.

'Slaves?'

The African nodded and pointed to Will's fetters.

At least he was going to be on land, Will reflected - and that meant there was a better chance of escaping.

The *Al-Shams* gradually slowed. They must be close to the harbour wall. Finally, the vessel came to a complete stop and Will heard the ropes being fastened to secure the mooring.

They had docked. The excited sailors were making a lot of noise and Will thought he heard the name Istanbul being shouted out. The notion of having arrived in the heartland of the Turks made his hair stand on end. He imagined a place of dark buildings, with fire-breathing dragons hanging off tall spires, roasting the unworthy at the command of the malevolent Sultan, who was King of the Turks.

The *Al-Shams* was emptying and it went quiet for a time, giving Will cause for concern that they were going to be left below deck. Then the hatch in the ceiling was opened, and light streamed in.

'Out!' a gruff voice commanded them. The small group of men around Will stood and started to ascend the ladder leading up to the deck. Will went behind the African. Out on deck, he screwed his eyes shut. As he grew accustomed to the brightness, he saw that the *Al-Shams* was a three-masted vessel, which could carry a few hundred men.

'Whoa!' said the African. 'Look at that!'

Will moved his attention away from the *Al-Shams* to gawk out at the city of Istanbul lying before them in the early morning light. He was immediately struck by the contours of the land, hills rising and falling across the skyline. Each hill had upon it the most magnificent mosque he had ever seen. Monuments and ornately carved sculptures sat close to the mosques, and streets formed intricate passages down from the hills, towards the river where the *Al-Shams* had docked. Bazaars bristled with merchants and customers, bargaining excitedly. Istanbul did not look like a wicked city; on the contrary, Will had never imagined something so wondrous could exist on earth.

'Come on, move it,' said the sailor with a slight smile, as he regarded the dazzled faces of the slaves, shuffling off the boat.

'Istanbul?' Will said dreamily, to no one in particular.

'Yes, my friend, welcome to the world's greatest city,' said the sailor, nudging him along.

Within moments of disembarking, Will was caught in a vast movement of people of all races, colours and ages, rushing past him as their small slave party made its way out of the harbour. The guards kept close to them, though in truth, Will could not imagine any of the slaves being able to run very far in chains.

They tramped away from the harbour and through an open square, where there was a small mosque with blue-tipped minarets, after which they passed a *Madrasa*, a college for Islamic instruction, in which Will observed students sitting cross-legged upon the ground. They began to walk up a steep incline. The road became narrower and rougher, and the hurly-burly of the promenade below was replaced by the sounds of young children crying, a goat bleating and two dogs fighting.

'Keep moving,' ordered one of the guards, who was dressed in a set of black pantaloons and a maroon tunic which came down below his hips. On his head he wore a covering which in part appeared to be a helmet, but was made of fabric. Will couldn't tell whether it provided any protection or was merely a ceremonial piece of clothing.

As they crested the hill, Will glanced down and could still see the *Al-Shams*, docked in the port, but she was now a tiny speck. He had been struck on disembarking by the diverse ethnic groups. Istanbul might have been the capital of the Ottoman Empire, he thought, but it was not only a land of Turks. It was as though the whole world had chosen to come and live here!

Will felt like an idiot for having been taken in by the lurid tales he had heard about the Turks. Marrakesh was a glorious city; as for Istanbul, there was no comparison.

They descended the other side of the hill and Will eyed a set of fortified buildings in the distance; the soldiers lining it were dressed like their guards. They must be going to a Janissary fort. Their journey took them through the gates of the fort, past the barracks of the Janissaries and out into the rear of the encampment, where they were told to sit on the ground. A pail of water was passed down the line, from which they could take a scoop and quench their thirst.

From behind the barracks strode a small troop of Janissaries, who were older than the regular guards. Will took them to be officers. Seeing their superiors, the guards ordered Will and the others up on their feet.

'Stand straight, chest out,' growled one of the guards.

The officers approached, most of them standing a short distance away, with one officer coming closer.

'My name is Kadri, Captain of the Twelfth Brigade of the Royal Janissary Force.'

Will noticed a white-skinned officer, whose fair hair was only slightly darker than Will's own. He was a man of middle years, who observed the slaves with a watchful eye. Could he be an Englishman?

'The Janissaries serve Sultan Murad III and his family. Some Janissary brigades consist of members who are not Ottoman, some not even Muslim. These men are chosen, so that the Sultan in all his glory can build alliances and treaties with the regions from which these people originate. We would like to give you the chance to join us,' Kadri declared as he surveyed them.

Will had heard about non-Muslims, such as himself, who made up part of the Janissary force.

Kadri continued, 'The choice is thus. You may join the Janissaries, to be trained and commit your life to Sultan Murad III and his family, thereby breaking the shackles of slavery.

You must be willing to spill your blood for the Sultan, at all times obey the orders of your superiors, commit yourselves to a wholesome life, train harder than you have ever done before, and never question your loyalty. Or you may return to the *Al-Shams* to become a galley slave.'

It didn't sound like much of a choice.

'All those who wish to return to the *Al-Shams*, take a step back,' said Kadri.

Silence. None of the men moved.

'Not all of you will pass the rigorous training it takes to become a Janissary. For those who do, it will be rewarding.' Kadri waited, staring at each man, locking eyes with them, then nodding to the group.

'Then it is done,' he said.

Will breathed a sigh of relief. He would train as a Janissary. He would mouth the oaths of loyalty. But at the first chance of escape, he would make a run for it. London still waited in his dreams. So did his beloved, long-lost mother.

6

BANDIT WAGONS

DARKNESS SMOTHERED HER SENSES AS the new moon shone dimly; even the stars seemed dull tonight. The caravan was halfway through its night journey, twisting through the Sahara. Awa noticed that the number of sick slaves had steadily multiplied in the wagons to the rear. In addition, those abandoned by the roadside had increased. Once they realised they were free, the uncaged slaves would try to haul themselves up and run, but being so weak and close to death, they soon collapsed and were still. Awa considered pretending to be sick and then dead, but if it meant placing her with those already infected with disease, it was not worth the risk.

'Awa,' hissed Wassa, pointing to something out in the desert. 'Look.'

Awa peered into the gloom and with Wassa's help was able to identify figures creeping up over a sand dune to her side. Bandits!

'Maybe they will free us,' said Awa.

'They will sell us,' Wassa told her.

The Moroccan soldiers had not caught sight of the approaching bandits and Awa was in two minds whether or not to alert them. Before she had the opportunity to decide,

Moroccan soldiers on camel-back close to them fell silently from their mounts. Arrows! she realised. Fired with incredible accuracy. The dromedaries continued plodding forwards, exhibiting no concern about whether their rider was still seated. Soon the soldier next to Awa's wagon was felled, as was their wagon driver, each with an arrow through his neck. Shadowy figures, dressed in loose robes, crested the dunes then started running alongside the wagons. Their faces were mostly covered, only the slits of their eyes showing. The bandits mounted the empty camels and slowly drew all of the wagons in the rear of the caravan to a halt.

As she watched, the bandits turned the wagons around and headed back the way they had come. Apparently, the theft went unnoticed by the Moroccans, so great was their caravan of treasures. Awa craned her neck to see the Moroccan caravan vanishing over the horizon.

The bandit-led wagons dipped to lower ground, continuing in the same direction for the next hour, before turning east to join a new track. Night passed into day. The bandits stopped, shaded themselves inside small tents, where they slept and woke once more before sunset. As they set off again for the evening, Awa recognised that one entire wagon had been left, containing the very sick. Even the bandits thought it better to abandon these Songhai than make the effort of selling them. Awa wondered if the woman who had been removed from her own wagon was one of them.

The food the bandits fed them was no different to what the Moroccans had doled out. Water was scarce, but there were fewer people in the new caravan, which contained about six wagons, with fifteen or so Songhai in each one. Two of the wagons consisted of women only, the others of men. At some point during the night the terrain changed; sand dunes were replaced by rocky tracts of land, views of mountains emerging

34

and vegetation sprouting at the foot of date palms. The caravan eventually rolled into a small valley where to Awa's surprise there was a *wadi* – a small valley with a streambed - with a substantial body of water.

'More bandits,' noted Wassa.

Those present greeted the newcomers but pointed in disgust at the wagons containing the women. A noisy conversation ensued; the bandits shouting angrily. The wagons were lined up and the ones containing the women were placed closer to the water. One of the bandits approached their wagon and smashed the lock with a hammer.

'Come,' he said, beckoning to the women in Awa's cage. No one moved. 'Come, wash.'

The prospect of water was very appealing. Awa knew she must stink as badly as the camels, but she was long past caring. Tentatively, one of the women slid out of the cage, followed by others. The bandit ushered them to the water to bathe. Awa didn't like it. There were too many men with hungry eyes staring at them. Torches lined the route to the water. She flashed a look over at the Songhai men, some of whom gripped their cage-bars, concerned faces looking in their direction.

'What do we do?' whispered Awa.

'We escape,' murmured Wassa.

It was a bold suggestion, and one worth considering. They were only let out of the cage by the Moroccans every morning, so they could relieve themselves. Even if they had made a dash for it, there was nowhere to go in the desert. Here, however, the terrain was more accommodating, with mountains to hide in, date palms and other vegetation to feed off. This might be their last chance.

Awa followed Wassa out of the cage, head down, pacing towards the large pool of water in one corner of the wadi. Some of the Songhai women had already gone in knee-deep and now sat down, the water covering them as they washed their faces and hair.

She entered the water, Wassa beside her. It felt so good that she quickly forgot about the men and dunked herself fully under the surface, cleaning the sand out of every crevice and pore. In Timbuktu she bathed every day, sometimes twice a day, and performed five ablutions for the five daily prayers. She had prided herself on cleanliness.

The women were left for some time and Awa sat, hands and feet resting in the water, her head tilted up to the sky, taking in the cosmos. With only the stars in her line of sight, she imagined being in Timbuktu with her father enjoying the celestial show . . .

'Out!'

The illusion was broken when one of the bandits ordered them to leave the watering-hole. Grudgingly the women began to rise.

'Now will be the time,' whispered Wassa. 'Camels are tethered to the rear - if we can get to them.'

Awa nodded covertly. The women came out of the water and to her surprise and relief the bandits ushered them back to their cages. The evening weather was hot, and their clothes began to dry almost immediately. The cage containing the next party of women was now readied. The Songhai men visibly relaxed when they saw the women return unharmed.

'Now!' said Wassa. She sprang forward, pushing the bandit closest to her to the ground, removing his sword from its scabbard in the same movement. 'Run!'

Awa darted in the direction of the camels. Bandits began to converge on them. The Songhai women screamed. The men, still caged, shook the bars of their prison. Awa scurried past the wagon in which she had spent the last eight weeks. When two bandits blocked her way, she sprinted at them. They looked surprised. At the last moment, she rolled forwards and went between the legs of one. She swivelled and kicked him in the rear, knocking him to the ground. The other made a grab for her, but Wassa was there and hit him with the flat of the sword upon his head.

More bandits appeared. The two runaways were surrounded, and then there was a series of screams and the clash of metal. Awa peered back and saw the other women attacking the bandits with their bare hands. Some of those surrounding her and Wassa went to quell the other rebels, but this diversion still left half a dozen armed men for the two of them to take on, with only one sword between them.

'Stay close, try and get a weapon,' Wassa panted as she lunged at a bandit who deftly blocked her, only for Awa to ram into him with her shoulder, knocking him to the ground, whipping his sword from his hand. Before she had a chance to stand, however, two meaty hands grabbed her from behind. She squirmed and wriggled but could not get free. Fortunately, the bandit had not trapped her arms and so she gripped the hilt of the blade and swung it back at her own head, moving at the last moment, so the blade caught the man full in the face. His grip loosened and he dropped her. She spun and cracked the weapon against the side of his jaw.

There was no time to feel relief, for she sensed somebody close and instinctively rolled away as a sword blade struck the ground where she had stood. She kicked out and struck her attacker behind the knees, and when his legs gave way, she was able to rise up and strike him under the chin with the hilt of her sword, knocking him out cold.

Wassa was on the ground and two bandits stood over her, one with a raised sword. Awa sprang forwards, driving her blade through his back. His sword dropped from his hand. The other bandit turned sideways, in which time Wassa was able to leap up and put her own blade through his belly.

Wassa grabbed her arm, nodding at the camels, but Awa shook her head and turned back towards the screaming women. They made their way around the wagon, fearful of what they might witness, but the rebellion was quelled. The bandits had most of the women back in the cage. There was nothing they could do for them.

Then one of the bandits spotted them and raised the alarm again.

'Run!' said Wassa.

They took off, heading for the tethered camels and leaped up on two of them. The saddlebags were empty of water, but there was no time to fill them. They would need to find a well on the way. Awa dug her heels in and her reluctant dromedary started to move, but rather too slowly, as one of the bandits was able to run up and grab her leg. She swung her sword down and he pulled away, just as the camel picked up pace and rode off behind the beast carrying Wassa.

Awa had no idea where they were headed, but exultation filled her. Surely anywhere would be better than here!

7

FREE AS THE WIND

WATER DRIPPED FROM THE TAP into the washbasin. Before the first drop splashed on the stone surface, the archer fired an arrow, striking a target dead centre, twenty yards away. Will, never confident with the bow, admired the man's skill. He had tried to master the bow, but when focusing on technique his aim was off, and when paying attention to where he was firing, his technique fell apart. No, Will Ryde was no bowman and he knew it. He continued running around the circuit, a dirt path winding its way through and around the perimeter of the Janissary fort. He was amongst a group of cadets and every so often they passed a rider upon a horse, using the parallel track.

Weeks had gone past, some of the best of his life. It felt as if he was back in Marrakesh with Hakim Abdullah. He almost felt safe. Yet, as during his time with the quartermaster, Will knew he was still a slave. The Janissaries might not treat him as one, but he was not free to leave the battalion. He belonged to them. Still, this was a world away from being a galley slave.

Each day started at dawn, with the Muslim members of the Janissaries participating in congregational prayers at the Mosque within the compound, and believers of other faiths encouraged to meditate and offer their own thanks and prayers. Will vaguely remembered going to a church service in London as a small boy, and in Marrakesh he had witnessed Christian gatherings, but had never participated. Now, being in an environment where everyone in the morning was praying or meditating, Will was inspired to do likewise. Kneeling at the end of his bed, he prayed to God for forgiveness and the salvation of his parents.

Three meals, at appointed times, were served. The food was remarkably appetising and Will marvelled at the range of fruits and vegetables on offer, as well as the succulent meat. The day ended at sunset when the cadets were sent to their barracks. The strict regime resulted in Will adding muscle and weight; his cheeks filled out and he felt stronger than before.

The daily circuit run followed two hours of book-learning. The tutors covered a range of subjects. Some had to do with the personal development of the soldier, such as self-discipline and patience. Others were to do with diet and how to manage on rations when campaigning. There were more philosophical subjects related to the ethics of war and how to lay siege to an enemy city. And then there was the study of military campaigns fought in the past. Will had not heard of the places they studied, but revelled in his tutors' depictions of battles fought in the Indus Valley, as far away as China and closer to home in Greece. Will was tapping into ideas he had never known existed and his brain gleefully absorbed the new material.

The instructor pulled them up on a hillock beside a pail of water, encouraging them to drink. Will wiped the sweat off his brow and took in the staggering view of Istanbul below. How could he have been so misled about the city? He ventured out once a week into town and had only just begun to discover its intricate paths and walkways.

'Will.' It was Gurkan, one of the other cadets in their cohort. 'Salaam.'

'Salaam,' replied Will.

'I hear you're good with the sword,' said Gurkan.

Will shrugged shyly. 'Not bad.'

Gurkan smiled. 'No need to be modest. Let's spar after the run.'

'Gladly.'

The instructor moved them on, down the circuit and back towards the fort. Following the exercise, they returned to the central quadrangle beside the store of the quartermaster. Of all the places in the fort, this was the one where Will felt most comfortable. The local quartermaster did not mind Will hanging around. He got useful work out of him, polishing and sharpening the weapons. It gave Will something to do and he knew he was a capable assistant. The quartermaster equipped the cadets with blunt practice blades for sparring.

Gurkan swivelled the hilt of his sword comfortably around his wrist. The young Turk from the province of Konya had an easy manner, the weapon appearing like an extension of his arm. Will had seen him spar; he was outstanding, likely the best in the group. Upon noticing Will pair off with Gurkan, the quartermaster smiled to himself. Some of the other cadets who spotted Gurkan and Will pair up, continued practising whilst keeping an eye on what was unfolding. Their circuit-instructor had returned to the mess hall, so there was an avid audience of cadets.

'English,' smiled Gurkan, raising his right hand to his forehead before flicking it away as a mark of respect.

'Turk,' said Will, bowing.

They locked their weapons before sliding them off one another and stepping back. Gurkan struck first, a swift blow which Will blocked with ease and countered by a sideways cut across his opponent's chest. Gurkan stepped back, out of the way of the blow, swinging his blade up, causing Will to leap clear.

'No need to hold back,' said Will.

'Really?' said Gurkan. 'Are you sure, English?' The young Turk barrelled forwards with the tip of his sword. Will side-stepped, tapping Gurkan on the shoulder with his blade as he went by.

'First cut to me,' Will grinned.

'Just letting you get ahead,' said Gurkan, as he switched the sword from his right hand to his left. Then, at Will's surprised look: 'I only fight left-handed with the better swordsmen.'

Gurkan bounded forwards. Will countered. Gurkan swiped low before going wide, then low again, catching Will on the shin with the flat of his blade.

'One apiece,' beamed Gurkan.

Will skipped away from his opponent, watching as Gurkan swivelled the practice-blade in his left hand as though he were twirling a piece of rope. This time Will sprang at him, blade coming down. Gurkan blocked, Will went high to the right, then low to the left, switching angles, trying to break through the Turk's defence, but Gurkan read him, knew where he was going to attack. Will then applied brute force; he was an inch taller than Gurkan and put his height behind the downward strike. Gurkan parried, then pushed Will away with the sole of his boot, causing Will to stumble backwards, losing his footing. Gurkan's blade was at him in a flash, and with its tip he flicked Will's own weapon out of his hand. Will's blade clattered to the ground and Gurkan placed his weapon against Will's shoulder.

'Two-one!' said Gurkan.

The ring of cadets applauded and Will couldn't help but join in. Gurkan held out his hand and Will took it, rising up with his support. He could learn from this man, particularly how he knew where Will was going to strike. He was fast - but no one was *that* quick. There must have been some giveaway in Will's technique.

'You are too good . . . for now,' Will told him.

Gurkan bowed, as did Will, when they noticed that the other cadets were no longer paying them any attention. Their instructor was standing close by, along with Captain Kadri, and beside him was the white-skinned Janissary officer whom Will recognised from his first day in the camp. Will and Gurkan spun to attention.

'Line up,' said the instructor. 'Row of two.'

They fell into line.

Captain Kadri strode forwards. 'This is Commander Mehmed Konjic,' he said, pointing to the senior officer. 'This fort and ten others are under his command. He wishes to address you.'

Konjic stepped closer to the cadets, saying pleasantly, 'At ease.' The Commander considered them, inspecting their numbers. His gaze wandered over to Will and Gurkan. 'I notice we have two talented swordsmen. I dare say others have skills in different areas. All will be useful.'

Will could not place him. He wasn't an ethnic Turk, nor was he English, French, German or from any other country whose accent Will recognised. Where was this fellow from - and how had he come to be so senior amongst the Turkish Janissaries?

'You all came here through an assortment of routes,' Konjic said. 'Some were recruited from the countryside,' he nodded at Gurkan. 'Others were rescued from slavery,' he nodded at Will. 'You are here now, and it is your good fortune to train as a Janissary, so you can serve the royal household.' He gazed in the direction of the main city. 'All of you were chosen because you are not residents of Istanbul. You have no ties to the royal court. You come to this city free of attachments. And for this purpose, you are being considered for a new branch of the Janissary force, called the Rüzgar - the Wind. Consider yourselves, like the wind, unattached.'

Konjic paused, before adding: 'We will share more details with you in due course. But for now, I am pleased to see you are making progress. Any questions?'

Will desperately wanted to ask him where he was from, but thought better of it. Konjic regarded them one more time, before marching back to the fort with Captain Kadri.

8

AN IMPRESSIVE CATCH

NIGHT VEILED THEIR PASSING THROUGH the mountainous terrain, but Awa knew it did not erase their footprints. Trackers would be on their trail. They needed to put distance between them, or risk recapture. It was so good to be free - but she hoped their escape had not led to repercussions for the Songhai left behind.

The camels were exhausted. Most likely they had been trudging throughout the day and were already in need of a night's rest when Awa and Wassa had escaped with them. Worse, much worse, as they already knew, the saddlebags were empty of any water or food. The women were aware that they needed to go south-west at some point, but the way was blocked by bandits. Their only hope was to use the vastness of the terrain to elude their hunters, before then swinging back south.

'We need to find water,' said Wassa, her voice hoarse.

They scanned the horizon. It was dark, and only the outline of a mountain range in the distance was visible against the night sky. Mountains might house springs of water - it was as good a place as any to search. Awa craned her head round. No one was following. Not yet. She dug her heels in and encouraged the weary dromedary to speed up. Reluctantly it complied, but not before baring its teeth and snarling.

'I know you're not happy. Neither am I,' said Awa, rubbing the animal on the cheek.

The mountains proved barren with barely any vegetation. The young women foraged some thyme leaves, normally used in cooking, but if things got really desperate they would eat them. Bathing in the *wadi* had given Awa a bolt of energy, but her belly was still empty. She alighted from her camel, to guide it through the more difficult terrain.

'Wassa, where do you think the bandits will take the people?'

Her fellow Songhai sighed. 'Most likely they will be sold in bazaars.'

The Songhai nation was being feasted upon by those vultures who prey on people who have lost everything. Anger towards King Askia welled up inside Awa once more. He should have protected them! What did this mean for future generations, for all those who lived on the western shores of Africa?

'If they catch us, what will they do?' she asked next, fearing the answer.

'Let's not give them the chance.' Wassa stopped her camel, staring up at the sky. 'When I feel that I have nothing left in this world, Awa, I look to the stars. There are so many, and they belong to everyone.'

Awa nodded, and was comforted.

They maintained their trek past dawn, until the sunlight became too overpowering, when they sought shelter in a cave. They took turns sleeping and then set off once more at night-time. The mountains had become taller and broader than before. Every time Awa thought they had reached a peak, there was a higher one to come. Surely there was no way for a tracker, no matter how good, to find them when they had taken such a convoluted path, crossing desert and mountains? They must be safe.

46

On the second day, they found a stream of clear water; it was only small, but enough to drink from till their bellies were full and the camels satiated. They filled their water skins and picked some figs and berries before setting off. The following morning, they rested and commenced at night once more.

Awa was feeling pleased. They had water and were finding provisions. Her strength was returning. The sheer joy of freedom was still fuelling her desire to keep running. However, the peaks were too high to scale, so they were forced to travel north-east, further away from their homeland.

As dawn broke, they found shade under a palm tree within another *wadi*. They ate dates, drank their fill of water. Awa took the first watch as Wassa slept. At some point in the day they swapped and Awa was soon asleep. Her peace, however, did not last.

'Wake up,' hissed Wassa, placing a hand on Awa's shoulder. 'Quiet.' The sun was going to set soon. She indicated the area of the *wadi*. 'People.'

Had they been found? After three days, when Awa was sure they had thrown their trackers off the trail, could it really be possible that they were going to be caged once more, enslaved - or worse? She rose quickly, wrapping her baggage and rolling it tightly shut. *No.* She was not going to be apprehended, like an animal. She would fight. She had a weapon and knew how to use it; she had already fought - and to her shame had killed - but there had been no other way. She never wanted to strike down another human being and if she was forced into combat again, she would attempt to injure, not to kill.

Drawing her sword, she crouched down beside Wassa. The women were hiding behind a palm tree, waiting to see who approached. Tethered close were their camels, entirely unperturbed by what was going on around them. Voices drew closer. They should have fled, she thought, got away before these strangers arrived. Awa peered around the trunk of the tree and saw three young men with walking sticks appear, emerging beside the dromedaries.

'Shepherds,' whispered Wassa.

Awa let go of the breath she had been holding.

The three shepherds came into the open area, peeking about.

'Hello, anyone here?' asked the tall, gangly one.

Awa eyed Wassa, who shook her head and put her finger to her lips.

'Hello?'

Silence. The young fellow shrugged, turned back to the camels and began to untie them, saying, 'Come, we will take them back to Tamdjert.'

'Thieving shepherds,' snarled Wassa, rising up. 'Come on.' They walked into the open. 'Stop!' she commanded. 'Those are our camels.'

The men turned slowly to look at them.

'Two women with two camels in Wadi Umar, beside the Tassili Mountains? Whatever are you doing here, my sisters?' asked the lanky fellow. At least his tone was friendly, not threatening or condescending.

'That is our business,' replied Wassa, approaching them and revealing the blade dangling at her thigh. 'And those are *our* camels.'

The shepherds took a step back, away from the camels. But they left them untied, Awa noticed.

'Now leave and let us go about our business,' ordered Wassa.

The leggy shepherd exchanged glances with the other two, and before the women could react, his companions had shoved their sticks into the camels' behinds, causing the beasts to kick out and run, sprinting away from the *wadi*.

48

Wassa glared at the shepherds. 'Collect up our things, Awa, we need to get our camels.'

Awa ran to the palm tree, where she had left the bedding. It was gone. She gazed around, her heart speeding up. She gripped the hilt of her weapon. Others were here. It must be the trackers from the bandit camp.

'Our things have been stolen, Wassa,' Awa turned and called. But she saw that the shepherds had run off - and now standing in their place was the lankiest man she had ever set eyes on. He carried a long spear, even taller than herself and his clothing resembled that of the people of the interior, where leopard and crocodile skins were commonly used. His head was shaved, as was the rest of his visible body. His eyes shone like pearls and when he smiled his teeth were like a moonbeam against his dark skin.

Wassa started to back off. Awa joined her, her weapon by her side. The giant strode forwards.

'Run for the camels,' said Wassa.

The giant was upon them as Awa scuttled away, scampering through the date palms, heading in the direction the camels had bolted. There was a scream behind her, and she whipped round to see the giant lift Wassa off her feet and remove her sword from her hand. He had her dangling upside down, holding her by the ankles, as she wriggled desperately to get free.

'No!' cried out Awa, stopping in her tracks.

'Run!' shouted Wassa.

Awa hesitated. She could not leave her friend. Not now. At that moment, she found herself confronted by a man with a crooked face; it drooped to one side, as though he had taken a blow there at some point. There was a nasty scar on his forehead and right eyebrow. He wore a leather belt which held various knives, and a curved sword was sheathed in its scabbard. His skin was dark brown.

49

'Odo is the name,' he said, rubbing his hands together. 'You may have heard about me?'

Awa shook her head, her weapon raised, as Wassa's cries rang out behind her.

Odo spat onto the ground and shrugged his shoulders. 'Uneducated sorts haven't.'

'Stay back. I know how to use this,' said Awa, brandishing the weapon.

'I know you do. It's why they sent me after you,' said Odo.

'They?'

'Bandits, thieves, desert snakes. They have many names. They're interested in making money. So am I. Defeating all those men with your weapon on your own - impressive.' Odo slowly drew the curved sword from its scabbard.

'And?' said Awa.

'And I don't get impressed so easily,' said Odo. His eyes flickering, he lunged at her with his blade. Awa blocked, he knocked her back then swung at her head. She ducked, heard the weapon strike the ground where she had been standing. He was quick. He swung from the right, she blocked, then kicked him in the stomach. He took a step back, smiled, and pounced once more, this time from the left. Awa parried, twisting around and under her blade, trying to force his curved sword out of his hand. He read the move, softening his grip on the hilt of his weapon, so it spun around in his hand, without breaking loose. They separated.

'Nice move,' said Odo. Once more he attacked and Awa brushed away, spinning past him. She sliced, aiming for his legs, but he pushed himself away, so her blade cut through air. 'Clever. Oh yes - they weren't wrong. You are skilled. More than you know it yourself.'

Awa suddenly felt herself being lifted off her feet. The giant! He had sneaked up behind her. She swiped the weapon at him,

50

but he wasn't within reach. So she swung her body instead, flicking into range with her weapon and aiming at his arm, whereupon he immediately dropped her, as the blade had missed his wrist by a whisker. She was rising when Odo stepped on her blade.

'Men like me survive in a world where dog eats dog,' he told her.

Then the giant hauled her up like a sack of potatoes and carried her away over his shoulder.

9

LOST MY SOUL

ONLOOKERS CRAMMED THE CENTRAL THOROUGHFARE which ran through the Fatih district of Istanbul. Will was amongst them, for Sultan Murad III and his vast entourage were due to pass through there on their way out of Istanbul for a hunting trip in the cooler interior. Citizens and visitors from all over the empire lined the streets, craning their necks in anticipation of seeing the Grand Turk himself in person. Business was healthy for traders, particularly merchants selling plums and cherries.

Will joined Gurkan at the front of the crowd beside a stall where the young Konyan purchased two coconuts They were joined by other cadets from their fort, all of them dressed in the loose trousers and tunic worn by Janissaries. Oddly, wearing a uniform helped: merchants knew you earned a living wage, which made them amenable. Officials acknowledged the cadets politely enough, but their expressions were wary. From what Will could see, the Janissaries aroused a mixed response, ranging from respect to hostility.

'The stallholder says these are the best coconuts in Istanbul,' Gurkan told Will, handing him a scalped fruit, with a small hole at the top of it.

Will placed it to his lips and tilted his head back; the refreshing coconut water went down a treat. 'Very good,' he said, swallowing, then added, 'but not the best. The fellow over at Suleymaniye has nicer coconuts.'

The fruit-seller overheard. 'My friend,' he called out. 'That rascal over at Suleymaniye is mixing sugar with his fruits. Do you really trust him, or me - a man with an honest face?' He smiled disarmingly, making Will burst out laughing.

'Dear sir,' he responded. 'You have the highest quality fruits in Istanbul, to equal those of the fruit-seller of Suleymaniye.'

The man bowed, satisfied, before turning to his next customer.

Will still had trouble absorbing how much his life had changed in the past three months. He had literally been at death's door - and now look at him - living happily in the world's greatest city. It was a sign: God was preparing to send him home to London! The smile then died on his lips as he reminded himself that if his world had changed so fast for the better, it could also swing back just as quickly.

The crowd stirred. The royal entourage was approaching. It was then Will noticed a strange-looking fellow, standing a little back from the crowd. He was watching the people, not the procession. How peculiar. The man was dressed in fine court robes, dark blue and grey in colour, with streaks of orange, red and yellow. Even his turban was colourfully decorated. The man himself was of medium height, with a long face, wide forehead, a narrow beard and moustache. But it was his eyes which were the most striking, for in them Will discerned mischief. In fact, the last time Will had seen eyes like that was in the seven-year-old nephew of Hakim Abdullah in Marrakesh. The boy caused his parents no end of grief with the pranks he played on people of all ages.

Sensing Will's scrutiny, the man looked up and caught his gaze before Will turned away, embarrassed.

'They're still far away,' Gurkan was saying.

Will took another swig of his coconut water - so refreshing in the late-summer heat – noticing that the mischievous-looking man had disappeared.

'Tell me again, where is this place you call England?' Gurkan wanted to know.

Will shrugged. Any description of his homeland always seemed to end with the Turks lumping England as a province of France. None of the cadets knew anything about England, particularly its Queen. By contrast, the names of the Hapsburgs, such as Charles I and Phillip II rolled off people's tongues in Istanbul. As did the names of al-Mansur, ruler of Morocco, and Shah Abas I of Persia. Cadets had even heard of the recently deceased Russian Tsar, Ivan the Terrible. Yet the name Elizabeth . . . well, you would be hard-pressed to find anyone who was aware of the Queen of England.

'It's to the north of France, across the sea,' said Will.

Gurkan nodded. 'I once saw a map of the world, a copy of the one drawn by al-Idrisi. I don't recall seeing England on it. But my friend, I hear there is a newer map in the Topkapi Palace, owned by the Sultan. Maybe on this map we will find your homeland.'

Will smiled. 'I can assure you it's there.'

Over the past two months Will had come to realise that the English were rather insignificant when it came to the powers living around the Mediterranean. He had met very few Englishmen whilst abroad and none so far in Istanbul. Yet he had encountered legions of Venetian, French and even Spanish merchants scouring the Ottoman capital for goods, mixing with local buyers. Earlier in the week, he had passed the Venetian Embassy, outside of which there was a trade fair. Even

Commander Mehmet Konjic had turned out to be a Bosnian from the Caucasus.

Excitement rippled through the crowd, and Will caught sight of the massive entourage of the Sultan. It went back as far as the eye could see. Cavalrymen wearing red robes with golden sashes rode decorative horses; there were at least a hundred of them. They were followed by foot soldiers, carrying ceremonial poles with the colours of the Sultan fluttering on flags. Behind them were German-manufactured horse-drawn carriages. Though the Hapsburgs were in an ongoing war with the Ottomans, this did not seem to stop commercially-savvy merchants from trading the most advanced modes of transportation made in Germany. The carriages were decked out in gold and brass, adorned with silken sashes, each steered by a driver sitting atop a gloriously-padded velvet cushion. The first few carriages contained lesser royals, their faces sober as they passed.

'It is Sultana Safiye, the consort of the Sultan,' said someone standing close to Will. The Sultana waved as she passed by, and the crowds responded by cheering her. She was sitting alone in her carriage.

'Where is she from?' asked Will, leaning on Gurkan.

'She is Albanian,' said Gurkan.

The next carriage was even more ornately constructed, with gold trimmings and embossed wheels. In it sat Sultan Murad III, also alone. His bearded face solemnly stared at the crowds. In fact, the Sultan appeared bored. Will imagined that travelling alone in such a mighty carriage with no one to converse with, would not be very entertaining. The crowds didn't seem to care that the Sultan was not giving them the time of day and roared their approval.

'My God, it's him, the Sultan,' said Gurkan, looking stunned. The young Janissary started jogging to keep pace with the carriage, as did others.

'Sultan Murad. May you live forever!' someone cried out, followed by others repeating the slogan.

Will watched his friend get caught up in the chants, as the crowds cheered and ran alongside the royal transport. Will was tempted to join him, but seeing the Sultan in the flesh didn't have the same appeal for him.

'His brothers didn't live long,' said a voice beside Will, making him jump. He turned to see the man in the court robes and colourful turban standing right behind him.

'I'm sorry, do I know you?' enquired Will.

'The name is Huja.'

'I am Will Ryde.'

'Ah, so you're English. Haven't seen an English since Harborne,' said Huja, rubbing his chin with his fist so the hairs of his beard poked in different directions.

'You said something about the Sultan's brothers?' Will reminded him.

Huja turned to stare after the disappearing carriage of Sultan Murad III. 'That one,' he said, 'strangled all five of his brothers when he ascended the throne.'

Will stared at Huja in shock.

'And his son will do the same,' said Huja. His hands clasped behind his back, he began to walk away from Will.

'Is that why he looks so indifferent?' Will wanted to know.

Huja stopped, turning around to look at him. 'All men are afflicted with some burden or the other,' he said, 'and one can be fooled into thinking a fellow is uncaring when all he is, is heart-broken.'

'Wait, who are you, Huja?'

'Men such as I, have no ambitions. All my actions must be for the sake of the Creator,' said Huja, setting off again. 'I am often told that the Sultan's greatest treasure is a wise adviser.'

'Are you his adviser?' Will asked, following him.

'The Sultan is the most powerful man in the world. His supremacy is based on winning wars, yet all the people want is peace. Whether he is adept at this . . . well, that is quite another matter.'

The fellow possessed an acuity of thinking which left Will completely confused.

'I lost it,' said Huja.

This fellow didn't make sense and kept shifting the conversation from topic to topic. Will didn't want to appear rude, but he had to know. 'What did you lose?'

'Something very important.' Huja got down on his hands and knees, fine robes dragging on the ground, and began to scramble about on all fours.

The fellow was surely crazy. Will meandered over, wary of being associated with a public fool.

Huja stared up at him. 'Will you help me find it?'

Will glanced around. No one else seemed to be paying much attention so Will also got down on his hands and knees and pretended to help Huja with his search, more out of pity than anything else. After a few minutes of going around in circles, he asked: 'Where did you lose it?'

'In the Topkapi Palace,' said Huja.

Will jumped up. 'Topkapi! But that's on the other side of town. Why are you looking here?'

Huja picked himself up off the ground, dusting his robes. 'Because the light is better here,' he said, pointing at the ground.

Will shook his head. 'The light . . .'

'Never mind,' said Huja, shooing Will away. 'It will turn up.' The strange fellow then did a little skip and walked away.

Will called after him: 'Wait! What did you lose in the Topkapi Palace?'

Huja turned back to look at Will with sorrowful eyes. 'Why, my soul, of course.'

10

MORE THAN A MATCH

DUST ROSE FROM THE MOVEMENTS of the gladiators practising their newly acquired killing skills. Before the sand particles settled, they thrust blunt weapons at one another in mock fight sequences. Awa was confident with her use of weaponry; other women at Camp Dido were not. She watched as many of the dark and brown-skinned combatants struggled with lances or swords. Taking a cupful of water in her hand, she poured it over her head, letting it stream down her face and neck. The weather in the north was cooler than in Songhai territory, but it was still brutally hot. She then drank, quenching her thirst, before collecting her wooden sword and returning to the practice area, where she set about performing the movements they had told her to drill. Thrust forwards, step back, swing right, leap into the air, crouch, turn full circle, pitch left, jump up, bring the sword down. Repeat.

Weeks had gone past, some of the worst of her life. It felt as if she was back in the slave wagon, penned in from all sides. She never felt safe. Yet somehow, she was still alive: the Creator had chosen to keep her in this world.

Each day started at dawn. The women were told to wash, before preparing themselves for early morning drills. Prayers were discouraged, leaving Awa and many others unsatisfied.

She took to waking up well before sunrise, meditating and praying before returning to sleep. Being in an environment where practising her faith was discouraged only made her more determined to cling to what she knew. So she knelt at the end of her bed every morning, praying to God for mercy and the well-being of her father.

After their capture in the Tassili mountain range, Awa and Wassa had been tied atop a single camel by Odo and the giant Ja, eventually arriving at a training camp in a nondescript dusty town. Odo said he would be back in a few weeks, when he would take them north where Awa would entertain paying onlookers with her martial prowess. Camp Dido, she was told, was named after a great Queen of the destroyed city of Carthage, and contained only women. They were fenced in by a wall made of stone and metal spikes.

It was abhorrent to ask any human being to maim and kill another for the pleasure and profit of the public. The scholars of Timbuktu had described the Romans' love of gladiatorial games, the purpose of which was to keep the populace distracted by the trivial. And now Awa herself had been drawn into the same kind of circus.

She twirled the hilt of the sword in her hand. The skin on her fingers was calloused from gripping a series of sword-hilts, lances and spears over the past few weeks. Mosquito bites followed by gladiatorial training had put paid to any notions of refinement she may have once possessed. Camp Dido drilled her hard, in running, lifting, pulling and weapon skills. They knew what it would take to survive in the arena.

The instructor called them over. He was a Spanish soldier of fortune named Tome, who had made his own mark in the gladiatorial ring and was now retained to train the women at the camp. He wasn't particularly tall, but his squat muscular frame looked powerful.

'Form a large circle, sit on the ground,' ordered Tome. The women complied.

'When you enter the arena, you will face an opponent in a fight to the death. To the *death*. Sometimes, those in charge like to make things harder. They'll pit you against two, maybe three or even four opponents at a time. Remember, the crowd want to be entertained, and this is your sole purpose in life now. Bring joy to the crowd and you survive another day.'

Awa smiled at Wassa. Odo had given firm instructions to keep them apart. They were allotted separate huts to sleep in and were only able to have brief conversations over meals. Awa knew that isolation was making her selfish. She had heard reports of what happened to those unfortunate women who failed to reach the standards required in the camp - and the stories were warning enough to make her concentrate on the task at hand. Her life depended on it, and the promise she had made to herself to one day return to the sleepy corridors of her father's university.

'You.' Tome jerked a thumb at Awa. 'Up here.'

She rose and joined him immediately, for Tome was quick to anger. She had seen him strike out at others when they dragged their feet or showed insufficient enthusiasm for the task at hand. He picked out two other women and told them to line up against Awa.

'Attack her together,' Tome ordered.

The women exchanged glances.

'Do it!' he snapped.

They lunged with their wooden swords. Awa leaped back and out of range, before circling right, creating space. She took a step forward and they both retreated. Awa skipped and lunged at one woman, before swerving and knocking the sword out of the hand of the other. She then aimed a blow at the legs of the first, pulling up at the last minute with her wooden sword, so as not to actually complete the strike.

'Good,' said Tome. 'She sensed hesitation in these two and acted on it. Awa, stay. You two, sit.' He pointed at three others and ordered them up. 'Repeat.'

Taking a deep breath, Awa faced her new opponents. They circled her with caution. One at the front, one behind and the other between. Awa stayed on her toes, ready to move when the first attack came. She would not strike first, for fear of exposing herself to a counter-attack. Her father said martial skills came naturally to her, as poetry to him. Was it really true? She wanted to be a mathematician and poet like him, not a fighter, but God had given her these abilities and she was grateful they kept her alive, even if the end was inevitable and she would die in the gladiatorial arena.

The first woman to lose patience rushed headlong, quicker than Awa anticipated. Awa twisted away from the sword strike, and as the woman went past her, she tapped the back of her opponent's neck with the edge of her wooden sword. The woman stepped out of the fight. Awa used her momentum to jump towards one of the other women, landing on the ground and hitting her on the back of her ankles, causing her to tumble, before Awa placed the tip of her blade on her neck. She too was out. Awa immediately snapped back, sensing the third woman was about to tag her with a weapon. Sure enough, the woman raised her weapon high and brought it down. Awa blocked. The woman swung from the right. Awa dipped under the blade and as the woman's momentum took her to the left, Awa went down on one knee and drove her wooden sword against the side of the woman's stomach. A real blade would have opened a fatal wound. The woman dropped her weapon in submission.

Awa breathed a sigh of relief, but then heard footsteps behind and instinctively rolled away from the attack as Tome came at her with a wooden sword, thrusting into the empty air behind her.

The Spanish instructor had not fought with any of them since she had been at Camp Dido. He had merely ordered them to drill with one another, shown them movements and gone through various routines. All the women sat up. Tome twisted his sword around.

'You may also fight with men, maybe more than one. You will need to be prepared.'

Sweat dripped from her brow as Awa skipped in a semicircle, reading the Spaniard's footwork. She waited, letting him strike. No reason for her to go on the attack against a stronger, more skilled opponent.

'Good,' Tome encouraged. 'You don't rush.'

He hoisted his weapon and brought it down. She jumped out of the way. He followed up, but this time she couldn't move fast enough and had to fend off the blow with her sword, feeling the pain shoot up her arm. She grimaced, staggering away as he launched another powerful strike. This time she planted her feet firmly and blocked, holding the weapon with both her hands. He kicked out at her, the sole of his boot striking her in the stomach. Awa fell back, rolled away as quickly as possible, twisting then leaping back onto her feet.

'Excellent,' said Tome. 'She controlled her fall, allowing herself momentum to rise.' The instructor backed away. 'Now Awa, you attack.'

Awa was grateful he had not persisted; she was not sure she would have been able to fend off another attack of such brute force. She took pigeon steps towards him, reading his movement, waiting till he was slightly off-balance - then she pounced, aiming for his chest. He pushed her weapon away with his own, before shoulder-barging her to the ground and placing the tip of his sword against her neck.

'Very good,' Tome praised her again. 'She waited till I was off-balance before attacking, but she did not compensate for my larger size and strength. If your opponent is stronger than you, do not fight close to them. You will die.'

Rising, Awa dusted herself off. The Spaniard nodded at her. Over the weeks she had spent with him, she'd come to recognise it was his way of saying well done.

'Take a break, get some water,' he said.

Awa trudged back over to the pail of water. She poured some over her head, before drinking. Wassa joined her.

'Well done, Awa. God has given you a gift.'

'I wasn't good enough to beat Tome,' Awa grunted.

'Don't be hard on yourself. I actually thought you might win. You beat five opponents! Why can't I believe you will defeat the Spaniard?'

'Even if I could, I wouldn't,' Awa told her.

'Why not?'

'How would he react? Most likely starve me and lock me in that metal box they use for insubordination. No, thank you. I've had enough of being confined in small spaces. I'm going to keep my head down and stay out of trouble,' said Awa. 'Returning home to Timbuktu is all I care about.'

Her friend placed a hand on her shoulder. 'You will, God willing.'

11

GRAND BAZAAR

THE GRAND BAZAAR OF ISTANBUL was visible on the horizon as Will passed through the city, leaving the Janissary fort. On Thursday after training finished, they were permitted to go into town, initially heading off to Shiraz the coffee-seller, before an evening meal of *borek* - filled pastries - and meat. Merchants did not work on Friday morning before the midday prayer, so trading on Thursday nights was extended.

The unforgiving training regime left Will exhausted most evenings, but his mental and physical abilities were vastly improved. He could now duel with two opponents simultaneously. Captain Kadri had complimented him on his skills. Only the talented Gurkan, who came from the province made famous by the Sufi poet Rumi, was his better within the cadet force. Will had met some gifted but arrogant individuals; fortunately, and would be the first to win promotion.

'The port is busy,' said Gurkan, pointing to the sea where there was a higher than usual number of vessels.

'Venetian delegation,' said one of the other Janissaries.

'Those Venetians are the best traders in the world,' Gurkan replied.

'How do you mean?' asked Will.

'They are Christians, yet defy the orders of their own Pope and trade with the Turks and the Moroccans.'

'The Pope doesn't want them to trade with Muslims?' Will enquired.

'Correct,' said Gurkan.

'Why ever not?'

'Ask the Pope.'

The longer he spent in Istanbul, the more confused Will became as to which empires and peoples were allied with whom. The Catholics of Europe were against the Protestants, primarily the English and the Lutherans of Germany. Yet the Catholics, or some of them at least like the Venetians, were comfortable trading with the Muslims. Equally the Turks, Moroccans and Safavids of Persia were at each other's throats. Will had seen embassies in Istanbul for the French, Spanish, Venetians. There had even been talk of an English merchant by the name of Harborne, who had tried but failed to establish an embassy in the past. The man Huja had mentioned him, Will recalled.

The path they followed wound down to the port, which joined the main thoroughfare of Fatih. The crowd swelled at this juncture, bodies from all nations clustered close as Will directed himself towards Shiraz, located outside the Grand Bazaar.

'Wait, I need to buy a new belt,' said Gurkan, stopping beside a stall. Will and the others hovered close, waiting for him.

A nearby brouhaha drew Will's attention. Passers-by leaped off the road to safety, as a group of Janissaries displaying the insignia of the Topkapi Palace streamed into the main thoroughfare. The soldiers were searching for someone, stopping random citizens. Gurkan joined Will.

'Come on, we should help,' said Gurkan, as he and a few of the other cadets headed towards the Janissaries. Will wasn't too sure about this, as the other soldiers seemed mightily annoyed and would not want some junior cadets getting in their way, so he stayed where he was. The crowd swelled in his direction and Will had to retreat into an alley.

Then someone dashed through the alley behind him. As he peered into the gloom, he saw three figures wearing dark trousers and close-fitting tops. Their faces were masked, only their eyes and foreheads showing. The Janissaries were still stopping and searching people. Were these the ones they were searching for?

'Over here!' shouted Will, but his voice was drowned out. He swung his gaze back towards the alley. Were they thieves? If so, they were getting away. There was only one thing for it. Will bolted down the lane after the men. The cobbled pathway was narrow and labyrinthine. He ducked to avoid lines of laundry drying overhead. A cat darted out of his way and hissed. He ran to the corner, turned - could just about make out the thieves up ahead. The one in the middle was carrying a long staff. Will sped up. Just then, a group of children skipped out in front of him. Will skidded, throwing himself against the wall on the right, before straightening and continuing to give chase. He would have a nasty bruise on his shoulder, but never mind that.

The three thieves paused at an intersection, where one finally caught sight of Will. He pointed him out, but the other two shrugged carelessly, before setting off to the left. As Will approached the intersection, one of the men was waiting for him. His assailant threw a knife. Will instinctively dived to the ground, the blade narrowly missing him, flying over his head. The man set off and Will retrieved the knife, fastened it to his belt - and gave chase.

After taking the next bend, he lost sight of them. Then a sound overhead drew his attention. The thieves had scaled the scaffolding of a building which was being painted: they were on the roof.

'Well, that's just wonderful,' mumbled Will.

He grasped the frame and swung himself up, ensuring he wasn't an easy target for a knife attack. At the second floor, he jumped onto the roof, only to see the thieves fleeing in the distance. His blood was up: he chased them hard, leaping from one rooftop to the next. The rooftops were mostly flat; some had junk lying around, including buckets with holes, masonry nails, pots, even a ship's anchor and chain, which created dangerous obstacles. The poor evening light didn't help.

Will scanned down to the left - to see members of the public pointing up at him accusingly. *Hey, I'm not the thief!* He put his head down and ran. The thieves were now racing across the rooftop of the Grand Bazaar, a rickety structure, when the one who had thrown the knife at Will tripped and went down, clutching his ankle. The other two halted, studying Will, before hauling up their colleague. They now moved at a slower pace and soon Will was right behind them.

'Stop!' he bawled. 'Give it back!'

'This is not your business, boy,' said the masked man holding the staff. As Will came closer he could see the man had very distinctive green eyes. The staff was wrapped in a cloth, fastened with three pieces of rope.

'You've stolen that staff,' said Will.

'No - we've *retrieved* what was stolen.'

The comment made Will pause. Sensing his advantage, one of the thieves whipped out a sword and went for him. Will dived to his left and almost went right over the edge of the tin roof, had he not grabbed hold of a timber strut.

The green-eyed thief helped his wounded comrade up. The swordsman swung his blade at Will, but he wasn't trying to strike him, Will saw, only fend him off so they had time to escape. Will charged forwards, tackling the thief. They clattered against the roof, but the thief was able to use his legs to push Will up and off him. Will flipped over and went off the edge of the roof, gripping it with his fingers at the last moment. The crowd below gasped. He peered down, hanging on for dear life: he could see Gurkan and the others amongst the crowd, as well as the Janissaries from the Topkapi. The swordsman reared above Will, weapon in hand. He put the blade against Will's neck.

'*Stay away, if you know what's good for you,*' he warned, then he turned and ran.

Will was now dangling by one hand, his lower body swinging from side to side. He heaved his other arm up and gripped the railing under the roof, before nimbly hoisting himself up and back onto the roof. His training had saved his life. The crowd below cheered.

The thieves were escaping in the direction of the Bosporus. They must have a getaway planned. The sun was setting in the background, the thieves silhouetted against it. Will charged on, gaining ground, as he observed the green-eyed thief with the staff vault off the side of the roof. What! The injured thief was standing on the edge, waiting to jump, as the swordsman leaped before him. They were going to escape. The injured thief hesitated. Will still had the knife: he drew it, aimed and threw.

The blade hit the man in the back of his right leg, causing him to collapse on one knee. He yanked the knife out and held it up threateningly as Will approached. But he was now in too much pain to fight, and Will kicked it out of his hand before punching him in the face, knocking him flat. Will then swung his gaze out towards the Bosporus, where the two escaping thieves had boarded a cargo ship, the crew oblivious to the presence of their new passengers. Whatever they had taken from the Topkapi Palace was slipping away from him – disappearing in plain sight.

12

KILLING FOR ENTERTAINMENT

I N THE WOODEN SHELTER BESIDE the arena, some twenty or so women sat on the bench, some rocking back and forth, others biting filthy nails as they awaited their turn to go through the doorway of death. Only Wassa sat calmly, her eyes closed. Awa followed suit, praying for God's protection.

Two women had already been paired and gone out to fight: only one had returned. The survivor sat, head in hands. Why were they subjecting women to this? Awa asked herself. The holy book made it clear that violence was only permitted in order to defend one's land: a believer is *never* an aggressor. Was God going to forgive her for what she was about to do? But if she refused to fight, what then?

Roars of approval erupted from the crowd outside. The amphitheatre held a few hundred spectators, but from the noise it sounded more like a thousand. Awa shuddered.

The door at the back of the cabin opened and two familiar figures entered - Odo and the giant Ja. They stopped beside Tome, and Odo spoke to him. The Spaniard acted surprised by what he said. Awa caught Ja staring at her. He smiled and his big teeth shone in the semi-darkness of their surroundings. Awa turned away, closing her eyes, reminding herself to breathe. Footsteps came down the line of women. *Don't stop beside me. Don't . . .*

'Awa.'

She opened her eyes to see Odo's crooked face. His thumbs were hooked into his belt, his blades and knives on display.

'Everyone's looking for gold. So, I'll be the one collecting the silver,' said Odo grinning at her. 'You're up next.'

Her throat went dry and she felt her heart quicken. Who was she going to be paired with? *Please let it not be Wassa.*

'The betting is going well, particularly when we announced you're fighting a man,' Odo said smugly.

'What?' whispered Awa. The women shuffled uncomfortably. They were making her fight a man!

'Oh, don't worry. You're more than capable. You took on all those men in the bandit camp and I've heard stories of how you slew ten Moroccan soldiers at the Battle of Tondibi. Fighting one man in an arena should be a piece of cake. The gamblers don't know this, of course, and they've put down big odds against you. Win this, Awa, and you'll make us a lot of money.'

Awa clenched her fists. Part of her wanted to lose to spite him.

'Remember,' he went on, 'this is a fight to the death. Don't let me down.' He gave her a chilling look, then turned and was gone, along with Ja, who stooped to go through the doorway.

Sweat dripped from Awa's brow. The woman sitting beside her said gently, 'I will pray for you, my sister.'

'Thank you,' said Awa, feeling stronger for those words.

There was a deafening uproar from the arena - the previous encounter had ended with the death of one participant. Awa heard the sound of a body being dragged across the earth. It was now her time.

When Tome approached and gestured to her, she rose and walked to the door. Through the gaps in the wooden slats, she could see the amphitheatre - circular, with five rows running

71

around it. Every space was taken up with bodies, jostling and harrying one another.

'Choose,' Tome commanded, motioning to an assortment of weapons hanging up against a wall, guarded by two men.

'Curved sword.'

Tome showed his approval. One of the men got up and handed the weapon over to her, along with a shield. She spun the hilt in her hand. It was light and flexible, the way she liked it.

'Remember, don't let him get close,' said Tome.

Awa nodded, recalling the manner in which the Spaniard had thrown her off on more than one occasion when they sparred. The door was unbolted and a moustached man poked his head around the corner.

'Ready?' he asked.

'Yes,' Tome told him. The door opened and Awa stepped through, hearing it lock behind her. Her opponent was a man of medium build, tight and muscular, brandishing a spear and long shield. He was much darker in complexion than her, so was probably from somewhere in the interior. Their eyes met and she noted how forlorn he looked.

'You will march to the centre and salute your lords,' cried a voice from behind them.

Awa did as instructed, taking ten steps to the middle of the arena and turning towards the right, where the patrons of this event sat with their bodyguards, their women and their colourful entourage. Awa and her opponent held up their weapons and saluted them. When the announcer clapped his hands together, her opponent took that as the start and immediately attacked her with the long spear, coming close to connecting. She jogged away.

Awa stared into the man's eyes, assessing him. She could tell he was not a trained killer. She twirled her weapon, acquiring a

72

feel for the hilt. He jabbed at her, the spear tip glancing to her right. She easily avoided it. Once more he plunged the weapon at her, but she dodged it.

'I'm sorry, my sister,' he whispered.

Awa gulped. He felt just as bad as she did. Two human beings, neither wanting to hurt the other, but forced into combat for the entertainment of these brutes. It made no sense. Jeers erupted at the lack of action. Neither fighter had struck a blow.

Then her opponent sprang at Awa. She deflected his spear upwards, then slashed right with her weapon, blocked by his shield. The crowd bellowed. This was what they wanted. Entertainment. Awa leaped slightly to the right, before twisting back and hammering her sword against his shield. The blow took him by surprise and he staggered. As he tried to poke her with his spear, she swept downwards with her blade; her weapon caught his exposed ankle, slicing the flesh. The crowd thundered in delight. He hobbled back, relying on his shield for support. Awa drove her weapon at him again. He blocked it with his shield, but as he raised his spear to retaliate, she slashed upwards and knocked the flint off the wood. The spear was useless. In a desperate bid to save himself, he charged at her with his shield, but his ankle was badly wounded and instead he fell flat on his face, on top of his shield. He lay there, his back to her, arms sprawled across the shield.

'Kill! Kill! Kill!' the crowd shrieked. Awa raised her weapon - just as the man rolled onto his back, his face exposed to her. She heard him praying and froze.

'Kill!' the crowd urged her on.

This man was like her, she thought, a breathing human being, reluctantly thrust into a fight neither of them wanted. She wouldn't do it.

Awa stepped away.

The crowd booed. Her opponent breathed a huge sigh of relief – but it was his final breath, for as he rose up, an arrow went straight through his chest and he crashed back onto his shield. Awa twisted round and saw that it was the giant, Ja, who had fired it. The next arrow was aimed at her. Ja looked at Odo, and Odo looked to the chief patron. After some thought, the crowd totally silent, the man pointed upwards with his thumb, to the noisy delight of the onlookers. Ja lowered the bow.

The door to the cabin opened and Awa saw Tome beckoning her in. She jogged across, as the crowd continued to cheer her victory. Awa handed the weapons back and was about to sink onto the bench with the other women when Tome grabbed her by the elbow and led her past a concerned-looking Wassa and out through the back door, slamming it behind him.

Awa looked around. They were in a small enclosed area, with stakes in the ground, penning them in. She turned to question the Spaniard, but his slap brought her to her knees.

'Stupid!' shouted Tome. 'It's a fight to the death. If you don't kill the opponent, the bets are scratched. Odo is going to be furious.' He spat on the ground beside her, just as a gate opened and Odo and Ja marched in.

'You just lost me a lot of money, girl,' said Odo, kicking her in the chest. Awa felt dizzy, the wind knocked out of her a second time. He raised his boot to stamp on her, but clearly thought better of it. 'You are skilled. You will make me money. But try anything like that again and I will personally cut off your head.'

Ja hauled her back on her feet and marched her out of the closed pen into a large courtyard. As they strode past some tethered goats, she could see where he was heading and tears rolled down her face.

13

FEED THE TURBAN

MILITARY BOOTS CLICKED AGAINST STONE as Will was led down a corridor in the Rumelihisarı fort, located on the shores of the Bosporus. The imposing structure, originally built to control traffic along the river, now also contained the offices of Commander Mehmed Konjic. The Grand Vizier insisted on the Rüzgar, the new covert Janissary force, being housed at a distance from the Topkapi Palace and its toxic atmosphere.

Beside Will strode Captain Kadri, whose silence since they took the short horse ride to the fort had struck a sombre note. Was Will in trouble? The previous night after he'd captured that thief, he had been applauded by onlookers around the Grand Bazaar. The Topkapi Janissaries, after initially grilling him, decided not to throw him in prison for questioning. Later in the evening when word reached Kadri, the Captain told him that by not imprisoning him, the Topkapi Janissaries were saying thank you. Yet this morning the Captain's expression was severe. Will didn't want to go back to the life of a galley slave, but knew it was in the power of these men to dictate such a future.

They emerged into an open space, beside which was a courtyard. Kadri asked him to take a seat then disappeared around a corner.

Will waited, listening to seagulls squawking overhead, perched on top of the walls of the fortress. The courtyard had a small fountain with water dripping into a basin below. Will sat with his fingers clasped reading a piece of Arabic calligraphy set into the wall: the words were from the last *Sura* of the Qur'an, in which mankind asks God for protection from the whisperer of evil. He was grateful to Hakim Abdullah for insisting he learn written Arabic as well as spoken, for the quartermaster often received detailed handwritten instructions, consisting of comments and measurements.

'Will Ryde,' said a familiar voice.

Will turned in his seat to see the turbaned Huja. For a moment, he failed to recognise him, for the man was dressed like a beggar. His clothes were ripped and stained, his sandals partly broken, his robe patched. Was this really the same man he had seen at the procession when Sultan Murad III had passed by? 'Master Huja?' he said uncertainly.

'I am the most unceremonial of the ceremonious, so do not stand for me,' Huja said, taking a seat beside Will on the stone bench.

'Sir,' said Will. 'I was left quite mystified by what you told me the other day on the road, about losing your soul.'

Huja gave Will an odd stare. 'I said that?'

'Yes.'

'Oh, I was smarting over some trifling matter. Best you ignore such frivolous talk,' Huja said, offering a languid wave of the hand.

It hadn't sounded trivial when Huja mentioned it previously, but Will decided not to press the matter. 'What happened to your clothes?' he enquired.

Huja held out his arms, the holes in his sleeves on display. 'Clothes are a fine thing, Will Ryde. They make us appear something we are not.'

'How do you mean, Master Huja?'

Huja tucked his legs up on the seat, sitting cross-legged in his beggar robes. 'I was once invited to a great banquet in a palace where all were welcome. Upon entering the magnificent hall, the ruler's chamberlain took one look at my ragged cloak and broken sandals and placed me at the furthest table, away from any important persons.

'Realising it would be hours before I received any food, I went home, dressed myself in a splendid cloak and turban, glittering with jewels, and returned to the feast. Upon seeing me, the heralds sounded the drums and I was welcomed as a visitor of high standing. Why, the very same chamberlain came out of the palace himself, and showered me with platitudes. He then proceeded to sit me in a position very close to the ruler himself.

'Waiters hastened to bring a delectable dish of food and placed it in front of me. Instantly I began to rub handfuls of the food into my cloak and turban. When the ruler asked what I was doing, I replied, "It is the cloak and turban which secured me the food. Irrefutably, they have earned their serving".'

Mouth open, Will was about to ask a question, when Huja announced that he was most urgently needed somewhere by someone important, yet he had no idea where the place was nor who that person might be. Before he disappeared from view, Huja spun around and said: 'Remember, Will Ryde, the human soul is like a torn garment, attached to the divine by a single thread, yet yearning for wholeness.'

And then he was gone.

Will was still feeling baffled when he noticed Captain Kadri approach, beckoning him over. Will rose and Kadri guided them down a series of corridors before halting outside a room with an oak door. He knocked.

'Come in.'

They entered. Lighting was poor in this western-facing room. Strands of sunlight crept through, spreading narrow spindly rays across the office. Mehmed Konjic sat on a chair behind a desk; two empty chairs with cabriole legs were set before him and a divan against the wall on the right.

'Will Ryde,' said Konjic. 'Please, sit.'

Kadri drew up the chair next to Will, opposite the Commander.

'I understand that some of the Janissaries from the Topkapi were rough in how they dealt with you,' said Konjic.

'I've had worse, sir,' Will replied carefully.

'I would like to thank you for apprehending one of the thieves. The man has been rigorously interrogated throughout the night and finally broke this morning. Though I do not approve of the methods used by my peers, they have borne fruit.'

'Who is he?' asked Will.

Konjic puffed out his cheeks, placing his palms down flat on his desk. 'Unfortunately, he is a Janissary.'

'What!' Will sat bolt upright in his chair.

'As were the other two who escaped,' Konjic said heavily.

Will looked over at Kadri. The Captain nodded, giving him permission to speak.

'Why? Who were they working for?' Will asked.

Konjic smiled. 'I see the inquirer in you. Good. We do not know at this time, but thanks to your brave work, we have a trail to follow.'

Will felt a great sense of relief. He wasn't in trouble – was not about to be sent back to the galleys.

'Commander Konjic,' he said, 'when I chased them, it was clear that the thieves were in possession of some type of staff. I'm assuming this is what was stolen. May I ask what it was?'

Konjic drew a long breath, before coming to a decision. 'Since you have been instrumental in capturing one of the thieves, it would pain me not to tell you.'

Will waited. He heard footsteps outside the door, but these continued on down the corridor. Konjic glanced at Kadri, who rose and went to the door, swinging it open and squinting up and down before closing it and taking his seat once more.

Konjic leaned forward, arms on the table, and said in a low but carrying voice: 'The Staff of Moses has been stolen from the Topkapi Palace.'

Will gulped. He knew of the religious artefacts within the Topkapi Palace. These had been brought to Istanbul from Cairo when Sultan Selim I defeated the Mamluks. Amongst the treasures were the Pot of Abraham, the Turban of Joseph, the Sword of David, the Scrolls of John the Baptist, the Banner of Muhammad.

'Understandably, the Grand Vizier is furious with this lapse in security and the Sultan will be informed later this morning, when a rider reaches him at his summer palace. His anger will know no bounds.' The Commander then revealed: 'The Grand Vizier has asked me to use my new Rüzgar unit to retrieve the Staff.'

Will recalled Huja's story about Sultan Murad III murdering his brothers when he ascended the throne. A man such as this should not be angered. Will felt sorry for the messenger riding to tell him the news. The Grand Vizier ran the Sultan's government and though Will had never seen him, he imagined an austere-looking fellow, accustomed to getting his own way. Yet there was something bothering Will.

'Begging your pardon, Commander,' he said, 'but aren't there more experienced Janissaries who can perform this duty?'

'That is a good question, Will Ryde. Yes, there are - but at this moment they cannot be trusted. Let us not forget, the thief was a Janissary and when confessing, he implicated others. The net has been cast wide. We have traitors in the Topkapi Palace and until we know who they are, this investigation will be conducted by an *outside* agency.'

The Ottoman court was a confusing place. Favours were given and received with an unending eye on jockeying for political favour. Losing favour, Will had heard, usually resulted in death or banishment. When the stakes were set so high, it was little wonder the worst traits of human behaviour bubbled to the surface. He himself had absolutely no intention of getting caught in these machinations.

'If you came across the other two thieves, would you recognise them?' asked Konjic.

Their faces had been well covered, but one did have green eyes. The chance of Will recognising them was remote, but if he said no, his usefulness to Mehmed Konjic was diminished, so he lied.

'I would.'

'I was hoping you'd say that, Will, because we're sending a team after them and we need someone who can identify the thieves. Someone we can trust.'

'I would be honoured to help,' said Will. Konjic had used the word 'trust', which made Will feel uncomfortable, for sooner or later he was going to sneak away, returning to London.

'Good,' said Konjic. 'I will lead the unit myself. It will be composed of some experienced Janissaries, who are part of the new Rüzgar force. Captain Kadri will remain in Istanbul, continuing to train the other cadets. I will train you as and when we have the opportunity - but I suspect most of your training will come about when you are in the field.'

The Commander pushed his chair away and stood. The meeting was finished. Will couldn't believe it: the chance to abscond might actually present itself earlier than later. Who knew what terrain they would be going into?

'Commander?' said Will.

'Yes?'

'I know the others in the team will be more experienced, and I still have a lot to learn. I think it will help me, if we could take one more cadet. At least I will have someone to train with.'

Kadri tilted his head to one side, considering the idea. 'Who were you thinking of?'

'Gurkan,' Will said. 'He is an exceptional swordsman and I've seen him defeat some of the full-time soldiers.'

Konjic rubbed his chin. 'I do concede that Gurkan is talented and will be good company for you both. Captain Kadri, what do you say?'

'He is the best sword amongst the cadets, and he is not tainted by court politics. I see merit in Ryde's proposal.'

'I like your attitude, Will. How you approach life in many ways determines how life approaches you. It is done, Gurkan will join us,' Konjic declared.

It was only then, after committing himself and Gurkan to the hunt, that it occurred to Will that he had no idea of their destination!

'Sorry,' he said, smiling apologetically. 'Where are we going?'

Konjic placed a hand on Will's shoulder. 'Alexandria, lad. The Land of the Pharaohs. The thief confirmed our suspicion that the theft of the Staff was most likely organised and financed by sympathisers to the defeated Mamluk empire.'

Egypt! The Bible recounted stories of the Israelites' struggle with the Pharaoh and how God commanded Moses to part the waters of the Red Sea with his staff. The very staff which turned into a giant serpent, swallowing the snakes conjured up by the magicians of the Pharaoh. The same staff Will was now going to seek.

The sea had parted for the Israelites. He needed it to part for him - to take him back to England.

14

GRAND VIZIER

SEAGULLS FLEW OVERHEAD, OCCASIONALLY
DIVING from the skies to swoop into the courtyard
when they spotted a potential meal. Konjic observed the
birds; the simplicity of their existence appealed to him. As a
boy growing up in rural Bosnia, Konjic had desired to leave
his village, make for the populated cities, become a person
of some standing. Now that he was here, in the milieu of the
Ottoman court, village life appealed to him once again, like a
lover calling from over the hill.

The Grand Vizier, Sardar Ferhad Pasha, had kept him
waiting far longer than expected. Konjic knew that with the
recent backlash against the Janissaries following the revolt by
many of his fellows, it was safer not to show his impatience
– if he wanted to keep his head. When the Grand Vizier
finally approached, his kaftan and turban were impeccable,
his posture erect. Like his predecessor, the Grand Vizier was
ethnically Albanian, and he greeted Konjic with a restrained
smile.

'Come, Commander, let us walk, for few conversations
within the Palace remain private.'

They descended into the courtyard and Konjic knew that
dozens of resentful eyes would be observing them, speculating

on what confidences were being exchanged with the Grand Vizier.

'My esteemed predecessor, Koca Sinan Pasha,' began the Grand Vizier, 'was removed from office for not adequately quelling the Janissary revolt. I do not intend for the same fate to befall me. Whilst I continue to admire the martial qualities possessed by your kind, Konjic, I have grown tired of the demands of the Janissary leaders, who seem to spend more time petitioning than performing their duties. It is, as you know, with this in mind that my predecessor started talks with you - a man removed from the politics of the Janissaries, not tainted by their whims and desires - to establish the unit we call the Rüzgar.'

Konjic remembered his surprise when Koca Sinan Pasha had approached him, asking whether he would establish a new covert force outside the ranks of the Janissary corps. One which reported directly to the Grand Vizier, avoiding the normal chain of command. Konjic had feared the backlash from the Janissary leadership when they discovered what he had been asked to do. Yet to his surprise they had left him alone. Perhaps they were certain he was going to fail and it would be better to let him hang himself, for all to witness. After all, without the support of the specialist Janissary units, what hope was there for one Commander, leading a rag-tag ensemble of new recruits, in a specialist unit called 'the wind'? It was laughable.

'You, Konjic, are a man known for his honesty and integrity, a rare set of virtues in these times.'

'Thank you, Grand Vizier.'

'It does not make a man immune to being corrupted, but you more than most are better equipped to swat away the temptations placed under your nose. Is your team assembled?'

'It is,' Konjic replied.

'I have prepared the requisite paperwork for you to travel as officers of the Balkan Trading Company.'

Konjic raised an eyebrow and the Grand Vizier smiled. 'I thought you would appreciate the ethnic reference.'

'I do.'

'You will be furnished with sufficient resources to follow these rogue Janissaries and hunt them down. Bring them back if you can, or remove them from the face of the earth. Either way we want the Staff back at the Topkapi.'

'We will do our best.'

The Grand Vizier stopped, turned to stare at Konjic. 'You will have to do more than that, Commander. If you are caught, we will deny all knowledge of your activities. If your team is enslaved or imprisoned, we will not be sending a rescue party to release you. Do you understand?'

Konjic didn't like this part of the arrangement. The Rüzgar would be operating independently, with no supervision but equally with no back-up or recourse. They were on their own. Was he, he wondered with foreboding, leading his unit to certain failure and death?

'I understand,' he said heavily.

'Very well.' The Grand Vizier removed a set of papers from within the folds of his robes and handed them to Konjic. 'Here are instructions relating to your departure: where to collect the resources you require, and also the names of operatives in countries outside the imperial realm, for I do not know where this expedition will take you. It could be east or west, north or south. Go in the name of God.'

The Grand Vizier made to move away, before stopping once more.

'One more thing, Commander. Return with the Staff, or do not return at all.'

15

CLOSE TO INFINITY

AWA WAS BEING COOKED ALIVE. She estimated nearly a day had gone by since her incarceration inside the tin box in the middle of the open field behind the camp. The box was about one yard wide and long, and less than one-and-a-half yards high. She couldn't lie down in it; she had to sit up at all times. It felt as though the burning-hot metal walls were falling in on her. Every so often, someone struck the box with a hammer or mallet, shaking her awake from a feverish doze. The first time this happened, she had thought they were going to release her, only to shrink back down in despair. Even her tears had dried up.

Anger had powered her through the first day. She swore vengeance on Odo and Ja, imagined committing terrible acts of violence on them before riding away into the sunset and returning to the Songhai nation. After the first day, however, her anger dissipated and desolation took its place. How much longer were they going to keep her here? How much punishment could her body take? She was pretty hardy, but the temperatures soared, the sunlight was overpowering and the dust suffocating. The lack of water and food made her head spin.

The second night approached. She heard the call to prayer. In the distance there were voices, laughing and joking.

She smelled meat being cooked on a grill; someone else was roasting corn, and late in the evening, the fragrance of jasmine seeped in and filled her with yearning. It was the flower her father loved to have around the house. The voices eventually died out and silence filled the tin box. She fell asleep, had a nightmare, then woke in pain from cramp. Her throat was dry, as though fiery sand had been poured down it, and white spots clouded her vision. She squinted, screwed shut her eyes. The spots vanished, then slowly returned. She was spinning. Awa placed her palms down firmly on the ground, yet inside her head, she swung like a monkey from a tree. Panic began to overwhelm her.

When she woke once more, it was from the sun beating down on the roof. She was being baked like a piece of meat on a spit, over a roaring fire. The throbbing pain which had pierced the right side of her head now stretched all over her skull.

Perhaps it was better to die, she thought: at least she would be reunited with her mother in the hereafter and they would wait together for her father to join them. A vision swam into her mind, of her father reading from the *Ihya ulum al-din*, by the eleventh-century Persian scholar, Al-Ghazali. And then he was there . . .

'Awa, my child.' It was her father's voice. He was standing at a distance from her, arms out, a white halo burning bright around his kaftan and turban. 'I miss you,' he said.

Her heart felt as though it was going to burst. 'Father!' she wept. 'Help me!'

He approached, bent down beside her. All was black around them and he was the only light illuminating everything. Taking her chin and tilting it up, so she was able to gaze into his radiant eyes, he said, 'In the depths of darkness, search for the heavenly light to guide you. Hold firm to the Lord of the Worlds. He will bring you back to us.'

Her father then kissed her on the forehead, before standing tall once more. As she watched, he floated away, taking the celestial glow with him, plunging her into utter darkness.

Awa woke, her face pressed to the ground. Her eyes flicked open and she could hear a beetle scuttle away from her. It was dark around her. She was still alive. How? Footsteps approached. Calmer now, she waited for death or deliverance. There was a screeching sound as the metal door was ripped open above and the cool evening air rushed in, making her blink. Ja bent down and thrust a lamp in to take a look at her sorry state.

'Humph!' he grunted.

Next to peer in was Odo. 'The world is agony Awa. When you die, you'll get some rest.' Then the opening slammed shut.

'No!' Awa croaked. She tried to raise her arm, to reach out to the metal door, but the limb did not move. This was it then: she would die. But wait! She heard other footsteps. Soon, the metal door was yanked open again, this time by Tome. She must be hallucinating: he was a heartless mercenary who would shed no tears to see her die.

'Get her out,' Tome said.

Two women came into view. They gasped at the sight of her.

'Awa!' whispered a familiar voice. It was Wassa, her friend. Wassa and the other woman pulled her up by the arms, trying to get her to her feet, but Awa's legs would not hold her weight and they collapsed with her. Awa groaned.

'Move away,' Tome commanded. He reached in, picked Awa up in his arms and carried her, with Wassa beside her.

'You will live, Awa, you are strong. God has willed it,' said Wassa, stroking her head.

The last thing Awa remembered before she slipped into unconsciousness, was being placed on a mattress in the dormitory where the women fighters slept. Someone pressed a damp cloth to her lips and squeezed a trickle of water into her mouth, moistening her tongue - her first drink for more than three days.

16

Λ SLY OFFER

THE SMELL OF SALTY SEAWATER hung in the air, infusing Will with memories of harsh days below deck on Moroccan galleys. He reminded himself that the *Misr* - the *Egyptian* - was an altogether different vessel, a commercial, not a military one, Turkish-owned, not Moroccan. And, most importantly, he wasn't a slave but a cadet in the Janissary force of the most powerful man in the world, Sultan Murad III.

They were halfway through their journey from Istanbul to the port city of Alexandria, and the sea was calm, clear and thankfully quiet. The Ottomans controlled the straits between Turkey and North Africa, with Jerusalem to the east. The *Misr* took a route hugging the coastline as the Captain felt there was little point straying too far west and falling foul of ongoing naval conflicts between the Moroccans and their European neighbours. Will leaned on the guard-rail, eyes peering down to the hull, where he viewed the oars in motion. Galley slaves were at work. He loosened his collar, as the thought of those men sweating below deck made him uncomfortable.

Will heard a groan and turned to see Gurkan shuffling along the deck, clinging queasily to the rail. His fellow cadet was faring badly on his first ever sea-voyage and Will felt a touch guilty for dragging him along for this mission. Originally, the Konyan had delighted in the news that he was going to accompany them, eager as he was to please Commander Konjic.

'Surely, this is a punishment from God. I have done some wrong,' he said piteously.

Will smiled. 'If God wanted to punish you, I'm sure there are worse things He could inflict than seasickness. Don't worry, it'll clear up the more time you spend out on the waves.'

The other man looked hopeful, then clutched his stomach. 'How long?'

Will considered bending the truth but thought better of it. 'Well, when I was drafted into the Moroccan navy as a galley slave, I vomited for one whole week.'

Gurkan moaned, his complexion green.

'But after that it was fine. My stomach became rock solid,' Will beamed, patting it.

Gurkan retched over the side.

'Come with me,' Will said kindly, taking him by the arm. 'I'll show you how to make it better.'

Mehmed Konjic had organised for them to travel on a merchant ship, so as not to attract untoward attention when they arrived in Alexandria. There were five in the team, the others with more field experience, plus there was Konjic, which made six. For the purposes of this assignment they were disguised as merchants from Istanbul. The passengers on board the *Misr* were primarily traders from what Will could see. The route between Turkey and Egypt was an active one for merchants plying their trade in coffee, citrus fruits, rice and leathers.

Will guided the sick Gurkan to a spot below the mast in the aft section of the *Misr*. He cleared some floor space, put down a tarpaulin and told him to lie flat. Then he picked up a wooden block and placed it under Gurkan's head.

'Shut your eyes and count to ten,' said Will.

The Konyan did as he was told.

'How do you feel?' asked Will.

'By God! The world is no longer tipping over. What did you do, Will?'

The crewman managing the rigging smiled, when he saw Gurkan flat out. Will reckoned every shipmate had experienced sea-sickness at some point in their time onboard, so all felt sympathy with the novice.

Will patted his friend on the shoulder. 'Stay there for as long as you want, old fellow. No one is going to disturb you.'

'My life is coming back to me,' said Gurkan, his voice returning to its lively tones. 'Perhaps once I get off this infernal boat I will hold a sword once more.'

'Yes, of course you will. Right - I'll come and check on you in a while. For now, just rest.' Will left Gurkan and headed off to the stern of the *Misr* to mingle with other passengers. He noticed Mehmed Konjic sitting on a stool opposite a finely-dressed gentleman, whose hair was speckled with grey. He wore a royal-blue doublet, burgundy-coloured Venetian breeches and a short black velvet cloak. The men were deep in conversation, but when his Bosnian commander spotted Will, he hailed him.

'Will, please join us,' said Konjic.

The young man took hold of a stool and sat beside his superior.

'This is my apprentice, Will Ryde,' said Konjic. Will kept reminding himself they had set off from Istanbul with false identification papers, describing them as merchants from the suburb of Fatih.

The man sitting opposite them held out his hand. 'Delighted to meet a fellow Englishman.'

Konjic must have noticed Will's eyes light up. 'This is Sir Reginald Rathbone,' said the Commander.

'I am honoured, sir,' replied Will. He would never have dreamed of encountering a nobleman. If only his mother could see him now, hobnobbing with a real English knight, she would be so proud.

'Since being in the East, young Will here has encountered few from his native land,' Konjic said smoothly.

'That does not surprise me. We are a fledgling nation with grand aspirations,' the other man drawled, 'yet if truth be told, we are only just starting to widen our horizons beyond our own shores. As for the Spanish and the Italians, they simply fill the waterways of Istanbul and the pathways leading to the Grand Bazaar.'

'May I enquire what brought you to Istanbul, sir?' asked Will.

'Profit,' said Rathbone, his eyes sharp. 'Istanbul is the centre of world trade; it is the artery which connects. If you are not under the patronage of the Great Turk himself, you are nowhere. My government understands this so we have been endeavouring to widen our commercial interests in Ottoman territories ever since William Harborne of the Levant Company arrived in Istanbul in 1578.'

'You also work for the Levant Company?' enquired Konjic.

'No, my patron the Earl of Rothminster has established his own concern, which goes by the name of the Orient Company. We are currently building trade routes, hence my trips to Istanbul and to Alexandria.'

A man approached, holding a portfolio of papers and a ledger. 'Sir Reginald.'

'Yes, of course,' said Rathbone, taking the quill from the hand of the officious clerk, who held the ink-pot, and signing the papers one by one before handing them back.

'Thank you, sir,' said the clerk, scuttling off.

'A merchant's work is never done,' said Rathbone, smacking his lips.

Konjic rose from his stool, placing a hand on Will's shoulder. 'Why don't I leave you with my apprentice, Sir Reginald? I'm sure he is eager to ask you questions about England. Besides, I need to check on another of my apprentices, who has fallen foul of a bout of sea-sickness.'

Once Konjic had departed, Rathbone fixed Will with a hard stare. 'Where are you from, lad?'

'London - just beside Smithfield Market. I was taken when five years old from my mother, who is a seamstress. I then worked for a Moroccan quartermaster in Marrakesh, before joining Mehmed Konjic in Istanbul, where I serve him in his trading ventures.'

Rathbone stroked his chin. 'Do you miss England?'

'Every day.'

'Given the chance, would you return?'

Will bit his lip. This was a dangerous question to ask. He wanted to shout out: 'Take me home!' but he did not know Rathbone well enough to be open with him. 'I serve Mehmed Konjic. I am at his disposal,' was all he said.

'I understand. Loyalty is an important virtue - I admire it. However, if the opportunity came up to serve England, would you consider it?'

Will wasn't entirely clear what Rathbone was getting at. 'How do you mean, Sir Reginald?'

Rathbone leaned forward and spoke in a softer tone. 'My patron, the Earl of Rothminster, is a rising star in the court of Queen Elizabeth. He may not hold influence over the Queen to the extent that Robert Dudley, the Earl of Leicester, does - but his word carries considerable weight. And one thing I know is that he is always looking for Englishmen abroad who are willing to share information with him which could be of political - and particularly of commercial - value. Hmm?'

Rathbone was asking him to spy on his behalf!

'Of course,' the man went on, 'the rewards for sharing sensitive information and documents would be quite handsome. A lad like you, if you played your cards well, could set himself up for life: a manor in the countryside, land to go with it, and maybe even a wench to keep you warm at night, what?' He chuckled softly.

Will disliked Rathbone's conniving tone, but his desire to be reunited with his mother was strong. Imagine if he returned to her as a successful gentleman! All the years apart would be worth it if he could save them from squalor. His mother would not need to sew garments for a living ever again.

'What do you say, young Will?' Rathbone asked. 'Will you do it?'

Will's palms were sweating and he wiped them against his breeches. 'I will.'

'Good,' nodded Rathbone, drawing a signet ring from within the folds of his doublet. 'There is a fellow by the name of Poulter based in Istanbul. He works for the British Ambassador, Sir Edward Barton, but the man is incompetent and Poulter's true loyalty is with the Earl of Rothminster. Whenever you have anything to report, go and meet with him. Show him my signet ring and he will know I sent you.'

As Will took the signet ring, Rathbone noticed Konjic circling back in their direction. 'Not a word of this to anyone,' he hissed, his expression forbidding.

Will nodded, still inwardly unsure. By accepting Rathbone's proposal, was he breaking his oath of loyalty to the Sultan? It seemed like it. If so, he was a marked man and his days were numbered.

17

CALL UP

WITH AGONISING SLOWNESS STRENGTH RETURNED to her limbs. It had been two full days and one night since they hauled Awa out of the tin box and placed her into the dormitory to recover. The dorm contained two rows of pallet beds running along opposite walls. At one end was a curtained-off area where the women could relieve themselves. In the midday heat it reeked. However, to Awa, after her incarceration, the dorm seemed like a palace.

Gingerly, she had started to walk, but she still felt light-headed.

'Here,' said Wassa, 'drink this. The Mandinka woman over there, Ida, says it's a remedy her mother used to make for her father when he was full of aches and pains.' Her friend was sitting cross-legged on the ground beside her bedding.

Awa lifted the herbal concoction to her lips, saying, 'I smell ginger, eucalyptus, and something else . . . I can't be sure.'

'Cinnamon,' said Wassa.

Awa peered over at Ida. Raising the cup, she acknowledged her gift. The Mandinka woman smiled and nodded, placing a hand over her heart. The company of strangers was proving to be kind, more so than Awa expected. Perhaps it was the situation they found themselves in which bound them together. The women were living on borrowed time, aware that their final hour could arrive at any moment. In fact, some of these women were going to die this very evening at the next contest.

'I was sure I was going to perish. I even saw my father, come to me in a vision,' said Awa. Her voice broke.

'I lost all hope. But he spoke to me, told me I should hold firm to the Lord of the Worlds, for He will return me to my parents. Why would he say that, unless he was dead too?' She wept.

'No! You must not think in such a way. Your father lives and waits for you in glorious Timbuktu. The daughter *will* return to her father. I promise you this, Awa, I will do everything I can. I will be your support when you need it.'

Awa took her friend's hand. 'You have already done more for me than you could ever imagine. Thank you.'

'You are my sister, you walk beside me. I will always be there for you,' said Wassa.

At that moment, the door at one end of the dormitory was unlocked, letting in sunlight and dust. The women quickly sat up; those who were partially dressed covered themselves and the room went silent. A man was about to enter. Everyone knew who it was going to be, for he had this habit of turning up when least expected.

Odo's form was silhouetted against the sunlight and at his side was Ja. The pair entered, smiling at the women, eyeing them rather too keenly for Awa's liking. They had not taken any for their own pleasure since they were, after all, trying to make money out of the women winning gladiatorial competitions. They didn't want any upset. How terrifying, Awa thought, if these two vulgar men suddenly changed their minds.

With his sword in its scabbard and a swagger in his step, Odo paced down the narrow space in the centre of the room. It was easy for a man with a weapon to look threatening amongst defenceless women. If Odo ever came in here without his sword, Awa reckoned they could collectively take him out, and Ja too. The women had all huddled together for protection; not a single one was by herself.

Odo stopped in the centre of the room, swinging his gaze to right and left. 'After this evening's competition, for those of you who make it through, there is good news. We're travelling north, to the port city of Alexandria, named after the famous Macedonian conqueror. You will compete in the glorious venue there and make me lots of money. Some of you will die and I am grateful for your sacrifice. For those who cannot bring excitement in the ring, we will find other ways for you to bring pleasure for paying customers.'

With a sadistic grin, he scanned the room and finally his eyes rested on Awa. He approached her. 'You made it out of the box, I see.'

Awa kept her head lowered, avoiding eye contact. She had learned her lesson - she was no longer going to be disobedient to Odo, other than when she had a dagger in her hand and his throat to slit.

'Ja,' said Odo, ushering the giant to his side. 'What do you think? Does she look well enough to compete today?'

The giant shrugged his shoulders.

'She is still very sick,' said Wassa.

Odo took a threatening step toward the young woman, brandishing his dagger. 'Silence! Did I ask for your opinion, girl?'

Wassa cringed and Awa clenched her fists. Odo noticed and was gratified. 'The rage returns. Good. Use it effectively next time I put you in the arena. Kill - or else Ja will string you up and cut you in half to die a slow death.'

He turned to the giant. 'Let's put this one,' he said, pointing at Wassa, 'in the ring tonight. See how she fares.'

Swivelling round to address the women, Odo warned them: 'If there is any insubordination tonight, the next person going into the tin box will be left there for a week. And trust me, I know you won't come out alive.'

He gave them one final threatening glare before departing with Ja in tow. Once they had gone and the door was chained shut, there was a collective sigh of relief, mixed with fear.

'Don't anger him,' said Awa.

'We have to stand up to him. How else will we escape?' said Wassa.

'Not when we have nothing at our disposal to fight with. Better to be submissive. When the right moment arises, then we strike.'

The afternoon stretched out. Half the women were summoned and they prepared themselves, putting on the clothes they had been given for combat. The apparel was deliberately revealing. As most of the women came from a background where modesty in attire was a virtue, this left them feeling humiliated. As they reluctantly lined up to leave, the chain was slipped away. Outside, Tome waited to direct them. He peered at Awa and nodded. She was left confused by his manner. He was brutal with her, yet she had seen concern in his eyes when he carried her from the tin box.

Wassa started to leave, but Awa pulled her back and hugged her tight. 'Be careful,' she cautioned.

'Remember, my sister, even the light of a thousand splendid suns falls short of the majesty of the Creator. He will save us,' Wassa replied.

Her friend departed and Awa said a prayer for her. Awa needed to sleep but rest would not come. Being unable to see what was happening made it all the more difficult. The sun went down and still the women did not return. Awa shared anxious looks with her companions. All had friends competing.

Suddenly, the chains were yanked off the locks. It was dark outside and Awa could not make out how many women had returned. Ten had left. One by one, the women entered, heads lowered. Some were still bloodied. Others had not fought. Only seven came back.

'Wassa,' said Awa.

None of the women replied.

'Where is Wassa?' asked Awa.

Ida, the tall Mandinka woman, entered last. She sat Awa down and took her hand, saying gently, 'I'm so sorry, my sister.'

'No!' Awa buried her head in the woman's shoulder, weeping. Ida held her, letting her grieve.

Why did it have to happen like this? Every time there was a shard of light, it was extinguished. For a time when Wassa was with her, Awa had not felt alone, but the truth was, she would always be alone. She continued to weep until the tears ran out, then she wiped her eyes and thanked Ida. If only she could go back into the ring right now, unleash her feelings on someone, fight the person who had slain Wassa!

The women around the room were silent. Two others had fallen: they also had friends. When everyone was asleep, Awa herself remained awake. She knew now that nothing mattered any more: they were all going to die. It was then she swore a solemn oath to herself that she would either die in the ring - or die trying to escape. Whichever came first, she no longer cared.

And if it involved slaying Odo and Ja, so much the better.

18

PERMISSIONS

RUINS OF GLORIOUS YESTERDAYS ADORNED the street corners of the world's former greatest city of Alexandria. From the Bibliotheca Alexandrina to the Roman amphitheatre, Will was filled with wonder at the achievements of peoples from so long ago.

When they arrived, Konjic divided them into three units. He took Kostas with him, since the black-haired Greek had a smooth tongue and a flair for negotiation. The merchants of Alexandria were notoriously difficult to deal with, Konjic knew. They still behaved as though their port city was the centre of the world.

Konjic and Kostas set off to meet local guilds and merchants, to see if they could find out whether the Staff of Moses was going to be handled by someone within this community prior to being sold. The two men wore headgear studded with gems and their tunics were heavily embossed in the Ottoman style: everything about their attire expressed wealth. Konjic said that despite the way these fellows blustered, they would nevertheless want to hear from businessmen arriving from Istanbul, to learn all about the requirements of customers further afield.

Mikael and Ismail meanwhile went off to mix with ruffians and petty criminals, to determine whether any of these undesirable elements were running the Staff through underground channels. They dressed accordingly, with an assortment of blades stuffed into their clothing. Will didn't envy them their dangerous task, but both young men were streetwise and knew how to look out for themselves: they came from less privileged backgrounds, so would fit in well with their roles.

As for Will and Gurkan, they were given freedom to roam the city, visit the stalls in the Souk, go to any other places where the public congregated. Primarily their role was to observe. The more people they encountered, the higher the prospect of them bumping into the green-eyed Janissary. Their day passed without success, however: there was no sign of the former Janissaries nor any whispers regarding the Staff.

As the Maghrib prayer after sunset was being recited, Will waited outside the Mosque of Sidi Gaber for Gurkan. He sat perched on a small wall, behind him the sound of a fountain trickling into a pond of water. When the prayer ended, the faithful came out in clusters, chatting and offering salutations of peace as they departed. Gurkan took a while to emerge and when he did he was with another fellow, who seemed to be trying to make a point to him. Will watched Gurkan hand over some dinars before finishing his conversation. Only after the other man had departed did Gurkan rejoin Will.

'Can you believe it!' he said, taking Will by the elbow as they left the mosque precinct. 'There's an illegal gladiatorial competition taking place near the docks.'

'You learned that in the mosque?'

'Yes - disgraceful. What's more, that fellow I was speaking with, he was selling tickets.' He shook his head. 'Can you believe it!'

'When is it?' Will asked.

Gurkan raised an eyebrow. 'You want to go?'

Watching a gladiatorial contest to the death did have a base appeal, Will acknowledged. He was training as a warrior, and watching live combat could prove a useful learning tool. He caught himself: was there really any justification for watching human beings kill each other for money?

'We might meet some interesting people, some of whom may know the Janissaries we're hunting,' he said aloud.

'Good. Because I bought two tickets.' Gurkan held them up. 'It's happening late tonight and could be the perfect place for our rogue Janissaries to meet potential buyers.'

Will grunted. 'I think they already know who their buyers are. Why come to Alexandria, otherwise? Right, for now, we need to get back to the lodging. Konjic asked us to return after Maghrib to compare notes.'

The walk to their accommodation took an hour. The others were already back and soon they all gathered around the table in the main living area downstairs. The small villa was sparsely furnished, with three bedrooms on the upper floor. Mikael had bought food and spread it out on the table: baba-ganoush made with aubergine, tabbouleh - vegetarian salad, humus, and harrias - flatbreads stuffed with minced meat.

As the six of them sat at the wooden table, tucking in to the food, it struck Will that the Janissaries were the closest thing he had ever encountered to a family.

When he had eaten his fill, Konjic dabbed his lips, saying, 'Kostas, why don't you share what we learned today?'

The young Greek finished his mouthful and addressed the group, speaking in a softer tone than usual. Will noticed that the windows were open; Kostas did not want his voice travelling.

'The merchants were cautious with the information they shared, although they were keen to understand how to secure trade routes to the Balkans. Commander Konjic being Bosnian

103

turned out to be very useful for us today. As for the Staff, no one let on they knew anything, other than the Hamidi family, who said they had heard of an unusual trade taking place in the city between a Venetian buyer and mercenaries from Istanbul.'

Konjic cleared his throat and took over the story. 'When we questioned them further, they clammed up, but we think the mercenaries they mentioned may well be our rogue Janissaries. Why buyers from Venice are interested is puzzling; we assumed the thieves came to Alexandria because of the lingering Mamluk factions.'

'Why would the factions want the Staff?' asked Mikael.

'Bargaining chip with the Sultan, perhaps?' Konjic suggested. 'Anyway, what did you two learn, Mikael?'

'We learned that loosening tongues isn't easy here. Some saw straight through us, so that was a waste of time. The ones who talked were those desperate for a few dinars. Mostly they gave us a load of rubbish, and the leads we followed ended nowhere . . . except for one unusual piece of information. Ismail, you take over,' Mikael said.

The curly-haired Ismail took up the story. 'There is a group calling themselves the Sicarii, who were referred to by more than one informant. We could see fear in their eyes at the mere mention of them.'

Konjic rubbed his chin.

'What is it, sir?' asked Mikael.

'The Sicarii are hired mercenaries. Originally, they were Jewish zealots, like the notorious Assassin sect that was an offshoot of the Ismaili Muslims. The Assassins were so resilient, even Saladin was unable to destroy them. It is said that after the Mongols defeated them at their mountain stronghold of Alamut, they just disappeared, reappearing when the need arose . . .'

Konjic went silent for a moment.

'Sir?' Kostas enquired.

'Considering we're investigating the loss of the Staff of Moses, and its connection with the Jewish faith, the Sicarii might be the buyers, or at least acting on behalf of them,' said Konjic.

'It might also explain the reference to the Venetian buyer,' Kostas replied. 'There is a strong Jewish presence in Venice, so perhaps someone from that community paid the Sicarii.'

'Could be,' Konjic acknowledged. 'Venetian merchants have been struggling to secure favourable trade terms with the Sultan, because we're trading more with the Safavids in Persia these days.' He turned to Gurkan and Will. 'You two: anything to report?'

'Nothing unusual,' Gurkan said. 'But . . . we are going to a gladiatorial contest tonight.'

Hearing this, the others sat up. 'Well,' said Will, trying to explain, 'these types of places attract all sorts - we might learn something.'

'How to kill someone with a sword perhaps?' said Mikael.

Will and Gurkan looked somewhat shamefaced: it did seem like a flimsy excuse.

'We have two tickets,' said Gurkan, waving the pieces of paper around.

'They won't let you in, you look too young,' said Ismail, smiling.

'I look older than I am,' said Gurkan.

'Me too,' said Will.

'You are both tall and broad, but you have baby faces,' argued Ismail.

'Baby faces!' Gurkan growled.

'It's a compliment,' said Mikael. 'Before you end up becoming a grizzled old misery like Ismail here.'

'Hey - watch it! I'm no misery,' Ismail began.

Konjic slapped the table and they all fell silent.

'Thank you,' he said heavily. 'Although I agree that our youngest members appear green behind the ears, I think it will do them some good to attend. Mikael and Ismail, I'd like you to accompany them. See if you can get tickets. If not, stay close to the venue. In an investigation such as this, taking the unexpected route may lead to results. The only problem is, these places are full of unsavoury characters who'll put a knife through you without a second thought.'

He turned to Gurkan and Will. 'Watch your backs.'

19

ROAR OF APPROVAL

HUNDREDS OF FEET THUMPED WOODEN benches, and angry cries erupted. The crowd was not satisfied with the previous gladiatorial contest, which had ended too quickly because one of the contestants gave up before the fight got properly started. It couldn't be called a bout, more a chase, with one gladiator trying to catch the other, who ran away until he tripped and fell flat on his face.

Tome led Awa from the holding shelter and down a narrow corridor lit by lanterns. They emerged into the weapons store. The quartermaster stood up when they entered, giving Awa the once-over with his one good eye, the other having a patch over it.

'Over here,' he said, beckoning.

The Spaniard was by her side as Awa carefully inspected the weapons stacked up on the shelves. Swords and lances were the most prevalent. There were long and short shields, as well as a war hammer, which was too heavy for her to even attempt to lift. She hoped her opponent didn't choose such a weapon. In addition, a clutch of daggers and knives were laid out on the table before her. She thought of stealing one, but Tome was keeping a watchful eye on her. The quartermaster presented her with a shield and waited for her to choose her sword.

'Let me try this one,' said Awa, pointing to a mid-length blade with a guard around the hilt.

Tome was a looming presence beside her. 'Also let her try the one with the curved blade and short handle,' he suggested.

Awa put her shield down and tested the swing and balance of both of the blades. The Spaniard was right, the curved blade suited her grip. She nodded at him. 'Yes, it's better.'

They turned and stood behind the door leading into the makeshift arena. Awa peered through the slats. The audience was a mixture of races, with a few faces whose skin was as white as snow. She had never seen that kind before, for though the Spaniard was naturally pale-skinned, his complexion had been tanned a leathery brown.

Awa had arrived in Alexandria the night before, but could not see much through the bars of a slave wagon. Still, she had gained the sense of being in a large city. If ever she was going to escape and disappear into a population, this would be the place. There were enough dark-skinned Africans for her to blend in, before she found passage out of the city - though at this moment she had no idea how. But it was essential to escape from this life of madness, where she killed for the pleasure of others, whilst risking the wrath of God.

Tome turned to her. 'The odds are high against you. Odo expects to makes lots of money tonight.'

'From my death?'

'No, from your victory.'

'Why would the bets be placed so high?'

The Spaniard inspected her, eyes narrowing. 'Because you're fighting two opponents.'

It was a shock. Awa exhaled deeply. She remembered how she had felt on the previous two occasions, first on the field at Tondibi, when she had little experience and her naïve approach carried her through, then when she had escaped the slave camp, with Wassa by her side. This time she was truly alone, with only her wits and limited skill to guide her. She prayed for self-preservation and forgiveness.

The arena master poked his head through the door. 'Ready?'

'Yes,' said Tome as he guided her out.

Immediately Awa was struck by the size of the crowd, larger and more diverse than before. They were in some kind of large store down at the docks. The ceiling was high, thick beams criss-crossing the roof above. The audience roared when they spotted her, alone with her shield and curved sword. Awa glimpsed Odo and Ja, standing to one side behind a barrier. The ranks of benches stretched back ten rows on four sides, giving the impression that at any moment, the audience could collapse in on the circle where the fighters were to perform.

Another door opened and a man, followed by a woman, entered the ring. He was of medium height, with stocky shoulders and thin arms. His moustache was narrow and his olive-toned body was well oiled. Beside him, the woman was taller than he was - darker too, with muscular arms. They both gripped swords but carried no shields. At least the organisers had levelled out the contest a little.

Sighting her opponents, the watchers scolded them, as though they were the villains, come to defeat the innocent young woman. It struck Awa that this was a piece of theatre, the crowd being entertained with the story of a weaker opponent overcoming a stronger adversary. Everyone liked this sort of tale, from when David slew Goliath. Only she was no David.

'Salute the crowd,' the ringmaster ordered.

She complied, as did her opponents.

'Now - fight to the death!' said the ringmaster, before scampering away to join Odo behind the barrier.

Awa spun the hilt of her weapon in her hand, her shield up, ready for an attack. Her two opponents fanned out to either side. She took small, light steps, bouncing around on her toes. *Let them come,* she told herself as she circled, watching for the first movement. The man darted at her with his raised sword, aiming for her chest. It was a clumsy manoeuvre which she deflected easily with her shield. He then swung low at her ankles. She leaped and brought her shield crashing down against his shoulder, causing him to stumble back. The woman's blade arced through the air, aimed at her neck. Awa ducked and smashed her shield into the woman's face. It cut her opponent's lower lip, blood turning her chin dark red.

The crowd thundered, but Awa barely registered the noise, for the stillness had come over her. She tracked the movement of her opponents, witnessing the world around her in a sort of slow motion. She twirled her sword, stepping towards the woman just as the man charged at her from behind. Rather than defend the blow, Awa dived onto the ground and rolled away - and the man's blade went straight into his partner's chest.

Awa was back on her feet immediately and as the man was pulling out his blade, distraught at having felled his ally, she pivoted and her weapon took off his head. Blood sprayed across the ground; the woman was covered in it as the man's body collapsed, falling into her arms. The woman stared aghast at his headless form, before she too toppled over dead. There were gasps from the audience, before they bellowed, hollered, *howled* their support for the victor. People danced up and down on the benches. They loved her display.

She loathed it.

Odo smacked Ja on the back with delight, as the ringmaster leaned over to ask Odo something before he entered the ring once more, staring at Awa with a mixture of respect and fright. She had given them a show, all right - and what a show.

'Awa of the Songhai!' the ringmaster announced, as loudly as he could.

'Awa! Awa! Awa!' The excited onlookers cheered her name, clapping with delight at the beautiful act of violence.

She stood statue-like, absorbing the praise. She would not fall into the trap of displeasing Odo again by throwing down her weapons in disgust, though it was what her heart desired.

Tome was by her side, ushering her back through the door. 'Come on, they need to clean up this mess,' he said.

Awa followed him back inside, showing no emotion whatsoever. The quartermaster was there to receive the weapons, and she noted that the knives and daggers were still laid out on the table. This was her chance. She approached, but tripped. Her sword went flying out onto the ground, while the shield scattered the knives and daggers, knocking many of them down.

'Sorry!' Awa cried. 'I'm feeling dizzy.' She placed her arm against the table for support, while Tome retrieved her sword and the quartermaster began to collect up the fallen blades.

'Clumsy girl!' the quartermaster scolded her. 'I have a mind to give you a taste of the back of my hand.'

'Hey!' shouted Tome at the man. 'You'll do no such thing, or you'll feel the back of *my* hand – and you won't like it!'

Awa was surprised to see the Spaniard defending her. But then, she was a money-making tool and it was in their interest to ensure she was well attended from now on.

'*Awa! Awa! Awa!*' The shouts of the crowd continued in the background.

'Hear that?' Tome said, jabbing his finger towards the audience. 'They love you. You entertained them.'

Awa clutched her head, pretending she was still feeling light-headed. 'It was too much. All those people calling my name – it made me come over faint.'

Tome grunted. Handing the curved sword back to the quartermaster, he said roughly, 'C'mon.' He led Awa down the corridor towards the holding-room, where the other women waited. What neither he nor the quartermaster noticed was the dagger she had tucked into the folds of her clothing.

20

CITADEL

B LOOD SHOWERED OUT OF THE headless corpse. Will swallowed hard. He had never witnessed a decapitation before. The gladiator, Awa, was a formidable opponent. When Will had seen the pairing against Awa, he had felt for her, but not any more. The stewards were in the ring, dragging the two bodies of the headless man and the impaled woman away. Others ran on, with buckets of water and mops, setting to work scrubbing the floor, readying it for the next contest.

'Filthy business,' said Gurkan. He jerked a thumb. 'Look at those vultures collecting their winnings.'

Close to the entrance where the contestants emerged, Will spotted an exceptionally tall man beside a shorter squat one with a nasty scar. They were Africans, though he was uncertain of their tribe or nation. They stood behind a barrier, the same position they had been in when the fight was taking place. Their smiles told Will the men were pleased with the result. A dejected queue of gamblers were lining up to hand over money to them.

'The girl doesn't get any of that,' said Will.

'She is their slave. She is entitled to nothing.' Gurkan shrugged.

Will nodded. 'I know what it's like. I spent years in the galley, chained down, beaten by oar-masters who took a dislike to me. As a slave, you live on a knife edge: any moment could be your last. I feel for her.'

'How did you not go mad?' Gurkan asked.

Will stared at his open hands, clenching and unclenching them. 'I thought about my mother, remembering her auburn hair and the scent of lavender. Whenever I come across lavender today, my heart quickens. Knowing my mother loves me, strengthens me. Knowing I love her, my courage grows.' It occurred to Will then that he had not shared this sentiment with anyone, not even his beloved former master, Hakim Abdullah. Why then was he confiding in Gurkan? Perhaps because the Konyan was of the same age. He hoped he hadn't said too much.

'You are free from the yoke of servitude now, my friend,' said Gurkan, placing a companionable hand on his shoulder.

Yes, he was, thought Will - but for how long? The world they lived in was so fraught with danger. He was a white-skinned English lad, living in a time and place where his nation was little known. If he had learned anything these past few years, it was that, other than the Spanish, power lay in the East - in Istanbul, Marrakesh, Isfahan and further east in Delhi. Until he was safely back in England, he would always be at risk of being captured, sold or worse.

Though Will himself was no longer enslaved, that poor woman down there was. He wanted to help her in some way, but how? What could he do in this alien city? How many others like her were present? Did they have a whole wagon of slaves lined up to be sacrificed for the enjoyment of the watching audience? The thought sickened him. He and Gurkan had paid to be present, but surely that was justified as they were searching for the thieves? Still, it left a knot in his stomach.

As he pondered the matter, a figure in the crowd drew his attention. The way he moved was somehow familiar. Will shuffled closer towards the man, all the while ensuring he was not seen. Was it him, the one from Istanbul? On that occasion, the man had leaped off the roof of the Grand Bazaar.

'Gurkan,' he muttered, 'I think I've seen the green-eyed Janissary!'

'Where?'

'In the queue, handing over his money to that tall fellow.'

The green-eyed Janissary waited his turn, before coming face to face with the tall African, to whom he reluctantly handed over a fistful of dinars. The giant smiled, his brilliant white teeth shining like the moon, and placed the coins in a metal box, jangling them with a heap of others he had collected. Green-eyes stared at his lost dinars, then eyeballed the giant, who beamed. Will didn't think the former Janissary had much of a chance going up against the colossus. Neither, so it seemed, did Green-eyes, for he turned and headed dejectedly for the exit.

'We need to follow him,' said Will, racing down the benches, ducking underneath, then sprinting over to the exit the former Janissary had taken. They emerged into the warm evening air. The street was silent. The chosen venue was barely visited after sunset, when the docks no longer operated and this type of illegal activity took place without any inspection from the city authorities, who were most likely paid to turn a blind eye. Mikael and Ismail were nowhere to be seen - they hadn't gained entry. Will had expected them to be outside as Commander Konjic advised. So, where were they? Perhaps they had returned to the guesthouse. Then he spotted Green-eyes turning a corner.

'There!' said Will.

'Let's keep our distance,' Gurkan advised as they pursued their target.

The rogue Janissary maintained a brisk pace, striding with a degree of purpose. He headed south into the windy streets of the Al-Attarin district, a warren of dilapidated buildings and cheap guesthouses. These contrasted with the plusher villa Konjic had arranged for them, given they were impersonating wealthy Istanbul merchants.

They remained about twenty paces behind Green-eyes; far enough to observe him, but not close enough to arouse suspicion. Will thought they had lost him at one point, but Gurkan caught his tail once more. Eventually Green-eyes came to a narrow building - a guesthouse it seemed from the sign swinging above the low doorway, which he stooped to go through. He entered, bounding up the stairs, and Will caught a glimpse of him on the first floor. He and Gurkan waited behind a wheelbarrow, two large barrels on top of it shielding them from being spotted.

'You sure it's him?' asked Gurkan.

'As certain as I can be.'

'All right, so we wait,' said Gurkan.

They sat with their backs against the alley wall, keeping watch. Will felt they might be mistaken for beggars. Time ticked by, till he began to wonder if the Janissary had gone to bed and they would be here all night. One of them would need to go and fetch Konjic and the others, but until they knew what the thieves were planning it was best they both remained.

'Why take the Staff?' he mused aloud.

'Who knows. Maybe someone offered a substantial fee to steal it?'

'But who?' wondered Will.

'That is the one-thousand-dinar question, my friend. It must be someone with the funds and influence to pull off such a robbery,' said Gurkan.

'And the guts.' Will shuddered. 'Crossing Sultan Murad III is not something to do lightly.'

'Yes. May his brothers rest in peace,' said Gurkan in a whisper.

There it was again, a reference to the Sultan's brothers, all of whom had been murdered on his orders, on the day he ascended to the throne. Will hoped he would never have cause to be in the presence of the Ruler. Huja's words echoed in his mind, about how he had lost his soul in the Topkapi Palace.

Will must have nodded off, for he jumped when Gurkan nudged him. He stared up and could see the green-eyed Janissary leaving the house, accompanied by another. By his height and body-shape, Will felt certain this new man was the second thief he had chased across the rooftops of the Grand Bazaar.

'It's both of them,' he said in a low voice.

The men were heading north, back towards the docks. Were they going to return to the gladiatorial games? If so, how odd. They weren't carrying anything.

'Should we check their lodging? Maybe the Staff is inside?' suggested Gurkan.

'Something so valuable?' Will replied. 'They wouldn't have left it in such as shabby billet, where anyone can take it. They would've hidden it in a secure location, till they were ready to trade. Besides, by the time we check the place out, we'll have lost their trail. We know where they are staying and can always return if need be.'

'Agreed,' said Gurkan.

They slipped out of their hiding position and followed the thieves. The men were now bearing towards the seashore - although there was nothing there but the Citadel of Qaitbay, built some hundred years earlier to keep the Ottomans out of the city.

The streets widened and a strong sea breeze cut in from the north, blowing Will's hair back and making his trousers flap like flags.

'They must be heading for the citadel,' he said. 'Why don't you run back and notify the Commander? I'll follow them and stay outside till you return.'

'We both know I'm the faster runner, so your suggestion makes sense,' said Gurkan with a smile, before shaking Will's hand and adding more seriously, 'Be careful, my friend.' Then he sprinted off, disappearing into the deepening dusk.

The wind rustled around Will as he pressed on, keeping low and edging along the side of the street, though the lack of buildings left him exposed. The citadel was sparsely guarded. Since the Ottoman takeover, the conquerors preferred to keep permanent warships patrolling in the bay, rather than fully occupying the citadel with troops. Lamps lit up its main entrance. Will watched the thieves swerve to the right of the structure. They hid as a guard passed in front of them and then sneaked in behind him. The thieves were inside the citadel.

Will lingered behind one of the stone blocks on a patch of land running up to the main gates. He was tempted to enter but thought better of it. Commander Konjic would want him to remain till reinforcements arrived. As far as Will could see, there was only one road in and out of the citadel, and he was on it, so there was no way the thieves were going to get away from him this time. Unless, of course, they were going to board a vessel . . .

'Oh damn it, don't get on a boat!' he muttered. If there was a boat waiting for them on the other side of the citadel, it would all be over. He had no choice but to emerge from his hiding place and jog down the path to the spot where the thieves had entered. There was a second guard doing his rounds. Will watched him and then slipped in behind his back, stealing though the same entrance as the thieves had done.

Inside, he saw wide hallways with ornate arches, lamps hanging at every turn, lighting the way. Ahead of him, two shadowy forms darted up a flight of stairs. Will checked behind: all clear. He followed, hugging the side walls and treading softly. He emerged on the first floor, scanning the hallway. Empty. No, there was movement at the far end. Someone came out under an archway. Will crept along, feet nimble, remaining in the shadows. When he turned the corner, he entered a vestibule which opened into an enormous hall, with an atrium rising up two levels. The chamber was lined with coats of arms, chainmail, scimitars, lances, war hammers, hatchets, bows, javelins, axes, and an assortment of knives and daggers. Around the walls were paintings and tapestries. This was some kind of quartermaster's museum. The weapons and equipment on display were old: an exhibition of grandeur from the past. Hakim Abdullah would be thrilled to see it.

The two thieves stood in an open space in the centre and before them were two men wearing black, with hoods and close-fitting trousers. Were these the Sicarii Konjic had mentioned? They looked impressively dangerous, as their reputation implied. The transaction was about to take place, and Will was alone and outnumbered. Reinforcements were not going to arrive in time.

He wiped his sweaty palms on his thighs, knowing he had to make a decision - but it must be the right one. Everything depended on it.

21

UNWANTED ATTENTION

COLD STEEL DUG INTO HER flesh as Tome marched her back to the dormitory, the stolen dagger shifting inside her cummerbund. Odo and Ja were occupied, collecting money. Now was the time to make a run for it. As much as she wanted to take all the women with her, Awa knew her chances were higher if she fled alone.

The Spaniard had his back to her when she drew the dagger. He immediately sensed the danger and spun away from her, raising his hands in submission.

'I wouldn't do that,' Tome instructed.

'I just want my freedom,' Awa said steadfastly. 'Let me go and I won't hurt you.'

'It's not so easy. Odo needs to make money from you.'

'What will he do with me? Tell me the truth!'

Tome lowered his hands and inspected her thoughtfully. 'You will either die in the ring, having made him rich, or if you survive, he will eventually sell you to a house of pleasure.'

'So either way I lose.'

He took a step towards her. 'Come on, end this nonsense. Hand me the knife.'

She backed away, stood up tall and firm, imagining herself in the ring once more. Tome stopped when he saw the look on her face.

'I don't want to hurt you,' she said, 'but I will if I have to. Now show me the way out.'

Tome shrugged. 'All right. In some ways, I daresay you deserve it. Come with me.'

He led her down a passageway. There wasn't much light, only a dim lamp placed at either end of the corridor. They came to a sharp turn, which the Spaniard took quickly, momentarily disappearing from view. As Awa turned the same corner, he barrelled into her, knocking her back, sending the dagger flying from her hand. She landed on the ground, sprawling on her back. Tome straddled her and grabbed her throat.

'Yes, you deserve this,' he said, a lewd smile crossing his face.

Awa gritted her teeth. Viciously, she rammed her knee into his groin. He curled up with pain, his grip loosening. She then gouged his face with her fingers, and watched blood trickle down the side of his right eye. He slipped off her. Awa was up. In a fury, she seized his head and banged it on the ground, over and over again. She snatched up her dagger and thought about stabbing him, but hesitated: that was when he grabbed her ankle. She swiped with her knife, slashing him across the face, and he fell back, holding his chin. She could have opened up his windpipe but showed mercy instead. She left him there.

The narrow passageway behind her led to a small door. She opened it, and a light breeze enveloped her. *Yes!* Awa ran out, to find the seafront on one side, the arena behind her. Before her was a storage area, packed with empty crates and containers - a loading zone for ships. Some vessels were moored up to her left. She needed to get on a ship, but these ones were too close to the arena; they would find her easily. A small cluster of men noticed her, still wearing her flimsy garments.

'Hey, sweetheart,' someone called out.

Ignoring the men, she sprinted off to the left, knowing she had to find proper clothing - quickly. The bay curved like a crescent moon and she observed structures up ahead. The road running along the coast was largely empty, but she did pass various individuals who stopped and stared at her. The night air felt good around her, the salt tang coming off the sea making her feel alive. But Odo and Ja would soon be on her trail. They had tracked her across a desert, so a city would be easy. The sooner she left Alexandria the better.

Tents were pitched by the side of the coast road. Awa could tell they belonged to Bedouins, passing through the city. Behind the tents, a line of clothing had been hung out to dry. Amongst them were a long tunic and matching pantaloons. Once she was sure no one was looking, she stripped off the vulgar costume and wriggled into the damp clothing. She kept the belt she had been wearing and was securing the dagger within it when she heard a voice.

'Sister!'

She turned to see a Bedouin woman, holding up the costume she had worn, looking at it with a puzzled expression. Awa placed her hand upon her heart, smiled and sped away, hoping the woman would forgive her for stealing her clothing and replacing it with such bawdy items.

Heading up towards the promontory, she saw a large building ahead and ran towards it. On the way she passed through a fish market. Though closed at this time, the smell lingered powerfully in the air. In a few hours, it would most likely be full of fishermen selling their previous day's catch. She turned, checking behind her. Silence. No one was following - for now. Slowing her pace, she studied the structure she was heading towards: it turned out to be some kind of citadel. Most likely it would be guarded, so not the right place to hide. Then she thought again. If she could sneak in and conceal herself, there would be supplies she could take and it was unlikely the guards were going to let the likes of Odo and Ja in. There were also some vessels behind the citadel and at least one of them had lamps lit. Maybe it would be her transport out of this place.

As Awa approached the citadel, she saw a guard patrolling up ahead. She hid, watching him pass, observing when the next guard went through. She timed her run, dashing into the building before the next patrol crossed. Once inside, she quickly realised she had entered the kitchens, for the heat from the furnace still warmed the room. There was no one present, but there was food in abundance. Some bread and a lump of cheese disappeared inside the pockets of her robe. She took a long, refreshing swig from a jug; the drink tasted like pomegranate juice. She left the kitchen and went charging up a flight of stairs to emerge in a wide passageway with high, symmetrical arches running along it, one after the other. It reminded her of the university in Timbuktu, a place of learning. But this was a citadel, built for war, not education.

A guard at the end of the corridor heard a noise and turned in her direction, but she ducked to the side and bounded up another flight of stairs. She wanted to find a quiet place to stay the night, hidden within the safety of the citadel. Surely Odo and Ja would not think to check in here?

She roamed until she came to a large hall filled with weapons and equipment from previous wars: a war museum of relics. She had never seen such a thing before, wondered how effective these ancient weapons were.

Awa eventually found a spot behind a statue of Alexander the Great. A thick velvet cloth was draped around its pedestal and swirled up in a pile behind, creating a safe and roomy hiding place for her. Someone could be standing looking at the statue, and not even know she was hiding only yards away. It also seemed like a comfortable spot to go to sleep in. Before she crawled beneath the covering, Awa thought to herself that if the Macedonian conqueror looked anything like the way this statue depicted him, then he was surely a hero of the ages. She ate the food and was beginning to feel drowsy when she heard voices. Terror seized her. Had they found her? Grasping her dagger, she strained to hear what they were saying.

'They'll be here soon,' said a throaty voice.

'You picked a good spot for the trade,' said the second man.

'It's the Staff, we should show respect,' said Throaty.

What staff? Awa peered through a small gap in the fabric and saw two men, both dressed in black trousers and tunic tops, their faces partially hidden by scarves across their mouths.

'Perhaps we should keep it within the community and not sell it to the Knights of the Fire Cross,' said Throaty.

'Moses did part the Red Sea and turned the Nile red with it,' said the second man.

Moses! The Staff of Moses! Awa caught her breath.

'God was responsible, not Moses,' said Throaty.

'Yeah, but He chose Moses to use the Staff.'

Just then, another two men entered the hall; both were of stocky build.

'Salaam,' said the two newcomers.

'Shalom,' replied the two men dressed in black.

'You have it?' asked Throaty.

'Yes, of course, but we weren't going to wander around Alexandria with it, so we came and hid it in here when we arrived in the city,' said one of the visitors.

'*You what?*' gasped Throaty. 'You left the Staff of Moses unguarded? Do you know what we'd do to you if you lost it, after all the risks we've taken?'

124

The man shrugged. 'The Janissaries can best the Sicarii any day.'

'Oh really?' snarled Throaty.

'Enough,' said his companion, and Awa realised they were part of some group called the Sicarii. The newcomers were Janissaries - the royal household guards of the Ottoman Sultan. What on earth were they doing in Alexandria, trading a religious object with the Sicarii? She leaned in, not wanting to miss anything.

One of the men strode in her direction, so close that she could see he had distinctive green eyes. She shuffled backwards to get away - and it was then that something jabbed her lower back. A long staff had been shoved under the velvet covering. The Janissary then moved the drape aside. Fortunately for Awa, he threw it across her, further covering her up. He reached down and yanked the item from its hiding place She had been sitting with her back against the Staff of Moses!

'Here it is,' said Green-eyes, holding the rod with great reverence.

The Sicarii viewed it with caution.

Throaty reached out, intoning, 'And thou shalt take this rod in thine hand, wherewith thou shalt do signs.'

'So said God to Moses,' Green-eyes agreed. 'But you aren't Moses. And we want our payment.' He drew the Staff back, holding it close to his chest.

It was then Awa noticed someone else sneaking into the hall - a young man of European origin. In fact, she recognised him because he had been in the audience at the arena. Immediately she took a dislike to him. He must be working for one of the parties, as a back-up in case things got nasty.

But on which side?

22

TOO CROWDED

WILL HID BEHIND A PODIUM in the great hall. For a moment or two, he gazed around at the displays of equipment, clothing and weapons from various nations and eras. There was a Dogon ceremonial mask, an Indian elephant mask for when the beast rode into battle, a curved Shamshir sword from Persia. There was even a Japanese Katana, he noted. Hakim Abdullah, who had once held one, had described it to Will as the most efficient blade he had ever come across. To the side of the sword was an imposing statue of Alexander the Great, behind which lay a crumpled velvet drape. To his astonishment, he thought he glimpsed movement from within it. Did one of these groups have a hidden assassin? If so, which side?

'This had better be the real Staff,' said a Sicarii with a throaty voice that reminded Will of a marsh frog.

'You are Jews - can't you tell?' jeered the green-eyed Janissary.

The two Sicarii stared at one another. 'Yes, we are Israelites, but let's just say we aren't as close to the Creator as our mothers would like us to be,' said the second.

'A common problem,' said the other Janissary. 'Now - do you have the money?'

They were about to make the transaction. He could not let it happen. The danger was, the Sicarii might take the Staff into the West - and the further west they went, the more the Sultan's influence would diminish. They had to keep the Staff in the East. Will tightened his fists.

'If you've deceived us, we won't hesitate to kill you,' Throaty was saying.

Green-eyes shrugged. 'You know precisely where we'll be - we're not looking to hide. We've brought you the Staff of Moses, from the Topkapi Palace. The very same captured by Sultan Selim when he defeated the Mamlouks. It left Egypt to go to Istanbul, and now it has returned.'

'Not for long,' snapped Throaty. 'This Staff is going to Venice.'

'Where you take the Staff is your business,' said Green-eyes. 'Now - payment.' He held out his hand.

Venetians! These were the men Commander Konjic had been tipped off about, Will thought. So it was true, the Staff of Moses was going to be taken to Catholic Italy - by Jewish mercenaries. It was uncanny, the sort of cross-religious dealings which were being carried out. The Protestant English were trying to set up in Turkey, as Catholic Europeans already had done. At the same time the Ottomans, Moroccans and Persians were involved in a three-way dispute with one another, constantly changing sides. Likewise, the European powers were in a permanent state of war.

Politics, Will thought, were the cause of so much conflict, and religion merely the banner under which men's ambitions were fulfilled.

He was about to reveal himself and create some kind of a diversion when he heard heavy footsteps approaching and ducked back into hiding. Marching into the hall were the two rapacious gladiator owners he had seen in the arena, collecting

127

the money: the very tall African and the squat, cruel-looking fellow.

'You!' said Green-eyes. 'What the hell do you want? Get out of here, this is none of your business.'

The Sicarius who was about to hand over a bag of coins, withdrew it, pocketing it safely. 'What is this, some kind of set-up?' the throaty Sicarius demanded, glaring suspiciously at the Janissaries.

'Odo is the name, famed tracker and hunter, you may have heard about me.'

And when the Sicarii and Janissaries looked baffled, he added: 'Or maybe not. This tall fellow here is Ja.'

The giant smiled, his white teeth gleaming.

'We don't care who you are,' Throaty snapped, and turned to the Janissaries. 'What do you mean by this? They're not part of the deal!'

'They're nothing to do with us,' said Green-eyes, raising his hands apologetically. 'I just saw this fellow in the arena this evening when I went to watch one of his gladiators. I'd never met him before.'

'Seems like he knows *you*,' Throaty said. The Sicarii were rattled, their hands on their weapons.

'What are you doing here?' asked Green-eyes.

'Oh, we mislaid something and we're looking for it,' Odo replied airily.

'Well, whatever it is, it won't be here,' said Green-eyes. 'Now get lost.'

The tall Ja moved around the hall, stealthily stepping behind and between the exhibits.

'You won't mind us investigating, will you? It's very valuable,' said Odo. 'Why don't you just carry on, pretend we're not even here? Maybe if I like what I see, I'll join your trade.'

128

Will dared not move. The giant swept around the hall, treading lightly for such a tall man.

Throaty lost patience. 'This is ridiculous. Get rid of this fellow, or else . . .' he threatened, drawing his weapon.

The green-eyed Janissary glared at Odo, who smiled unperturbed, as Ja stole around the hall. Reaching the statue of Alexander, the giant paused, sniffing the air. Odo slunk forwards, as the others watched. Whatever these unsavoury interlopers were looking for was behind the statue. Was it a thing, or a person?

The two men suddenly reached out and yanked the drapery away, revealing a young woman - the very same, Will saw, who had won the gladiatorial contest by decapitating her opponent. Her name, if he remembered correctly from the chants of the crowd, was Awa. She must have escaped somehow. Wide-eyed with shock, she bolted out from behind the statue, making a run across the hall. The Janissaries blocked her way, as did the Sicarii. Odo and Ja came up behind her. The six of them cut her off, forming a tight circle around her.

'We've found what we're looking for,' said Odo, beaming widely. 'We'll be on our way.'

The others relaxed. Awa whipped out a knife, pointing it at Odo and Ja.

'Tut tut,' said Odo. 'Come along quietly now. Tome is looking forward to having his way with you.'

The young woman wasn't going to get out of this situation without help. What could he do, on his own? Will's legs felt paralysed with fear. Then he remembered the kindness First Officer Said had shown him on board the *Al-Qamar*. It had made a colossal difference to his life. To hell with it! Will leaped out from where he was concealed and ran - barrelling into the back of the man called Odo. He took him down.

'You!' screamed Green-eyes.

Will squinted up at the Janissaries. 'Hello there.' He rammed Odo's face into the ground, hearing a bone crack. Rising, he felt an enormous hand grab the back of his tunic, lifting him clear off the ground. Will kicked out at the giant as he was lifted, but Ja blocked him with his other arm. Awa rolled under Will and plunged her dagger into the rear of Ja's knee, causing him to stumble and drop Will, who immediately sprang up and kicked the rising Odo in the face. Will then spun with his own sword, aiming the weapon at Ja, when someone caught his arm. It was Green-eyes.

'Oh no, you don't, sonny,' said the former Janissary, punching Will in the face as the second Janissary launched himself at Will with his weapon. Will blocked, going down to one knee, before countering. Awa flashed past, her blade slicing Green-eyes on the thigh, before she yanked the Staff from him, darting over to the statue of Alexander and leaping up onto the pedestal where it stood, clinging to him for balance.

The Sicarii hadn't entered the fray but stood observing. Odo ran at Will, who ducked at the last minute, causing the slave owner to crash into the giant.

'Stop! Or I'll break it!' screamed Awa. She held the staff horizontally. 'I will snap it in half!'

Everyone stopped still.

'He,' said Awa, motioning towards Will, 'and I get to leave, or else I split this Staff.'

'That's the Staff of Moses!' Throaty cried out. 'You won't do such a thing. You mustn't!'

As Awa stood, waiting for them to make up their minds, Will manoeuvred his way over to where she stood on the podium. They really needed Commander Konjic and the other Janissaries to turn up and make this an even fight.

Ja sluggishly rose to his full height. A line of blood dripped down his leg, as he dragged himself in her direction.

'Stay back!' Awa warned him.

The giant ignored her command.

'You're dead,' growled Odo, pointing at Will with his weapon.

Awa raised the Staff over her head, ready to smash it to pieces.

'Wait!' shouted Will. He could not let her destroy it. Sultan Murad III would be furious, the Grand Vizier would be livid. Any chance of him returning to England would be over. He would end up incarcerated in an Ottoman dungeon for the rest of his days.

Awa paused. She was bluffing, Will realised. Ja must have known it as well, for he took another bloody step towards her, grimacing with pain, then collapsed.

'Damn it,' said Awa, throwing the Staff like a javelin, high into the air, before leaping off the pedestal, landing in a crouched position.

Everyone stared up as the Staff sailed high over them. Ja made a grab for Awa, but she rolled under his outstretched hand, only to have Odo block her way. The squat man rammed his weight into her, causing her to lose her balance and slip on the blood pool left by Ja. Will's gaze flicked from the Staff to the young woman – and he chose. He sprang at Odo from behind and brought his sword down hard, driving the other man to his knees. Awa jumped up and stabbed Odo in the shoulder, causing him to drop his weapon.

'Don't ever come after me again,' she hissed.

It was then that Will, panting, realised the Sicarii and Janissaries had left the hall – and the Staff had gone with them.

'Come on,' he urged Awa. 'Let's get after them.'

Awa had her dagger poised to thrust into Odo's neck. The man gasped out: 'Hard times don't last for ever, hard people do. You'd better do it to make sure.'

Awa's hand trembled . . . but then she plunged her weapon into his thigh, ripping the blade back towards her. Odo grabbed his leg, screaming, as Awa did the same to the other leg. Cursing, he toppled to one side, in agony.

Will considered the young woman. 'My name's Will,' he said.

'I'm Awa.'

'We need to go, I have to get the Staff back.'

As Will and Awa hastened out of the hall, they heard Odo shouting after them, his voice fading.

'I will find you, Awa. I will follow you to the ends of the earth, and I will find you!'

23

INVITATION TO RIDE

AWA WAS NOT SURE WHY she was following Will. True, he had helped her out of a tight spot, but she had reciprocated by throwing the Staff, helping them escape. Was it truly the Staff of Moses, that had belonged to the great Hebrew prophet? A quiver ran down her spine at the thought of having held the same piece of wood which Moses had used to marshal the Israelites, and by which God had parted the waters of the Red Sea.

Will had run into trouble - two guards, waiting at the exit.

'Halt!' ordered one with a spear in his hand.

In the distance, Awa could see the Sicarii and the Janissaries. Having somehow eluded the sentries, they were sprinting down the coast road.

'We don't have time for this,' muttered Will. 'Sorry!' And he ran straight at the guards, rolling under the sword swipe of the first and striking him on the back of his head with the flat of his own weapon, sending the man sprawling. Will kicked the other guard in the stomach. He doubled over as Will jerked away his spear and hit him on the chin with the hilt of his weapon. The guard wobbled, and then he smacked the ground.

'Come on, Awa,' said Will.

She followed, desperate to put distance between herself and Odo. Otherwise why was she going with this young fellow? Could he be trusted? Pelting out of the grounds of the citadel, the pair rejoined the coastal road, this time heading away from town. The paved roadway soon ended, and they were slower over shingle laid on sand. Up ahead, the four men got into a waiting carriage and sped away. The chase was over.

'Damn it!' said Will, sliding to a halt and trying to catch his breath.

Awa mopped her brow, glad of a rest. He really was concerned about the Staff, she saw, as though it meant something to him personally. Why? Who was he?

'Will,' she said, 'thank you for saving me back there, but I need to be on my way now.'

'Wait! Why the hurry?' Will asked, loath to see her go.

'Whatever you're involved in is no concern of mine. The only thing on my mind is to survive this night and to live another day, and maybe one more,' she said, turning to leave.

'Whoa! Just hang on. If they catch you, it will be bad news for you. Why not stay with me - we can protect you.'

'We?'

'The Ottoman Janissaries.'

Awa shook her head. 'Like those Janissaries you are chasing?'

'No, not like them. They were Janissaries once, but now they're common thieves and mercenaries.'

The sound of a large carriage drawn by two horses made Awa jump; she whipped out her dagger.

'Kostas? Yes!' Will shouted.

The carriage skidded to a halt beside them, and an older man alighted. He was dressed in a kaftan over a tunic, with a sash around his waist; on it was tied a scabbard for a sword. The man was of average height, but appeared taller due to his powerful presence. He surveyed the scene, before turning to Will, then Awa, examining her. She saw concern in the way he observed her, and it made her want to stay.

'We need to get after them,' said Will, pointing towards the fast-disappearing Sicarii transport.

'And this young lady is?' said the older man.

'She helped me,' Will said. 'I would be dead otherwise. Her name is Awa, and she can fight - I mean *really* fight.'

'Well then, Awa, please join us,' the man said, before climbing back into the carriage.

Awa gripped the hilt of her dagger, gazing back at the citadel. How long did she have till they came after her? How long could she survive by herself? Whoever Will and these people were, they had resources and were organised. If by joining them in their quest it meant that she lived another day, it was one more chance she had of returning to the Songhai nation.

'By yourself you are but one woman, together we are a unit,' Will urged.

She nodded, then sheathed the dagger and got into the carriage. Will came in after her, shutting the door, and the vehicle began to move.

It was then Awa realised there were four others in the carriage, sitting on the bench opposite to her.

'We have a lady in our presence,' said the one on the right, who seemed like a Turk.

'Awa, this is Gurkan,' said Will. The Turk possessed a charming smile and he used it to good effect. It made her blush.

'This is Mikael and Ismail, up on top is Kostas. And most importantly, may I introduce you to Commander Mehmed Konjic,' said Will, indicating the man next to him. 'Everyone, this is Awa.'

'Commander?' asked Awa.

Konjic gave Will a hard look. Perhaps he had spoken too much.

'Awa overheard more than I did back there. She knows who we are,' said Will.

The carriage surged along the shingle and sand track, the sea to the right, the citadel a distant blur behind them.

'May I enquire what you learned from the conversation you listened to, Awa?' Konjic asked.

If she informed them of everything she had overheard, would they still need her? Awa wondered. Perhaps it was better to be cagey with the truth, only reveal some of it now. No. Though she had only just met this crew, there was something about them which made her feel comfortable, even safe.

Instead of replying directly, she asked: 'Are you all Janissaries?'

They all nodded.

'Serving Sultan Murad III,' said Konjic.

The carriage jolted, sending her flying into the arms of Gurkan.

'Sorry!' came the voice of Kostas from above. 'Stray goat on the road.'

The Turk helped her back to her seat; both she and Gurkan were bright red.

'Best hold on,' he said rather sheepishly.

The carriage continued at a breakneck pace, smooth and straight this time, picking up speed on the open road. Awa cleared her throat.

'The Sicarii are taking the Staff of Moses to Venice, where they will be selling it to a group called the Knights of the Fire Cross.'

As she spoke, the carriage skidded to a halt. Kostas jumped nimbly down from his seat, landing on shingle. 'Everybody out!' he called.

They had stopped before an enclosed section of the seafront, at the end of which was a pier, with a vessel moored by its side. The gates to the section were guarded by a row of warriors dressed in dark robes, armed with swords, lances and spears. Awa could see the two Sicarii and the two ex-Janissaries hurrying on foot towards the pier. One of the Sicarii held the Staff. They were going to get away, unless . . .

'Remember, a person who shows courage is a person who has mastered fear, not banished it,' said Konjic as he led the Janissaries forward. 'Gurkan, Kostas, you are the fastest runners, we will create space for you. Draw your weapons.'

Awa watched them depart. 'What about me?' she called after Konjic.

'This is not your fight,' the Commander called back, without turning round.

Will gave her a reassuring nod and Gurkan smiled, making Awa's heartbeat speed up. She had never experienced such a thing before and longed to embrace it.

'Attack!' yelled Konjic, leading the charge, with Will, Mikael and Ismail alongside him. Gurkan and Kostas tucked in behind them.

The warriors guarding the storage area remained where they were, letting the Janissaries come to them. Swords clashed, metal on metal, sparks flashing bright in the evening air. Awa observed how the warriors held their ground. The Janissaries fought, hard, but they were outnumbered twelve to six. Meanwhile, the Sicarii and the two thieves were going to get away, unless there was something she could do. But what?

One of the horses neighed behind her. She turned and studied the carriage, then squinted back towards the pier. *Could she?*

Awa untied the harness attaching one of the horses to the carriage. She mounted the mare, grabbing a tuft of hair on the mane and stroking her, whispering into her ear: 'Swift as the wind.' Then, digging her heels in, she swung the mare in the direction of the narrow gate, urging the animal into a gallop. Seeing her approach, the soldiers were distracted, allowing Will and Mikael to strike their opponents down. Gurkan and Kostas shot through the space.

'Out of the way!' shouted Awa, charging through the gates, knocking aside one of the guards, avoiding the Janissaries, as her horse galloped towards the pier at full speed.

'*Steady now,*' she whispered to the horse.

The Sicarii had boarded, as had one of the Janissaries, but the other was left behind. Her steed hurtled along the pier, the sea on either side of her, the wind billowing through Awa's hair. She felt *alive*. The end of the pier fast approached. She hadn't worked out what she was going to do - but her mare had. Deciding this was far enough, the horse pulled up short. Awa flipped over its head and onto the pier. The Janissary was only yards away. Readying herself, she took aim and threw her dagger. The blade buried itself into the back of the Janissary, who fell.

Awa ran past, kicking him in the head, knocking him out. As she stared up at the vessel on the left of the pier, she saw three archers with flaming arrows drawn. They fired at her. She threw herself to the ground, as the arrows whizzed over her, then rolled off the pier and into the sea. More arrows rained down. She dived under the pier and came up for air. There were voices overhead.

'Awa, Awa!' cried Gurkan.

'Awa!' echoed Will.

'Down here,' she shouted, slapped by the waves.

In the next moment, she saw the smiling face of Gurkan pop his head around one side of the pier and the concerned face of Will from the other.

'I'm fine,' she said.

A rope was thrown down and they hauled her out of the water. The vessel with the Staff had departed, sailing away into the Mediterranean, but the ex-Janissary she had wounded and knocked unconscious was still lying there, Commander Konjic standing over him. She gazed back, to see that the warriors who had been guarding the pier had dispersed. Their task was done; they had provided safe passage for the Staff of Moses to leave for Venice.

24

STRONG CUP

THE AROMA OF COFFEE PERMEATED the guesthouse. The Turkish Janissary called Ismail was very particular about the brewing process, but now it was done, he tasted and pronounced himself satisfied.

'You like it?' he asked Will.

'I do. I used to drink it in Marrakesh when I was apprentice to a quartermaster,' said Will, savouring the drink.

'Coffee is the lubricant of the soul,' sighed Ismail.

The front door opened and a haggard-looking Konjic returned with Kostas, Mikael and Gurkan.

'I could do with a cup of coffee, Ismail,' said Konjic as he and the others flung themselves into chairs around a dining table.

'Right away, sir.' Ismail hurriedly placed a freshly filled pot and a set of cups on the table.

Will pulled up a wooden chair and stared at Konjic expectantly. Far from being discreet, they had created a significant commotion the night before when trying to stop the Sicarii, and it left a whole lot of administration and bureaucracy to deal with it, when it came to the city authorities.

'What happened, sir?' he asked.

'It took some convincing and the production of the Seal of the Grand Vizier himself, to prevent them from arresting us. After that, it was a matter of telling them a story which avoided any mention of the Staff of Moses. Imagine what the news could do! The Topkapi Palace, home to the most powerful man in the world, broken into? No, that must never be made public. Anyway, we are in the clear. As for our new friend . . . will you ask her to join us, please?'

'I'll fetch Awa,' said Gurkan. He bounded up the stairs to collect Awa.

When Awa came down, she was dressed in men's clothing; they had given her a white kaftan, trousers, and even a turban, for when she went out. The girl was being hunted by ruthless slave traders who seemed to possess a knack for finding her. Disguising her as a man might help keep them off her trail.

'Awa, please join me,' said Konjic, ushering her to the table. 'Everyone else is dismissed.'

Exhaustedly, the others trudged upstairs to their rooms. 'No, Will, I'd like you to stay,' the Commander added. Gurkan gawped at him, desperate to remain, but he reluctantly obeyed orders.

'Coffee?' asked Konjic. 'Ismail brews a wonderful cup.'

'Please,' said Awa.

Konjic passed her the drink. '*Shukrun*,' said Awa in Arabic. *Thank you.*

'Awa, last night you helped us when there was no need to do so. You fought with tremendous skill and bravery, unlike any other young woman I have seen. I can understand why those slave traders caged you in the gladiatorial ring and why they are so desperate to find you. But rest assured, we are not going to let them,' said Konjic.

Awa's shoulders relaxed upon hearing his words.

'That is good to hear,' she said gratefully.

'I would like to help you, Awa,' Konjic went on, 'but before I commit to such a thing, I need to know who you are. Tell me how you came to be here today, sitting across this table.' He smiled encouragingly as he sipped the contents of his cup.

As both men listened attentively, Awa recounted her story.

Will's own recent past was pretty torrid, involving enslavement and adversity - but after hearing Awa's story, he realised he'd got off lightly. She was a high-ranking educated woman from a noble family, whereas he had always been on the periphery of society. It had been difficult enough for him, but it must have been intolerable for her. Somehow, through strength of character, she had retained her dignity during the trials and tribulations.

Konjic remained silent, rubbing his beard, deep in thought. Eventually he said: 'Awa, your tale is engrossing, to the point of it being a story one would tell one's grandchildren. My heart urges me to believe you. But for a man in my position, my rational faculties must also align with my emotional ones. If you have no objection, I would like to ask you one or two questions.'

Awa looked taken aback. 'Very well,' she whispered.

'Do not worry. Any elementary student will know the answers, and since you have a more formal education and broad range of subjects at your disposal, you'll be fine.'

'Please go ahead,' said Awa. Her voice trembled. Will liked her, he wanted her to get all of the answers to this test Konjic was setting her right, but he also knew the Commander had to ensure they were not being tricked.

'Are you familiar with the *Muqaddimah* of the fourteenth-century Tunisian historian, Ibn Khaldun?'

'I am.'

'Good. How does he describe the rise and fall of a dynasty, and what is the element which binds a group of people together?' asked Konjic.

Awa smiled. Will breathed a sigh of relief. He had no idea what the answer was, but from the expression on her face, she did.

'The thing that binds is the *'aṣabiyyah*, which can be described as a coming together, or solidifying around a certain idea. This *'aṣabiyya,* then propels a particular group into power, but it also carries the seeds of the group's eventual downfall.'

Will frowned. He didn't understand how a thing which drove a group or tribe to power could also result in its downfall.

'As for the rise and fall of a dynasty, Ibn Khaldun says the first generation of conquerors tend to be hardy tough desert travellers or Bedouins, who come from out of town and take over a city. The people of the city cannot put up a resistance to the barbarians and so submit. By the second generation, the conquerors have taken on the trappings of those they conquered, adopting their art, music, literature and culture. The third generation grows up, having lost nearly all connection with their desert roots. Decadence creeps in. The fourth generation is over-indulgent so is conquered by a sturdier force of Bedouins. And so the cycle continues.'

'An accurate summary of the idea,' said Konjic. 'Another question if I may. Ibn Sina, the Persian polymath of the tenth century, wrote *The Book of Healing*, which is a scientific encyclopaedia. However, as a teenager, which work was he so troubled by that he read it forty times before he finally understood it?'

Awa was unflustered. 'It was the *Metaphysics of Aristotle*, which Ibn Sina was finally able to understand after reading al-Farabi's commentary.'

Once more there was a smile upon the face of Konjic. Will felt like a dim-witted simpleton, if these were topics an elementary student knew about!

143

'Thank you, Awa. Clearly your father is a learned man and has given you the basis of a sound education. You have indeed satisfied my intellectual curiosity.'

'My father always says, to know a man, you must visit his library, for the contours of his mind have been shaped by the words on his bookshelf,' Awa said.

'I agree with him,' Konjic replied.

Will peered at the Commander. Was he now willing to trust Awa? The young woman had grown in confidence as she spoke about familiar topics. It must have been comforting, after the last few months of madness in her life. Her intellectual reach was beyond Will, but as he listened to her he made himself a promise: he was going to learn, become educated.

'We still have a challenge to overcome, Awa. What do we do with you?' said Konjic.

'She can come with us,' Will blurted out, then realised he should have kept his mouth shut, as Konjic stared repressively at him.

'What would *you* like, Awa?' Konjic asked.

The young woman gazed out of the window, across the balcony of the guesthouse. 'I wish to go home, to the Songhai nation.'

The Commander nodded. 'We all wish to return home.' He went on: 'You strike me as one who is patient, so you will know that things don't always happen in the sequence you want them to. I would like to offer you the opportunity to return to Timbuktu, but you must earn it.'

'How?' asked Awa.

'Join us. We could do with your martial skills and sharp mind. A rare combination. We may also need the guile and deftness of a woman for where we're headed next.'

'As a Janissary?'

'No. Women have not been entered into the Janissary corps and I would not possess the authority to break this tradition.

144

However, I invite you to join my unit, the Rüzgar, as an associate, a free agent if you will. I will pay you - the same as our cadets. You will remain under contract to work for me for three years, after which you may go.'

Three years! Will was expecting to be long gone by then. If Konjic wanted Awa to remain with them for that period of time, how long did he expect Will to serve? He waited with Konjic, as Awa considered the proposition.

'I agree,' she decided.

25

PREVENTION

WAVES THUMPED AGAINST THE VESSEL'S hull. The sea became clearer the further north they sailed up the Adriatic, away from the coast of Africa, away from the plains of the Sahara . . . away from the lands of her fathers.

With the vastness of the Mediterranean behind her, Awa's mood grew sombre; her heart numb at the thought of being in exile for three whole years. But if she had said no, the Rüzgar would have left her in Alexandria to fend for herself, to run the gauntlet of being re-captured by a vengeful Odo and Ja. With the Janissaries, she would be starting afresh in a foreign land.

The four-masted ship they had taken from Alexandria to travel to Venice was one owned by the Venetian authorities. The crew of the *La Liona* were Italians, Spanish and Portuguese. It was strange to see men devoid of colour. Awa had to remind herself that these men, like her, were the Children of Adam, all from the same origin. God had scattered people across the vast regions of the world, and part of His test was for peoples of different tribes and nations to understand one another by showing compassion. It seemed to Awa that this tenet of the Divine was often forgotten, trampled under man's insatiable pursuit of power.

In the morning, they sailed alongside the island of Corfu and straight into the Adriatic Sea. They cruised close to the eastern shores of Italy; ships heading south hugged the Balkan coast. Merchants and tradesmen made up the bulk of the passengers. As one of the few women on board, Awa caught unwanted stares wherever she went. After leaving port, she had decided to take off the men's clothing the others had given her, for it seemed unfitting for a woman to be wearing such garments. Earlier she had purchased, with an advance Konjic gave her, an outfit more suited to feminine tastes, but one that allowed her to move freely in conflict. Her curved scimitar was strapped to her waist, as were two knives; one she kept hidden, strapped to her ankle below her white trousers. To complete the outfit, Awa wrapped a long scarf around her neck; when she prayed, she used it to cover her head. She liked her new clothes, as they were practical, and she purchased two matching sets.

She noticed Will approach. He came to stand beside her at the aft of the *La Liona*, leaning against the railing and staring out at the clear waters of the Adriatic. She liked Will. From what he had shared about his life, his past was a troubled one. Despite his lack of formal education, of all the Janissaries, he understood her best. The pain of parting, the humiliation of enslavement, the plight of becoming destitute and then the crumbs of hope to hold onto, when all was lost. He knew all about that.

'Is Gurkan still ailing?' she asked him.

'Yes, he's lying down, incapacitated for now.'

Awa could tell that the Konyan had taken an immediate liking to her, and she did feel a mutual attraction; her heart always beat a little faster when Gurkan was close. But she was in no position to foster such feelings towards anyone in this turbulent world. The only certainty was the promise of

Konjic to release her after three years so she could return to the Songhai nation.

'The sea divides Africa from Europe,' Will mused. 'Yet the people who live in those lands need not be divided. I've lived in both places and I know from experience we are more alike than we'd care to believe.'

Awa nodded. 'I have never been so far from my home,' she sighed, as a breeze cut in from port, causing her scarf to billow out before her.

'And I have never been so close to mine,' said Will.

'I always wanted to travel, but now that I am, all I want is to go home,' she confessed, and Will laughed. Then she asked: 'Where is England?'

He explained: 'On the western side of Italy are the French. Beyond their lands, across a small body of water we call the English Channel, though the French may call it by another name, lies the land of the English. It is an island, made up of the Scottish, who live in the north, the Welsh in the west and the Irish, who lie on an adjacent island, further west.'

'The English rule over these other peoples?'

'At times, yes. Other times, no. At this moment, I'm not entirely sure. We have a Queen on the throne of England, her name is Elizabeth. She has been the monarch for many years and is fighting the Catholics of Europe.'

'She does not follow the Pope?'

'No, she does not.'

Awa glanced over her shoulder, leaning in a little. 'What of the Turks and their land?'

Will puffed his cheeks out. 'Istanbul is a city unlike any other. When you arrive, it shines like a jewel. The hand of the great architect Sinan is everywhere. As you approach along the Bosporus, you cannot but be amazed at the glories of the city and the reach of the Sultan, the most powerful man in the world.'

It sounded quite incredible, yet anything so phenomenal was bound to have a darker side to it. 'What troubles you when you are in the city?'

The question seemed to catch Will off-guard, for he too checked over his shoulder before replying and lowered his voice. 'Slavery. The Ottoman Empire, like the Roman Empire before it, is fuelled by slave labour - unpaid men and women who are worked into the ground. I see them on building sites, at the port, in galleys; their eyes devoid of hope, their spirits crushed.'

The young Englishman fell silent, and Awa recalled her time as a slave. She was still in servitude to another, though she earned an income from her efforts. It was a marked improvement on where she had been, but she was not free, as she had been in Timbuktu.

'The Moroccans enslaved the entire Songhai nation when they defeated us at the Battle of Tondibi,' she told Will. 'Our treasury was emptied, our gold and silver shipped to Marrakesh, our crops and food stolen, and my people made destitute.'

'What was it like at Tondibi?'

'It was the first time I had killed a man. I was left sickened by what I had done. Life and death is for God to decide.'

'You were defending your homeland,' Will said gently.

'Our scholars issued a ruling with the same advice, but it did not make me feel any better. Even the pleasant recollections I have of my family fade beside it. It's the vilest memories which remain.' Awa gazed away, remembering the face of the man she had slain. Will remained silent.

Eventually, she cleared her throat then changed the subject. 'You grew up in Marrakesh, Will. You must be close to the Moroccans?'

He shrugged. 'They're like everyone else. You have good and bad. My master, Hakim Abdullah, was a quartermaster, and always treated me with dignity. I served him, ran errands for his family, was spoken to with respect. Never did he raise his voice against me. Hakim was a common man but he had a noble spirit, which made him a greater human being than most I have met.'

'You miss him?'

'Yes, I miss my time with him, but not the situation I was in. Commander Konjic is also a kind man. We are fortunate to have found him when we did, for I fear I would not have lasted much longer in the galley.'

Awa gripped the handrail. She had conjured an image in her mind of all Moroccans being vile and cruel. Yet she knew from her own education and upbringing that this was never the case. Every tribe and nation held within it the capacity for good and evil. Still, it troubled her deeply.

'God is most merciful. Why then,' she asked passionately, 'did He let the Moroccans destroy my people and create such misery?' Her father would be mortified to hear such an utterance. Yet this was how she felt.

Will listened, then turned to the sea once more, to think how to reply. In the end, he said: 'One time I was with Hakim Abdullah, and we were travelling to a neighbouring town. Upon the road, we came across a merchant, flogging his slave for insubordination. Around him were his personal bodyguards, also kicking the poor fellow, for the merchant was rather corpulent, unsteady on his feet.

'Hakim hesitated. I sensed that he wanted to intervene, but after assessing the situation, he decided to move on. Later that evening, after we had eaten our meal, I asked my master why God permitted cruelty to be inflicted by one person on another. He told me that when there is injustice in the world, we should not blame God. We need look to ourselves, for God has appointed men and women as His stewards upon the earth and it is for us to help others when we are able to do so. God will ask us, "What did you do, when you witnessed injustice?"

'I said to my master, "It is not always possible to intervene, if one fears for one's own safety and livelihood, such as the encounter we had with the merchant on the road." My master smiled, for he realised that what was really troubling me was witnessing his urge to do something, then his failure to intervene. He related to me a saying of the Prophet Muhammad: "Whosoever of you sees an evil, let him change it with his hand; and if he is not able to do so, then let him change it with his tongue; and if he is not able to do so, then with his heart - and that is the weakest of faith".'

Will was about to add something, when a familiar voice interrupted them. It was Gurkan. 'How you two can keep so steady is a miracle,' he said, stumbling his way towards them.

He gripped the handrail and stared out at the horizon. 'Oh dear, just looking at the waves is making my stomach churn.'

'Why did you get up then?' said Will.

'I was going mad lying in the same position. Besides, I need to get used to staying onboard when we get to Venice. Commander Konjic says Turks are presently not welcome in Venice, so Ismail and I will need to remain on the *La Liona*.'

'What about the rest of us?' enquired Will.

'He's worked out new identities for you, including one for Awa,' said Gurkan with a smile.

26

BASILICA

DONG WENT THE BELLS OF the Basilica of St Mark's in Venice. Evening mass was in progress, and the faithful had gathered to pray for salvation. They had come from near and far, for this was a special week for the city state. Congregational prayers were held for Doge Pasquale Cicogna, whose leadership kept Venice at the forefront of trade in the Mediterranean. His position was an unenviable one, for he had to continually balance political, religious and commercial interests.

Will wanted to join the congregation but Commander Konjic had called a meeting and their small crew was assembling, taking chairs onto the patio of their guesthouse, which was located off one of the side streets near St Mark's Square. Gurkan and Ismail were absent, left on the *La Liona*, moored in the port. The Venetians had no problems in trading with Turks, but during this important week they did not want to see any Turks in their city state.

Venice, like Istanbul, was a cosmopolitan city of diverse cultures and beliefs, driven by an insatiable appetite to trade with the world. Will had seen Cypriots, Greeks, Danes, French, Spanish and the odd Englishman, transacting deals in the markets and exporting goods from the port. He had even heard of a vessel arriving from the exotic eastern market of India. The Venetians were Catholics but never on the best of terms with the Vatican, for they continued to trade with Protestants as well as those from rich Muslim lands.

Will poured the coffee. It was his first attempt to make it without the supervision of Ismail. He filled the cups of Kostas, Mikael and Awa, and when Konjic entered the room, one for him, before pouring his own. The five sat in wicker chairs around a circular table, and Will observed them discreetly as they sipped the drink. No adverse reactions. He drank from his own cup. It was quite good. Not as sweet as Ismail's concoction, but that wasn't such a bad thing.

'Tomorrow afternoon is the official opening of the newly reconstructed Rialto Bridge, which spans the Grand Canal,' Konjic announced. 'This bridge is built of stone, not wood - and Doge Cicogna has invited many dignitaries to the ceremony. All of the resident ambassadors, leaders of merchants' guilds and notable foreign visitors will be in attendance. Through some connections, I have managed to reach out to Antonio da Ponte, the architect who designed the bridge. Antonio very kindly met me this morning and provided three tickets to the opening.'

Despite political differences between Catholics and Ottomans, artists were relatively free to exchange ideas. Will had seen Christian and Jewish artisans in Istanbul, plying their trade and, in some cases, being given patronage by the Sultan. If Konjic said he had three tickets, no doubt he and Mikael would be left out. He was right.

'Kostas and Awa will join me at the ceremony. Mikael and Will, you will be patrolling the public spaces. This is the most significant event in Venice this year, and it's no coincidence that the Sicarii have arrived at this time. Whoever is buying from them will be at the opening. I need you all to be vigilant,' said Konjic.

153

'Aren't we looking for the Knights of the Fire Cross?' Mikael asked.

'Like the Sicarii themselves, they are merely handlers,' replied Konjic. 'The real buyer sits behind them, shielded in the shadows. Their identity and intentions are a mystery. If we are to stop the transaction, we will need to discover who they are and where the Staff is going next. If we miss this opportunity, I fear it may slip out of our hands.' Konjic paused, glancing down at his cup of coffee. 'The Grand Vizier was very clear when he told me: *"Return with the Staff, or do not return at all"*.'

It had never occurred to Will that the stakes were so high. He felt tension seize the back of his neck, as though a hand were squeezing it. It was the same feeling he had had when the oarmaster was about to whip him. Will did not want to disappoint his Commander; if Konjic were removed, what would it mean for him? A return to the life of a galley slave? It seemed to Will in that moment, that those at the bottom of the pyramid, such as galley slaves, were powerless; while those near the apex, close to power, lived on the edge.

'Kostas, you and I will continue to maintain our Balkan Trading Company identities. It has served us well to date and the papers have passed inspection in Alexandria, as well as the Port in Venice. Remember, we are visiting to see how we can facilitate trade with the Balkan regions, through our Turkish entities. Now, to Awa.'

Will and the others turned to look at their newest recruit. If they floundered, what would it mean for her? Every day Will spent with her, he came away feeling he knew so little of the world compared to this Songhai woman. Not only was she sharper of mind, her martial qualities also outstripped his own.

'Yes, Commander?' she said.

'You will be impersonating a noblewoman from Gao. Your father is a wealthy landowner from the province. He has appointed me, in my capacity as an officer of the Balkan Trading Company, to identify suitable Venetian products which can be exported to West Africa. He is particularly interested in luxury items, which are highly sought after amongst the affluent and which fetch a healthy profit. Unable to travel due to his commitments, he has sent you on his behalf.'

Awa lowered her head. 'Gao has been destroyed by the Moroccans.'

'I know, because you told me. News has not reached Ottoman lands, however, and it will not have been heard about in Venice,' said Konjic, who observed Awa with a sympathetic eye. 'If you impersonate a character whose background you are familiar with, there will be less opportunity to make a mistake.'

She nodded, trying to smile.

'Any questions?' asked Konjic.

'I will need to be suitably dressed,' Awa told him.

'A dressmaker has been arranged and will be arriving shortly with a number of costumes in the latest Venetian fashions for you to choose from. I leave the matter entirely in your hands. My only advice is to select something elegant, but which does not draw too much attention to yourself.'

Konjic went on: 'If someone asks about your family, such as how many siblings you have, improvise. Don't go into detail, keep it superficial. Try and meet as many people as possible, ask them what they trade in. Mention that your father is personally very interested in acquiring rare religious artefacts. See if anybody latches on, mentions that they know a seller. The Sicarii after all are handlers, and like any mercenary organisation, may switch allegiance - if offered the right price.'

'And what would be the right price?' Awa was curious to know.

'Don't worry about particulars, focus on articulating your intentions. Detail can be filled in afterwards. Besides, you're

155

far too important to worry about such trivial concerns as cost. Your administrators, myself and Kostas, will take care of such matters.'

Awa nodded. She was remarkably composed, Will thought admiringly. He had seen her in action in the field. He remembered the way she rode the horse along the pier, showing courage and intelligence. She almost caught the Sicarii.

On Konjic's prompting, Kostas wrapped up the briefing with additional information about the key personalities they were going to meet. Every notable person in Venice was likely to be in attendance. After Kostas finished, Konjic dismissed them. As he did so, there was a knock on the door and the dressmaker arrived. Two servants hauled in a heavy trunk, stuffed with clothes. Awa and the lady disappeared upstairs, and the two servants vanished, leaving Will to heave the trunk up the flight of stairs.

He knocked on the door. 'Trunk is here,' he said breathlessly.

'Good,' said the dressmaker. 'Now off you go, young man, we have work to do.'

Will trudged back down, returning to the empty table. He was about to sit when he remembered St Mark's Basilica. Perhaps there was still time to attend the service? He nipped out and strode down the narrow street linking their guesthouse to the main square, and soon found himself standing beside the four bronze horses at the entrance to the basilica. He stopped to marvel at the craftsmanship.

'Brought over from Constantinople,' said a crackly voice behind him. Will turned to see an old man, hunched, sitting on a pedestal with a bowl beside him. 'You been there, young feller?'

'Constantinople?' said Will.

The old man nodded.

'Briefly, for business, but of course not at the moment. Things are a little tense, what with the Turks and all,' said Will.

'Excuse me, I'd better be getting in for the service.' He turned to go, but the old man coughed and motioned with his eyes towards his begging bowl.

Will thought for a moment. He was in a church and God instructed people to be charitable. He took out a coin and dropped it in the bowl, before smiling at the old man and entering through the left doorway. He came to a halt in the foyer before the main church and was overwhelmed by the finery and magnitude of the mosaics. There were thousands of them, carefully placed, telling numerous stories. Gold shone off the tiles, glittering in the reflection of a thousand candles. Within each cavernous dome in the roof was a story: above him was the tale of Noah and the Flood. The marble floor was designed in geometric detail.

As he approached the first archway, two replica griffins glared at him. Will slipped onto one of the benches, lowering his head. He reminded himself he had come to pray. He wasn't a Catholic or a Protestant. He was simply a Christian. Will then sank to his knees on the cushion placed on the marble floor. He prayed for his mother and the father he had never met. He prayed for England, the country he never knew, and the Queen, the monarch he would one day serve. He prayed for his safe return to London, the city he was taken from. He prayed for Istanbul, the city which took him in. And he prayed for Commander Konjic and the Rüzgar unit he served, for they were akin to family.

As he started to rise from his position, he noted a hefty-looking fellow, martially dressed. The man wore gloves, but as he knelt down, the sleeve of his tunic went up, to reveal a tattoo - of a burning cross. The Knights of the Fire Cross: handlers who were going to receive the Staff from the Sicarii. The man became aware of Will's interest, so Will quickly rubbed his knee, feigning discomfort as his reason for being slow in rising.

In case the Knight looked again, Will limped off the bench, then scuttled to the back of the cathedral, keeping out of sight. He was in time to see someone approach the tattooed man and tap him on the shoulder; the two men turned and left the church together. Will darted after them and saw they were headed in the opposite direction to the guesthouse.

He mustn't miss this chance: he had to follow them. Will knew that his disappearance would cause concern to the Rüzgar, but that couldn't be helped. He would say sorry later. Lifting up his collar, he shadowed the men, away from the Basilica.

27

BRIDGE TOO FAR

THE ROAD FROM ST MARK'S Square to the Rialto Bridge was packed with excited crowds. Their progress in the cramped carriage was slow: it would have been quicker to walk. However, it was not befitting for Awa, Konjic and Kostas to be seen walking amongst the throng in their elaborate evening wear. In some ways it suited Awa to sit in the dawdling transport, as it was hard to move in the elaborate floor-length bright blue gown she wore. Her breathing was constricted by the corset, and the embroidered partlet covering her neckline made her want to scratch. Upon her head she wore a cap, lined in silk and attached to a band, pinning her hair up. It was all so uncomfortable.

The trio finally alighted and made their way to the marquee set up for dignitaries, who would be the first to cross the bridge following the grand opening by Doge Pasquale Cicogna. Afterwards, the people of Venice would be able to cross the new bridge.

'Any news from Will?' asked Konjic.

'No, sir. He seems to have disappeared after this afternoon's briefing,' said Kostas.

Will had spoken to Awa about his desire to return to England. Had he already fled? she wondered. In Venice, he was closer to home than he had ever been, so perhaps the temptation to run was too great.

The Commander nodded. 'I'm sure he will show up.'

'Yes, sir,' said Kostas, but Awa detected uncertainty in his voice.

Guards patrolled, keeping unwanted guests out. Entering the marquee, Awa was struck by the range of nationalities present, all wearing the traditional clothes of their country. She herself wished she was wearing the regal dress of the Songhai women.

'Remember Awa, you *are* a noblewoman,' said Konjic in a soft voice.

Only weeks before, she had been a slave, living in squalor, surrounded by sickness; death in the arena a constant threat. It was all a long way from her beginnings in the noble city of Timbuktu. Now here she was, swanning about in the high echelons of Venetian society in a dress fit for a queen. It made her giddy thinking about it.

The Rialto Bridge was adorned with a series of lamps, illuminating its grandeur as the sun set. The bridge had been cleverly designed with two inclined ramps meeting in a portico in the centre of the bridge, allowing for the passage of tall ships.

'Life is made of moments, each moment an opportunity. Come,' beckoned Konjic. He took them towards a frail-looking man. '*Buongiorno*, Antonio!' he said, shaking the man's hand.

'*Salve!*' the man replied.

'Antonio, this is Awa Maryam al-Jameel, whom I mentioned when we met yesterday.'

'Enchanted to meet you,' said Antonio, with a courtly bow.

'Awa, this is Signor Antonio da Ponte, the architect who designed the new Rialto Bridge, and who kindly invited us to the opening,' said Konjic.

'Thank you for allowing us to view your marvellous creation, signor,' said Awa, curtseying.

'Kostas, my bookkeeper.' Konjic introduced him in turn.

Da Ponte asked a server to return with three glasses of pomegranate juice for his guests. While they sipped, he explained the intricacies of creating the new stone bridge. The previous one had been built of wood and regularly collapsed. This one he expected to last a thousand years, he told them - unless an earthquake sank it, which he could do nothing about since it was the will of God. His competitors were jealous of his work, he confessed, for he was a man of humble origins. Fortunately, despite these people plotting against him, filling the Doge's ear with doubts about his abilities, Cicogna had remained loyal to him and da Ponte had repaid him with this fine bridge.

'Here comes His Eminence now,' the architect said. An elderly man with a long beard, dressed in immaculate cream robes and draped in a red cloak, was walking towards them: he was wearing the distinctive horned ducal cap. Behind him were two hefty guards.

'Antonio, I will need you for a moment,' said Cicogna.

'Yes, of course, my Doge. May I introduce Mehmed Konjic of the Balkan Trading Company? He is facilitating access for our merchants to the East.' The architect chose his words carefully, not mentioning Turks or Ottomans.

'We are always grateful to those who provide our merchants with openings to new markets,' said Cicogna.

'Venice is a diamond, its merchants jewellers. It is we who are honoured,' Konjic replied humbly.

The Doge was pleased with the comment. He and da Ponte then moved to the far corner of the marquee, the two bodyguards trailing behind them.

Awa meanwhile was regarding everyone there with suspicion, however rich and well-favoured they might be. Was the mastermind present, the one who had planned the theft

161

of the Staff? She was a skilled fighter, but spying on others like this made her uneasy.

'Konjic! Lovely surprise,' drawled a man dressed in an outfit with wide shoulders and puffed sleeves. He wore an embroidered doublet with silver buttons, and a blue gemstone was sewn beside his collar. His tall felt cap sparkled with jewels.

'Sir Reginald Rathbone!' said Konjic, shaking the newcomer by the hand.

'What brings you here, my good man?' Rathbone asked.

Awa noticed a large bearded fellow standing a few feet away, clearly with Rathbone - perhaps a bodyguard. He was immaculately dressed in black and grey from head to foot, and his neck was the width of a tree trunk. When he locked fierce eyes with Awa, it sent a shiver down her back.

'We've been doing business with the Venetians for years, you know how it is. Officially the Ottomans are at war, but not when it comes to making money.'

Konjic was about to introduce Awa, but Rathbone was too full of himself to notice. 'I heard the Moroccans made a huge profit by raiding those savages, the Songhai,' he was saying. 'Imagine, King Askia was stashing away more gold than in al-Mansur's entire treasury in Marrakesh. They acquired plump war booty and the Earl of Leicester is a happy man as it means the Moroccans will likely pay him for his next shipment of steel. Trade has been poor since the Battle of the Three Kings.'

Awa clenched her fists. Fortunately, they were covered by the embroidery around her wrists.

Despite Konjic's assurance, news *had* already travelled about the destruction of her people . . . As before, Rathbone was oblivious, but Awa saw that the bodyguard was watching her carefully. She immediately unclenched her fists and released her breath.

'I see,' said Konjic, glancing at Awa. 'Are the English doing much business with the Moroccans?'

English! Rathbone was from the same land as Will? How could that be? Will was gentle and thoughtful, while this man was pompous and arrogant.

'Only through Leicester. It's an interesting market, but they don't pay on time. Ottoman and Safavid agreements are key to opening up doorways to the East.' It was at this moment that Rathbone noticed Awa, raking her from head to toe with a hard stare.

'Allow me to introduce Awa Maryam al-Jameel, who is acting on behalf of her father, a person of considerable wealth. And you know my bookkeeper Kostas, whom you met aboard the *Misr*.'

Rathbone acknowledged Kostas, then turned to Awa. 'And where might you be from, Awa?' he asked condescendingly.

'West Africa,' Awa replied.

'That's a big area, where specifically?'

Awa was trying to keep calm in the face of the inquisitive Englishman. 'You won't know it.'

'Try me.'

'Yes, well,' Konjic interjected. 'Her father's shareholdings and lands stretch across many territories. Sir Reginald, if I may enquire, what brings you to Venice at this time of the year?'

Rathbone's stare lingered on Awa a moment longer, before he turned and replied with a smile: 'Oh, Stukeley,' he motioned with his head to the large bodyguard, 'and I are in town to collect an item.'

'It must be very precious if it needs you to collect it in person,' Konjic said carefully.

'One of its kind,' Rathbone agreed.

Konjic exchanged a look with Kostas and was about to say something, when Rathbone asked: 'Where is young Will Ryde?'

'Just out on an errand,' said Konjic.

'Shame. I'd love to have met him. Please convey my best,' Rathbone said in a laconic manner.

'Gentlemen, ladies, please come.' They were being ushered towards the Rialto Bridge for the opening ceremony. The guests moved to the St Mark's side of the bridge, everyone keen to try out the stone walkway.

'No doubt we'll be seeing you, Sir Reginald,' said Konjic.

The Englishman studied the Commander, taking his hand and shaking it. 'I'm sure,' he said, before departing with Stukeley.

They watched the two Englishmen move on up ahead, before the Commander murmured, 'Kostas, follow them. I want to know who they are going to meet after the ceremony and what they have come to collect.'

'Yes, sir.' Kostas split away from them and surreptitiously began to trail behind Rathbone and Stukeley.

'You did well not to react,' Konjic praised Awa.

Awa still brooded, however. She had been tempted to draw the blade she had strapped around her ankle and put it to Rathbone's throat, for the manner in which he spoke about her people.

She and the Commander followed other dignitaries along the canal bank, forming an orderly line to cross the bridge. Everyone stopped as the Doge waited at the foot of the bridge. He turned to the Patriarch, who led a small prayer. The guests bowed their heads. The blessing given, the Doge led the visitors across the stone structure, accompanied by roars of approval from the ordinary Venetians watching from both banks.

Awa approached the bridge with some caution, as her dress made it difficult to ascend the stone incline. She urged Konjic to go on ahead. Soon she found herself next to a man who was clinging to the side of the bridge, looking down at the Grand Canal with a great deal of trepidation.

'Sir, are you all right?' Awa asked.

The fellow shot her a look. 'Madam, how can anyone be all right? This bridge will collapse at any moment. I predicted it, when they gave that amateur da Ponte the contract to build the new Rialto.'

'And you are?' asked Awa.

'Vincenzo Scamozzi! Venice's number one architect.'

She watched him scurry across the bridge as quickly as possible. He seemed genuinely convinced that the bridge was unsafe. Konjic was waiting for her when she reached the other end.

The Commander beckoned her close. 'Awa, you and I have more people to meet and questions to ask. We will listen and we will learn. Remember - no one can be trusted. We must keep our wits about us at every moment.'

28

GHETTO

LIGHT AND LAUGHTER FLOWED OUT of the inn. Will had followed the Knights from the Basilica of St Mark's to a wine house and was now hanging around outside, waiting for them to reappear. Twice so far, he had sneaked up to the narrow windows to take a peek inside. The men were seated at a corner table, their backs turned to the entrance. On the third occasion, Will saw that they had been joined by two more Knights.

Finally, after spending more than an hour at the inn, the men departed. When they left, they appeared remarkably sober.

Their next stop was at a guesthouse; they vanished inside and came out only moments later, wearing black cloaks and hoods. Will could see swords concealed beneath their clothing, strapped to their belts. He was mulling over how to get word to Commander Konjic when he spotted a sprightly young lad sitting on a crate.

'Here, lad,' said Will. 'Can you deliver a message for me?'

'Right away.'

'I need you to find a man called Konjic. He is staying at the Blue Flag guesthouse, off St Mark's Square. I need you to tell him: *Will Ryde has found the Knights. Not sure where they are going, but is in pursuit.*'

The lad peeked at the four burly men, disappearing down the street. He repeated what he had been told, took part payment from Will and scurried away. The Knights marched at a brisk pace, but kept a constant lookout, forcing Will to stay further back than he would have liked. Once or twice he thought one of them had spotted him, so he lingered before hastening to catch up with them. The four men stopped at the Chiesa dei Santi Apostoli; the church was still open, and they entered. Will assumed they had gone inside to pray. Afterwards they continued north-west, following the curve of the canal, and then summoned a boatman to row them down the Rio dei Servi. Will followed suit.

The Knights alighted and made their way to the upper tip of Venice. As the buildings and roadways grew dilapidated, Will realised the men were heading to the ghetto, the Jewish quarter. He pulled up, uncertain about entering an area which after dark had its gates shut. He observed the men speak with the Venetian guards on patrol outside. One of the Knights paid them, after which they were allowed entry. Will checked his pockets: he had coin, but what was he going to tell them?

As he pondered what to say, he noticed a young man walk by, one arm steadying an awkward load stacked up above his head. With his other arm he was pushing a wheelbarrow containing curious glass globes, the insides of which were hollowed out to reveal intricate metal lattices. Will took him to be an apprentice of some kind, possibly to a metal-worker.

'*Shalom*, my friend,' said Will, coming out from his hiding place.

The startled young man spilled what he was holding, before nearly tripping into his own wheelbarrow. Will dashed forwards, helping him to collect up the items he had dropped.

'Sorry, my friend,' said Will. 'Allow me to lend a hand.'

The fellow eyed him with suspicion. 'Are you going to rob me?' he asked nervously.

'No, of course not. You looked like you were about to drop your load and might need help,' Will said.

'Well, I did drop it, didn't I,' the young man said resentfully, 'having borne it successfully for the past mile.'

'That was my fault – I do apologise. My name is Will. You are?'

The fellow sighed then cocked his head to one side. 'You do want something, don't you? Come on, speak up.'

Will scanned the entrance to the ghetto; the Knights would be well on their way to their rendezvous with the Sicarii. He must be swift. 'I need to go into the ghetto, but . . .'

'Yes?'

'I'm not Jewish.'

'No one's perfect.'

Will did a double-take, then noticed the young man was joking.

'Come on, who is the Jewish beauty who stole your heart? She had better not be a cousin of mine!'

Will hesitated. 'Um, it's meant to be a secret, but . . . if I tell you her name, will you help me enter?'

'No,' said the young man, taking his items from Will.

'Wait,' said Will. He saw he had no choice but to be honest. 'I'm following four men, they're part of a group called the Knights of the Fire Cross. They've just gone into the ghetto. I think they're meeting with the Sicarii.'

The apprentice inhaled sharply. 'Not good.'

'No, not good at all. I need to follow them, because they are in possession of something which doesn't belong to them. Something so precious that I'm not permitted to tell you what it is, but if you can help me get in, then I'm sure my master will be very satisfied and will offer you any assistance you might need,' said Will.

'What is your master's designation?'

He didn't have time for this, but if it got him into the ghetto . . . 'He is a very prominent merchant of Istanbul who is in Venice conducting business with the Doge himself.'

'Really? Where was he this evening?'

'At the opening of the Rialto Bridge. He was a special guest of architect Antonio da Ponte,' said Will.

The young man considered. 'Very well. My name is Anver. Stick close to me, keep your head down, don't look the guards in the eyes and play along with what I do.' Anver dumped all of the metal objects into Will's arms, then told him to follow. They approached the entrance, Anver striding ahead, leaving Will to push the wheelbarrow as well.

'Hurry up, you fool,' said Anver, motioning for Will to keep pace.

Will could barely see where he was going in the evening murk, but he succeeded in passing the guards without incident. Once inside, they turned a corner and Will handed back the items to Anver.

'Not so fast, Will,' said Anver. 'I'm coming with you. This is a Jewish quarter and I don't want you stumbling into some kindly old couple's house with your talk of crusading Knights.'

Will thought Anver seemed a decent enough fellow. He needed a guide, and this peculiar lad with these metal contraptions was likely better than most.

'Thank you,' he said simply.

'First, we need to drop my belongings off,' said Anver.

'But the Knights are going to get away!' Will fretted.

'Everyone knows the Sicarii stay in the kosher butcher's house, in the western quarter. Besides, my place is on the way. Come on, we don't want to be late.' And Anver zipped off with the wheelbarrow, leaving Will to trail after him, his arms still full of junk.

Crumbling buildings loomed over them. The pathways were empty as the hour was late. Anver cut into a narrow side street, the wheelbarrow barely fitting as he trundled it along. There was an open drain on one side, which stank. Will was shocked. The ghetto was a far cry from the grand walkways of St Mark's. It was difficult to believe they were in the same city, barely half an hour's walk from the Basilica.

Anver opened a door and piled his wheelbarrow in, took the items from Will and stacked them inside.

'Wait a minute,' the young Jew instructed, before disappearing further within. Will could hear metal objects being lifted and moved about, before Anver resurfaced with a sack slung across his shoulder, saying, 'Let's go.'

They moved more quickly without the wheelbarrow, running along deserted streets before approaching the kosher butcher's house, distinguishable from the outside by its arrangement of terracotta pots containing sea grass, as well as goats tied to one side, inside a locked enclosure. The animals were silent. Lamplight illuminated the interior. Will crept closer to the structure, Anver beside him, the sack on his back rattling with the sound of objects clanging together.

'Who are the Knights?' whispered Anver.

'I don't know, but they're about to take possession of the . . . of an item which belongs to my employer.'

Voices could be heard, but not clearly, and visibility was poor. Will moved around the edge of the building, considering a way in. There was only the main entrance. Cautiously, his heart in his mouth, he nudged the door open. The voices grew louder. Keeping low, the young men padded along the corridor, lit by a solitary lamp at the end. When wooden panels creaked, Will clutched Anver and made him stop. At the end, the corridor turned right and led into an open courtyard with rooms branching off on either side. It smelled of meat: this must be where they sacrificed the animals. Herbs were planted in the ground at one end, otherwise it was partially-paved with cracked slabs.

As they crept around the corner, they saw the four imposing figures of the Knights standing not too far from them. On the other side of the courtyard was a large group of the Sicarii, including the two Will had encountered in Alexandria. Throaty was gripping the Staff of Moses, holding it with reverence before him.

'It is with a heavy heart I hand the Staff of Moses to you,' he announced.

Anver jerked with shock beside Will, and for a moment he thought the young man was going to keel over. Will grabbed him, looking him in the eye and placed a warning finger over his lips.

One of the Knights, wearing a red glove on his right hand, removed a bag of coins and held it out.

'Count it,' said Throaty, motioning to one of his companions. A thin man stepped forward and poured the coins out on a table. Gold glittered, as he fingered his way through them. Eventually he nodded.

'Here, take it,' said Throaty, handing over the Staff to Red-glove. 'And treat it with care.'

Before Will could react, Anver leaped from his hiding place. 'No!' He still had his sack flung over his shoulder and it clanged about.

'Who are you?' cried Throaty.

The Knights drew their blades, pointing the weapons at Anver, who stumbled, stepped back and tripped.

'An imbecile,' snorted Throaty. 'Take him away,' he instructed the Sicarii around him.

Gripping his weapon, Will revealed himself and drew the blade from its scabbard. He came to stand by Anver.

'Janissary!' said Throaty, his eyes widening. The Knights spun, searching for others.

'We have the place surrounded,' said Will in a ringing voice. 'Hand back what belongs to Sultan Murad III, custodian of the religious treasures of the Topkapi Palace, and we will let you live. Defy us, and face the wrath of the Ottoman army.' Will was bluffing, but he hoped the Sicarii and the Knights would fall for it.

'You idiots, you've alerted the Janissaries and brought them here!' Red-glove barked.

'No, of course we haven't,' Throaty growled, furious.

Red-glove motioned for one of the Knights to go and look outside. Only moments remained before the game was up. Whatever Will was going to do, he needed to do it *now*.

29

MESSENGERS

THE RIALTO BRIDGE CEREMONY HAD passed triumphantly: the patrons were lavished with praise, the guests replete with fine food, and the public delighted at having a new crossing over the Grand Canal. Only the Janissaries were down-hearted, for they were no closer to solving the theft of the Staff of Moses.

The boatman dropped them off close to the Basilica, since their guesthouse lay nearby. The piazza was vacant but for a drunk staggering back to his lodging and a couple rendezvousing under cover of darkness. Awa spotted an evening patrol - two uniformed members of the Venetian guard, circling the Basilica.

'I found the Spanish Ambassador much too full of himself,' Konjic was telling Awa and Mikael. 'All he spoke about was their kingdom's conquests over the Inca and Aztec peoples in the Americas. The *conquistadores* have plundered gold and silver from these societies and to be quite frank, I fear the effect such an influx of gold will have on Ottoman trade. But despite his self-centred view of the world, I doubt he has anything to do with the theft of the Staff.'

Awa thought of Tome, who had been her trainer, jailer and in the end her would-be rapist. Because of him, she would forever hold a grudge against the Spanish, though she knew it was irrational to condemn an entire race of people on the basis of the depravities of a few.

'What of the Portuguese?' asked Mikael.

Konjic shook his head. 'Still recovering from the humiliation of losing at the Battle of the Three Kings. They are no more than a vassal state for the Spanish. Their fleet has seen some action against the plucky English, but they are in no position financially to acquire the Staff, nor do they have the resources and influence.'

Konjic turned to her. 'Awa, what was your impression of the Venetians?'

'It seems to me that buying and selling is in their blood. Their aim is to keep all parties happy, which in turn keeps trade buoyant. Why would they want to anger any commercial partners, especially the Ottomans, by stealing the Staff? It does not make business sense.'

'Well put. I agree with you,' Konjic nodded.

'But,' Awa added by way of a caution, 'there was a Cardinal in attendance, and it occurred to me that the Vatican may have an interest in acquiring the Staff.'

Konjic said thoughtfully, 'They certainly have the money and influence. They might be using the Knights of the Fire Cross through one of their proxies, but we don't have any evidence for that, so it's merely conjecture. Let's do some more digging - there might be a lead to follow.'

In truth, Awa wasn't sure how useful she had been at the big event, since she was rather reticent about approaching people she did not know. The most fascinating conversations of the evening had been with the Africans from the continent's interior, who described the lush fauna of their homeland, the wild beasts and colourful jungle creatures. Had she not had work to do, she could have listened to them all night long.

174

Their route took them past the Basilica, now an imposing shadow looming large behind them. They strode across the Piazza in the night chill.

'Mikael, what did you observe?' asked Konjic.

'Not much, Commander. I located a couple of handlers of stolen goods, but these were freight gangs who specialise in avoiding taxes set by port authorities. No one seemed to know anything about religious artefacts being traded in Venice.'

'Let's see what Kostas has to say. I asked him to follow Sir Reginald Rathbone.'

'That fellow we met on the *Misr*?' asked Mikael.

'The very same. My suspicions were aroused when he said he was here to collect something which was "one of its kind". What is his role in this game, I wonder.'

When they turned into the alley where the Blue Flag guesthouse was located, they found a boy dozing in the porch. Mikael shook him. 'Wake up, laddie.'

Startled, the boy sat up, stuttering, 'I'm waiting for a man named Konjic.'

'I am he.'

'I have a message.' The boy screwed up his face, remembering. *'Will Ryde has found the Knights. Not sure where they are going. But in pursuit.'*

Konjic exchanged glances with Mikael and Awa. 'Was it Will himself who gave you this message?'

'Yes, sir, I believe so, sir. Tall. Fair hair, pale white skin.'

'Yes, it's him. Where were you when he gave you the message?'

'Over by the San Apostoli Church.'

Konjic paid the lad generously and sent him on his way. He then turned to Mikael, saying, 'If the Knights and Sicarii are getting together, we will need the support of Gurkan and

Ismail. Go and fetch them from off the *La Liona*; ask them to be hooded, faces hidden. It's dark so they should be all right, but I don't want to take any chances and cause a diplomatic incident when Turks are not permitted in Venice at this time.'

'Yes, sir,' said Mikael, scooting out.

'Awa, you need to get changed for action.'

Awa nodded, pleased. What a relief, to struggle out of these restrictive garments and get back into the comfortable attire she had purchased.

Awa and Konjic were both back downstairs, armed and waiting for Mikael to return when there was a knock on the door. Mikael had the other set of keys to the front door - so who else would be calling at this hour of the night? Awa's hand went to her weapon. Could it be Odo and Ja, intent on snatching her again?

'Who is it?' Konjic enquired, approaching the door.

'Message for a Signor Konjic.' Another young lad.

The Commander pulled open the door to reveal a scrawny freckle-faced boy with an untidy mop of hair. 'I am he.'

The boy scanned him up and down. Konjic pulled his cape around him, concealing his weapons.

'Message from Kostas: *Rathbone has gone to the ghetto. I am here. Come immediately.*'

'Describe Kostas to me, lad.'

'Greek chap. Curly black hair. Was wearing a grey cloak. Mighty fine piece of clothing for the ghetto.' The boy made a face.

Konjic gave the lad a coin and sent him on his way. He was about to shut the door, when they heard light footsteps heading in their direction. Mikael had returned with Gurkan and Ismail.

Gurkan exchanged a beaming smile with Awa, who was happy to see him.

'We had a message: Will has located the Knights and was following them. We don't know where,' Konjic informed them. 'Kostas meanwhile has followed Sir Reginald Rathbone to the ghetto, a most peculiar location for a distinguished gentleman to be frequenting at this time of night. We know the Knights are due to meet the Sicarii, to purchase the Staff. If the meeting is taking place on Sicarii terms, it might be in the Jewish ghetto, which implicates Sir Reginald by his presence there, and in turn his patron, the Earl of Rothminster.'

'Kostas and Will might both be at the ghetto?' Mikael asked.

'It's a possibility,' Konjic replied. 'We need to get there as quickly as possible.' They left the guesthouse, racing across St Mark's Square as the ruddy moon cast a weak aura around them.

'Amazing place,' Gurkan noted, hastening past the Basilica for the first time, keeping his face hidden.

'Quite a sight,' Awa added, running beside him.

'Been inside?' asked Gurkan.

'Haven't tried.'

'We should go together,' Gurkan said.

A gondolier rowed them close to the ghetto. The evening air was muggy, the streets empty. They approached the ghetto from the east, winding past decaying frontages and open drains. In a clearing surrounded by rubble and undergrowth stood an ornate carriage, entirely at odds with the location. *Rathbone.* Was he waiting for the Knights?

'*Psssttt.*' Awa spotted Kostas hiding behind a disused red and white awning, which could have belonged to a shop at one time. They joined him, moving noiselessly.

'Greetings, Kostas. What do you have for us?' Konjic whispered.

'Not much, Commander, save that Rathbone is in the carriage with that muscle-headed bodyguard, Stukeley. They seem to be waiting for someone.'

'We believe it could be the Knights,' Konjic informed him. 'Will has been following them. We need to gain entry to the ghetto, but if we go in through the front, Rathbone will see us.'

'There is a side entrance. It's guarded by one man,' Kostas replied.

'All right, lead the way. Ismail, I'd like you to remain here to keep watch. If they leave, do your best to follow them.'

'Yes, sir.'

They trailed after the Greek, ducking and keeping low, making not a sound, as he dodged around broken carts and disused pallets, then past an abandoned foundry. Rusting bars and tubing lay scattered across the ground, creating a hazardous obstacle to traverse in the moonlight. The ghetto walls were on their left. The side entrance became visible where a solitary guard sat on a wooden chair outside, half asleep.

The unit settled behind a sheet of metal.

'Allow me, sir,' said Kostas.

The Commander nodded and Kostas ambled over towards the guard. He spoke in a jovial manner, though Awa could not hear what he was saying. The guard got up from his chair, greeted him. Kostas slipped him some coins and the man momentarily left his post and sauntered away. Kostas waved them over.

'Nicely done,' murmured Gurkan to the Greek. 'You have a golden tongue.'

'I am from Athens, my friend, home of Plato. Dialogue and dialectics run in my blood.'

'It's why the Commander keeps him in the unit. He's got the gift of the gab, although his martial skills aren't quite up to it,' said Mikael, a grin upon his face.

'I'll show you what's what with the sword,' said Kostas, gently barging into Mikael with his shoulder as they strode onwards.

'I'll remember to ask for you, friend Kostas, next time I'm in a tight spot,' teased Gurkan.

30

CRACKING FIRE

WILL KNEW HE HAD NO back-up - that there was no one out there, ready to charge in at his command. The Sicarii and the Knights didn't know that, however. At least, not yet.

The Knights peered out into the moonlight, scanning the scene outside. Throaty gripped the Staff. Other Sicarii, nervous at what was coming, rushed into the corridor through which Will had entered only moments before, while others shot upstairs. Will stood unmoving, his weapon raised, as did Red-glove and Throaty, in a three-way stand-off.

Anver. He had forgotten about the blacksmith's apprentice! The young fellow had half-crawled inside the sack he'd brought. What on earth was he doing?

'It's a bluff,' scowled Throaty. 'Ain't no Janissaries out there.'

'Better be sure,' said the red-gloved Knight.

'They're . . .' Will started to say, when there was a blast from behind him. Anver's sack went flying into the air and there was a cacophony of explosions, streaming red and green lights, blinding smoke and what seemed like white snow dropping around them. Fireworks, Will realised – and just in time.

'We're under attack!' one of the Sicarii screamed out.

'God's punishment!' shouted one of the Knights.

Bang! Bang! The eruptions had caused chaos. This was the perfect moment. Will made a grab for the Staff. Throaty pulled back.

'The Staff belongs to the Jewish people,' said Throaty through gritted teeth.

'Why are you selling it, then?' said Will.

'The Knights of the Fire Cross have paid for custody. Give it to me!' shouted Red-glove.

'The Staff of Moses belongs in the Topkapi Palace, from where it was stolen,' Will shouted back.

Each man pulled the Staff towards him. The Staff began to glow, as if it were on fire. The Sicarii, the Knight and Will stopped pulling, but each still gripped the holy relic, uncertain what was happening. *Bang.* Flames erupted around the staff.

'A fiery serpent!' screamed Throaty.

'The wrath of God!' wailed Red-glove.

Ka-boom! All three let go at the same time. The Staff remained upright, spinning on its tip, as the firecracker which had been let off at its base engulfed the ancient artefact. Sparks ran up the shaft, before there was an explosion and the firework went off. In the next moment, as they shielded their eyes, Anver shot forwards, grabbed the Staff in a single daring move, and dashed out of the kosher butcher's courtyard.

Will was the first to react. He leaped up, kicked the Knight in the face and swung round to hit the Sicarius in the chest with the underside of his boot, knocking the man back onto the ground. A group of Knights were approaching, so he dashed into the corridor, crashing into two Sicarii who were surprised when he barrelled them down, and burst out through the porch onto the street, as the explosive pyrotechnic show continued. One of the goats had managed to free itself, and Will ran straight into it, righting himself and running for his life.

'Get them,' shouted Red-glove, emerging from the building.

'*Feh! Amoretz!* You idiots!' Throaty bellowed.

Will tore down the street, chasing after the fast-disappearing Anver. The explosions had brought local residents out; they were staring around, confused by the light and sound show from the butcher's shop. Will took a sharp right and collided with someone; they both ended up on their backsides on the filthy ground.

'Will!'

Gurkan! The others were also here: Konjic, Kostas, Mikael and Awa. Finally. Was he glad to see them. But there was no time to hang around.

'What's going on?' said Konjic.

'The Staff of Moses is with . . .'

'*Get 'em!*' a voice bawled from behind.

'Why are fireworks going off?' asked Mikael.

'Some very angry Sicarii and extremely upset Knights are about to come around that corner. Let's go!' cried Will, shooting off before Konjic had a chance to respond. The others hesitated, then he heard them pounding after him. Gurkan caught up with him.

'Where's the Staff?' asked Gurkan.

'Anver.'

'Eh?'

'Just met him - blacksmith's apprentice, Jewish - from the ghetto. Helped me out, but made off with the Staff.'

'Another thief then,' Gurkan retorted.

'Not necessarily. A well-wisher, I think.'

The road narrowed and they emerged into a small square, at the end of which was the main entrance to the ghetto. Will saw the guards' bodies lying slumped to one side.

They left the ghetto and came out by the canal, where a black carriage waited. Will pulled up, the others skidding to a

182

halt around him. An enormous fellow, dressed in pristine black and grey, was holding Anver by the collar over the canal, about to throw him in.

'Will!' screamed Anver, when he saw him. 'I can't swim!'

The hulk pulled his arm back and propelled Anver into the water, the young blacksmith's apprentice landing with a fearsome splash. Dusting off his enormous hands, the brute jumped into the carriage. As the door opened and shut, Will glimpsed Sir Reginald Rathbone, sitting on a leather-upholstered seat, clutching the Staff of Moses. Their eyes locked. Rathbone smiled and nodded politely, before the carriage shot off down the narrow roadway. Without a moment's delay, Will ran to the edge of the canal and dived in. Anver was splashing around, his panicked movements making him sink further.

'Help!' he gurgled, surfacing.

Will was beside him in a moment. He placed Anver on his back, told him to stop moving, and swam back to the bank. He couldn't see any of the Janissaries waiting by the edge to help them out. Fortunately, there was an iron ring, used for tethering boats. He latched onto this, before guiding himself and Anver over to the rung of a mini-ladder fixed against the inner canal wall. The young Venetian clambered up, streaming with water, coughing and retching, Will behind him. As he hauled himself back to land, he saw the Janissaries standing in a line, their backs to him. Ahead of them, spread out, were at least ten Sicarii and four Knights. The Staff was gone, taken by Rathbone. It had been so close, nearly in his grasp, yet once again they had been outwitted. What could the Earl of Rothminster want with the holy wood?

'Nice you could join us,' quipped Gurkan, as Will took his place beside the Konyan.

Anver scrambled to one side, still spluttering, eyes full of tears. A small crowd of residents gathered by the walls of the ghetto.

'Draw your weapons,' Konjic said with calm leadership.

The Sicarii and Knights charged, running straight at them, weapons swinging. Quicker than anyone else, Awa shot forward - striking her sword into the midriff of a Sicarii who went down. Will was fixing his aim at Throaty, who wore an expression of demonic fury on this face.

'You've caused me a lot of grief,' snarled Throaty, as their weapons clashed, sparks flying. Their blades locked. Will pushed downwards, but Throaty was stronger than him and held his position, before he started to shove Will back. Suddenly Red-glove was at his side, about to strike the killing blow - but his sword was blocked by Gurkan's blade.

'Oh no, you don't,' Gurkan muttered, just as Will kicked Throaty in the chest, knocking the air from his body and causing him to stagger back. Another Sicarius attacked with two swords, blades criss-crossing at all angles in a dazzling display. Half-blinded, Will retreated, his steps uncertain. He was on the bank now, the canal behind him, when the Sicarius swept low with his blade. Will jumped, clearing the sword, and in the same movement swivelled his own weapon, striking his opponent on the wrist, causing one of the Sicarius' swords to clatter to the ground. In doing so, Will's own weapon flew from his grip, so that by the time he landed he was unarmed and defenceless. The Sicarius bared his teeth in a rictus smile, which disappeared when Will butted him in the stomach, sending him flying backwards. Will then snatched up his weapon and flicked it behind him at the Sicarius, who toppled into the canal.

He watched Awa driving her opponent back. Gurkan was still engaged in a duel with Red-glove. Konjic and Kostas were fighting, backs against one another, seeing off a couple of opponents. Mikael was by himself, but becoming surrounded. He needed help. Will dashed over, but was met halfway by Throaty, chopping wildly at him with his sword. Will avoided it by a hair's breadth as he skidded to a halt - but he was being driven back towards a pack of Sicarii behind him. Will leaped forwards, his blade aimed at his opponent's heart; the man blocked it. Will followed up with a knee in the stomach, before ramming his elbow into his enemy's Adam's apple, sending Throaty, choking and clutching his throat, to his knees. Will raised his weapon to finish the job, but thought better of it.

By now, Mikael's opponents had pummelled him to the ground. Will charged into the pack, scattering them, allowing the Janissary to get back on his feet. In the next moment, Gurkan joined them. The Sicarii were about to attack, when one of them pulled the others back. Hesitating, they glanced over at the Knights, who were down to their last man. The sole Knight contemplated the scene, before fleeing by leaping into the canal and hiding under the bank, clinging to the ladder, weighed down by his clothes and sword. Once he had gone, the Sicarii collected up their fallen, including Throaty, who remained unconscious. Giving a last threatening look behind them, they trudged off in the direction of the ghetto, where the crowd abruptly dispersed.

Mikael and Kostas took a step in the direction of the Sicarii, but Konjic pulled them back. 'No, leave them, we know the identity of the puppet-master,' he said.

'Turks!' someone shouted. The voice came from the canal area. 'Turks!'

Will looked - the voice was coming from the water. The Knight was hollering at the top of his voice. 'Turks!'

Lamps came on, doors opened, a bell was rung. Konjic ordered: 'Back to the Blue Flag. At the double.'

'Will!' Anver cried out.

Will called back, 'I'm sorry, friend Anver, I have to leave. Come with us!'

Anver took a step towards him, then halted, peering back at the ghetto. Sadly, he shook his head. Raising his hand in farewell, Will pelted off to join his unit as the cries of *'Turks!'* spread through the streets and canals of Venice.

31

CHALK AND CARRIAGE

WHITE CHALK CLIFFS LOOMED AHEAD. Awa and the crew had packed up and left Venice immediately after returning from the ghetto. Konjic's idea of retaining a vessel, ready to depart at a moment's notice, had proved to be sound. Upon receiving word, the Captain mobilised his sailors, who ensured that the vessel was soon out of port and into the calm waters of the Adriatic.

Fortunately, the rumour that Turks were in the city had not yet reached the harbourmaster, so a close inspection of the vessel was not required. Prior to leaving, Konjic composed a letter to the Grand Vizier, notifying him of developments and informing him that they were heading to England to track down the Staff, now with the Englishman, the Earl of Rothminster.

Their voyage took several days, sailing around the coast of Italy, then past Malta, before approaching the narrow Straits of Gibraltar which separated Africa from Europe. As their ship cruised past Jebel Tariq, the mountain after which Gibraltar was named, Awa peered south to the continent where she longed to be, while Will was drawn to what lay north. The irony of the situation was not lost on Konjic, who smiled in an avuncular manner when Awa mentioned it to him.

Thereafter the sea grew stormy, the wind blustery. Awa's skin became dry and flaky, as though it were crumbling from the cold. It was late autumn, yet in this place it felt like winter. She pondered what the weather was like further north. Her father had read to her from the journal of Ahmed ibn Fadlan, a tenth-century diplomat from Baghdad who had travelled to the land of the Volga Vikings. In it, he described a Viking Chief's burial, longboats, mist-monsters and the near-death episodes he had experienced amidst these martial yet unsophisticated peoples. Was she about to experience something of the same in her voyage north?

South or north, the world was a dangerous place wherever you went. Only when one returned to the Creator of the Worlds did the soul attain peace – one's worldly existence was a struggle. Awa had come to realise the truth of this over the past few months, when everything she knew had been turned upside down, every bond broken, all hope scattered. Living day-to-day, how could she ever plan ahead, when recent experience made her wary of becoming reliant on anything or anybody?

Sailing in from the English Channel was a choppy affair, as strong gusts pitched their vessel side to side, reducing Gurkan's sea legs to jelly once more. The port at which they docked was called Dover - a remote outpost on a distant island, bordered by white cliffs. The bleakness weighed heavy on her, yet Awa consoled herself with the knowledge that above the clouds, somewhere the sun still shone.

Upon encountering the first English people, Will was very excited, like a child being given sweetmeats. His dream had come true: he was back in the land of his fathers at long last.

Konjic assumed Rathbone had returned to England. If so, he wouldn't be far ahead of them.

Kostas set about organising accommodation for their first evening in a town called Canterbury, a carriage-ride away from

Dover. Their transport was large enough to hold all six of them and their luggage. It was drawn by four horses, with a driver sat outside, wearing a heavy overcoat against the chill. Awa felt her skin crawl when his ratty gaze swept her from head to toe, as if he were pondering what lay beneath her outer garments. Konjic was last inside and sat beside the door, Awa next to him and Kostas on her other side. Opposite sat Will, Gurkan in the middle and Ismail beside him. Mikael sat on the floor in the space between the two sets of seats.

'You comfortable down there?' Kostas asked Mikael.

'Not really, but don't worry, I'll swap with one of the cubs soon,' Mikael replied.

'Let me know, I'm ready,' Gurkan offered.

'Give it a bit more time, especially after you spent the entire sea voyage heaving your guts up,' said Mikael.

Gurkan's face went pale. 'Best not to remind me of that episode in my life.'

'We have a return voyage, my friend,' Mikael reminded him innocently.

The harmless banter continued amongst the Janissaries, their Commander content to remain silent, listening to the camaraderie. They all seemed like genuinely nice people, Awa thought. Konjic was a good leader; she had never seen him behave in an arrogant or dismissive manner. If only this peaceful moment could last - but she knew the world did not work that way.

She noticed Will watching her, as though he could read her thoughts and shared them. Was he going to abscond if he found his mother? Awa wouldn't blame him if he did. Who would? Blood was closer than all other bonds, Janissary or not, promises or not. Awa could not remember her mother, but her father had described her in intricate detail and always said that Awa bore a striking resemblance to her. If her mother were alive today, Awa too would long, like Will, to be reunited with her and to rest her head upon her lap.

The carriage sped away from Dover, rattling through villages, past farmers at work in the fields. Clouds hung heavy, wrapping the sky in a grey blanket. It was a depressing sight.

'Will, how does it feel to breathe the air of England?' Gurkan enquired.

'Good,' said Will, his grin wide.

'Don't get too used to it, we'll be heading back soon,' added Ismail.

Will nodded, catching Awa's eye. Did the others know of his plan to run?

'We will soon arrive in Canterbury,' said Konjic. 'Tomorrow, we journey to London, where we will meet with our associates at the East Mediterranean Company. We will maintain our roles as representatives of the Balkan Trading Company: Kostas the bookkeeper, Mikael the scribe, Ismail, Will and Gurkan, my apprentices. Awa, you get to wear your costly clothing once more and impersonate the daughter of a wealthy merchant from West Africa.'

'Yes, Commander,' said Awa, sighing at the prospect of donning restrictive European clothes again.

'We are far from Ottoman territories. The Sultan does not have an Embassy here, for this nation is not yet mature politically and commercially,' Konjic went on. 'By coming here, we have entered the lair of the Earl of Rothminster. These are his people, many of them are likely in his pay, so wherever we go there will be spies and informants. We must remain vigilant, or we won't be getting off this island alive. As your Commander, I remind you that we must work together, as what holds a unit together is trust, built on integrity.' Konjic's gaze rested for a moment on Will.

'What of the Knights of the Fire Cross - should we expect to encounter them?' asked Mikael.

190

At that moment, their coach veered violently right, before straightening once more. They heard the driver's boots scrape against the iron plate fixed at the foot of the box seat. 'Pardon me,' he shouted out.

Konjic glanced behind him, to where the coachman was sitting, then leaned forward and spoke in a softer tone. 'Like the Sicarii, the Knights are mercenaries for hire. I suspect through Rathbone, the Earl has procured their services. Whether we encounter them or not, the Earl will have his own bodyguards, which will make getting through to him difficult. What he plans to do with the Staff of Moses remains unclear. Whatever it is, it's not in the interests of Sultan Murad III.'

'Where do we find the Earl?' Gurkan asked.

'Most likely at his country residence,' Kostas replied. 'Our chances of taking back the Staff are much slimmer now. The Earl and his allies will have roads and paths to the ports guarded, and we could become stuck on this island for a very long time. After a short taste of the weather here, I'm not one for staying longer than we need to.'

'What then?' Mikael wanted to know.

'We need to expose the Earl to his Queen for what he has done,' Kostas suggested.

'Why?' asked Will. All heads turned in his direction, making him go red in the face. 'What I mean is - don't we risk incurring the wrath of the Sultan by letting the nobility here know how he has been robbed?'

'It's a moot point, Will,' interjected Konjic. 'You see, as we know, Queen Elizabeth is terribly isolated by the Catholics of Europe and is therefore anxious to create a working relationship with the Sultan. Her previous attempts were met with lukewarm reactions in Istanbul. However, since the defeat of the Spanish Armada three years ago, the reputation of the English Queen has soared. I even heard that the court scribe of the Moroccan ruler, al-Mansur, composed a poem in her honour, referring to her as Sultana Isobel, and saying it was God Who sent a sharp wind against the fleets of her enemies.'

Kostas looked to the Commander for permission to continue, then told them all: 'The Queen wishes to strike a favourable deal with our Sultan. If we expose Rothminster to her, she can contain the situation before it gets out of hand. Our mission in England requires discretion. Will has a point: news must not leak to the English nobility of the Staff being stolen from the Topkapi, as it will reflect badly on the Sultan, particularly if people discover that former Janissaries were involved.'

They all thought about it for a moment.

'Commander,' Will said, his voice high, 'we can't just walk up to one of her palaces and ask to see the Queen. How are we going to get her attention?'

Konjic smiled at him. 'Good question, Will. Lord Burghley, presently Lord High Treasurer to Her Majesty, has in the past been in touch with the previous Grand Vizier. I am aware of the correspondence between the two men. Burghley is a strong advocate of trade with the Ottomans. I will approach him when the moment is right.'

'Commander Konjic,' Awa interjected, 'why would Sultan Murad be at all interested in establishing diplomatic and commercial ties with England, when this nation has so little to offer?'

'I am not a man of politics, but the Grand Viziers are, and I have learned some matters of statecraft from them. Presently, who are the greatest enemies of the Sultan?'

Awa pondered the question. 'The Catholics in Europe, closely followed by the Safavids in Persia and the Moroccans.'

'Quite right,' said Konjic. 'And who are the most active enemies of the English Queen?'

'The Catholics of Europe,' Will answered for her.

'So, in the estimation of the Grand Vizier, my enemy's enemy is my friend,' said Konjic.

'I see,' said Awa, and they all absorbed this information.

'Exposing the Earl's reckless behaviour, which runs contrary to the strategic goals of his Queen, will mean we gain her support. By returning the Staff of Moses to the Sultan, through discreet diplomatic channels, the Queen will gain favour with Sultan Murad, and her chances of signing attractive commercial agreements will only be increased. Whereas if it emerges that an English Earl has stolen the Staff from the palace of the Sultan . . . well, I imagine His Excellency will block all attempts by the English to trade in Ottoman lands.'

'Just one more question, Commander,' Awa said slowly. 'What if, after we expose the theft by the Earl, Queen Elizabeth does not want to return the Staff of Moses. What happens then?'

32

MATTER OF TRUST

NIGHTINGALES SANG IN A COPSE close to their accommodation in Canterbury. The birdsong reminded Konjic of his home town of Konjic in Bosnia, a mountainous place of dense woodland. Outings with his parents and siblings beside the Neretva River were enduring memories, nourishing him through difficult times in the frenzy of Istanbul.

Konjic sat down on an old tree stump. Their stay in this ancient cathedral town was for one night only, before he took his unit to London. The Commander had never expected the chase to be such a protracted one when they set off from Istanbul, heading to Alexandria. Had he known their journey was going to bring them to England, he would never have brought Will. He knew what it felt like to return home after an extensive period away; the pull of home distracted from the work at hand.

A twig snapped and Kostas approached. The Greek was a reliable and resourceful number two, and Konjic would not have attempted this mission without him. He trusted all of his team, but he trusted Kostas most and needed to speak in confidence with him. He glanced around; the copse was deserted.

'What is it, Commander?' said Kostas, positioning himself on a rock, his back to the inn.

'When we arrive in London, I will need you to take the team to the East Mediterranean Company's offices in Chancery Lane. I am told it's close to the centre of the city. Use discretion, arrive early, avoid crowds. Our men, Briggs and Furrows, are the officers,' said Konjic.

'Have you met them, sir?'

'No, not personally, but they have been vetted by the offices of the Grand Vizier and their names appear on a register of agents provided to me. The Grand Vizier gave me a list of the names and details of all Ottoman operatives in territories outside of direct imperial control.'

'I see,' said Kostas. 'If I may ask, where will you be going, sir?'

'I am paying a visit to Lord Burghley, the Queen's Lord High Treasurer. He has been an advocate of trade with Ottoman lands for many years. The briefing notes sent by the East Mediterranean Company state that he has accommodated all of their requests and is keen to secure a commercial and political alliance with the Sultan. As I mentioned previously, there has been some correspondence between Burghley and the previous Grand Vizier. My impression is that he will be very distressed to learn about the actions of Rathbone and Rothminster and the difficulties which may occur as a result.'

'What if Rothminster is operating with the Queen's approval?' Kostas suggested, his voice low.

'It is a possibility,' Konjic shrugged, 'and if that is the case, our mission will end in certain failure. For now, we must take the view that Burghley is advocating the wishes of the Queen, not Rothminster. Our intelligence suggests this, and the political situation confirms that the Queen is isolated by the Catholics of Europe. At such a moment, she will not want to invoke the Sultan's wrath. I'm sure she will rather sacrifice one of her nobles, than a potential alliance with the Sultan.'

Kostas sighed, scratching his curly black locks. 'Our opponents are always one step ahead of us, Commander. I feel as if we have been led by the nose along this journey, as when the wolf entices the sheep - before killing it.'

It was an interesting thought. Konjic did indeed feel that he was chasing, never quite catching up. 'One more thing, Kostas,' he said.

'Yes, Commander?'

'Keep a close eye on Will.'

Kostas gave him with a quizzical stare. 'Sir?'

'Rathbone has been trying to get to him, to use Will against us. Returning to England may trigger patriotic fervour in young Master Ryde. I know how it feels: the first time I returned to my home town of Konjic, I also felt a stronger affinity with those I had left behind, than the Janissary Order to which I had pledged my life. I don't want to lose him. He is a good lad, his heart is in the right place, but the temptation to betray us may be deeper. I pray this is not the case, but with all of our lives in the balance, I can't take any chances.'

'Anything in particular you had in mind, Commander?'

'No. Just watch him and . . . watch out *for* him.'

33

LAVENDER

LAVENDER LINING BURGATE LANE TRANS-PORTED Will back to the time his mother took him from their humble dwelling near Smithfield Market, to the heath at Hampstead. The journey required an entire morning of riding on various carts, and walking on his short legs, but it was an outing he never forgot. His mother, Anne, had been there once before, and even though it was a good five miles to the north, she wanted young Will to run and play there in the sun, away from the dirty streets near their home. He remembered her instructing him to breathe in the scent of lavender planted on the heath, for there was nothing else in the world quite so uplifting. After eating a piece of the pie she had brought, he pocketed a few sprigs of lavender, but by the time they got home they had crumbled. *Nothing lasts forever*, his mother said, when she saw the tears in her little boy's eyes. And then she cuddled him, and he smelled the lavender again; the scent had perfumed her skin.

When the crew entered Canterbury, the first thing he saw was the lavender along the Burgate. Inhaling its scent, he thought how close he was to being reunited with her . . . With luck, he could fulfil his obligations to the Janissaries before leaving them. But that didn't feel right. What about loyalty?

he asked himself. Their weeks on the road together had forged a lasting bond between them all; never could he betray them.

Lodgings belonging to the Cathedral extended down the Burgate; there was also a metalsmith, blacksmith, butcher, grocer and fishmonger. A sizeable stonemason's workshop on the corner was crammed with headstones. Further into town was an inn with stables for horses. Despite his Ottoman clothing, folk approached Will with friendly nods; perhaps they considered he was a gentleman who had done well in the land of the Turks, and who was now returning home. It wasn't that far from the truth - apart from the lack of material wealth. Still, what did that matter? He was on English soil, and it put a spring in his step. He sorely missed the sun, it was true - but he had missed England more.

'Been to foreign parts, 'ave yer, sonny?' a grey-bearded man said, leaning on a walking stick and looking ready for a chat.

'Yes, sir. Land of the Turks,' Will replied, stopping outside the metalsmith's shop, where various swords, shields, a shaft from a carriage and numerous iron rings and other items were on display. The sight brought a smile to Will's face and made him feel at home as he recalled his time in the workshop of Hakim Abdullah.

'The Great Turk himself, eh?'

'Yes.'

The old man stroked his beard. 'Fella once told me they drink the brew of the devil there; it's as black as tar, bitter as charcoal, can make a man lose his sleep and his faith. Is it true?'

Will chuckled. 'The beverage you speak of is called *kahava* or coffee. Having drunk it on many occasions, I can safely say it's quite delightful. The aroma is enchanting, the taste, though I admit it is bitter at first, grows pleasant on the palate. As for losing sleep, it can be useful when you need to keep active until late into the evening.'

198

The old man wrinkled his nose at Will, shuffling closer. 'Are you one of 'em - you know, a believer of Mahomet?'

Will said patiently, 'No. I am a Christian.'

'Good. Well, don't let 'em go converting you, my boy, or it'll be damnation for your soul.'

'There isn't much difference in our beliefs . . .' Will started to explain, but then saw the old man wave his stick to halt him.

'The devil's brew has glazed your tongue, lad.' He patted Will kindly on the shoulder and lumbered along the road. Will watched him go, pondering why it was that people who had travelled the world and encountered other faiths were more tolerant, able to accept difference. He set off down the Burgate, the Cathedral to his right looming large, its enormous stained-glass windows depicting scenes from the Bible.

When Will returned to their lodging, he found Awa sat on a stool out on the terrace behind the building. It backed onto an open field, where a herd of cows grazed. In her hand was a quill, and she was writing on parchment.

'How does the lavender smell?' she asked with a smile.

'Just like I remember it, thank you. Here, I brought you a sprig to put in your clothes-chest. What are you writing?'

'A journal. You see, all the travellers I have read about, such as Ibn Battuta, or Ahmed Ibn Fadlan, wrote journals of their adventures, first to remind themselves of what they had experienced and secondly to leave a body of knowledge for future generations. My people have been scattered from our homes, and I have travelled to cities perhaps no other Songhai has ever visited, so these are encounters to treasure, to conserve in a book.'

Will studied her handwriting. It was beautiful, the Arabic script flowing from right to left, as though an artist had painted the letters. 'What have you written?'

'I'll read it to you someday.'

But would that day come? Will wasn't sure how long he was going to be with the Janissaries. Awa herself was committed to a three-year term, and by the manner in which she conducted herself, Will believed she would fulfil her covenant with Konjic. Will too had made a pledge, but the temptation to leave continued to gnaw at him. This was his country - he could disappear amongst its people, wait it out, let Konjic and the team return to Istanbul before he resurfaced. Konjic himself had said there was no formal Ottoman presence in England, so there was no one to check on him. Yet, watching Awa now brought something else into focus. He *liked* being a Janissary. Konjic was a valiant leader, the crew a hearty set of individuals who had made him welcome, made him one of them. What's more, he had learned so much and been given extensive responsibility in a very short space of time. What kind of man was he, if after all they had done for him, he betrayed their trust?

Mother waits for me, whispered a voice in his mind.

'I look forward to hearing it,' Will said, before starting to move away.

'Will?' Awa delayed him.

'Yes?'

'Are you staying?'

Looking his friend in the eyes, Will murmured, '*Inshallah*.' He knew that she understood his dilemma. Consigning his decision to the will of God was often a reason to say, 'No.'

For their evening meal, Mikael booked them a table at the Stag, where the fare had been strongly recommended to him. The place was doing good business, particularly with fellows who had the weathered appearance of men-at-arms. This was surprising for a small town, pondered Will, who had expected such places to be full of farmers and the odd man of religion, not soldiering types.

The presence of so many men attracted a clutch of harlots, bright with powder and rouge, their necklines low. Roars of laughter erupted every now and then, as these women frolicked and drank with potential clients. The Stag was square in shape, with a large dining area in the centre containing some twenty tables, with several chairs around each one. A solitary candle was placed on each table. Drinks were served along a bar opposite the entrance. Kitchens were to the rear, and accommodation took up the first floor, where a balcony ran all the way around. Will lowered his gaze whenever one of the women took a leering fellow up the stairs and along the gallery to a room.

Konjic sat them at a table close to the entrance so they had a good view of the inn. The place was so busy, there was scarcely a seat left. Earlier, Ismail had purchased two chickens and made them *halal*, after which the innkeeper agreed to cook them in a stew. The meal was surprisingly agreeable, accompanied by barley bread which they dipped in the chicken broth.

Awa sat beside Konjic, her hood up. Her looks attracted curiosity wherever she went, and Will could tell the attention was beginning to bother her. he knew how it felt, having been the only European living in the neighbourhood his former master occupied in Marrakesh.

He noticed a group of men sitting on stools at the bar, tankards of ale placed on the counter before them. The one in the centre was a large fellow, broad-backed, wide-shouldered. Will couldn't quite see his face.

'May I join you?' Another man approached, a mug of mead in his chunky hands. Will could smell the fermented honey from his cup. The fellow smiled, but Will saw the way his face twitched nervously.

201

'Please do,' said Konjic.

Will drew up another chair, placing it beside him.

'The name is Cleaves. I'm a blacksmith, way over the other side of town. You folk passing through or are you here to see where the Saint was buried?'

'Just passing through,' said Konjic.

'Where you heading?' Cleaves persisted.

'We have business to attend to in London. My name is Konjic, these are my associates.'

Cleaves skimmed each one of them, before his gaze came to rest on Awa. 'Ah. Associates.'

'Yes,' said Konjic. 'Forgive my lack of knowledge about your town, but who is the Saint you refer to?'

'Saint Thomas Becket. He was the former Archbishop here, till King Henry the Second's knights came and murdered him in his very own church. Terrible business.' Cleaves took a swig of mead, wiping his lips with the back of his hand. 'Well, they all got their come-uppance.'

'Does the Queen visit?' Konjic asked.

'Once, I think, about twenty years ago.' The fellow spat. 'We don't need the Crown here, we have our own supporters. Besides, the tide will soon turn.'

'How do you mean?' Konjic asked.

'The Queen doesn't have any heirs. She's grown long in the tooth. Change is coming,' said Cleaves, rising heavily from his chair. 'Be wishing you a good end.'

What a strange parting comment. Will observed Cleaves walk briskly away. Konjic was about to say something, when Will saw the blacksmith raise his head towards the gallery and make a sign. Four men who had been dallying with the harlots now pushed the women aside to reveal deadly crossbows - loaded and ready to fire. The large fellow at the bar also spun round, revealing himself to be Stukeley, the personal bodyguard of

Rathbone and the man who had thrown Anver into the canal in Venice. The Knights of the Fire Cross!

'Down!' Will shouted, ramming into Awa. As they went to ground, he heard the *whoosh* of crossbow bolts fly past. Will scrambled under the table, knocking it over to shield them, as bolts flew from several positions in the inn, thudding into the wood, some piercing through it. The projectiles were deadly - could cut someone in half.

'No!' Awa screamed.

Will whirled round. A bolt had pierced Kostas' chest. Another had gone through Mikael's neck, a third had hit Ismail straight in the heart. All three were motionless. Konjic had taken a bolt through his left shoulder and was slumped in his chair. Gurkan scrambled along the floor, tucking in beside them.

Will was in a state of shock. He had always wanted to die on English soil - but not like this. Dear God in heaven, *not like this.*

34

ENTRAPMENT

KONJIC LAY ON THE FLOOR of the Stag Inn. He was still breathing. Gurkan had pulled him out of the line of fire, so he was shielded by the dining table, but how long were they going to last? It seemed there were dozens of assailants, hitting them from all corners.

'Commander,' Awa whispered, as she crouched over Konjic. His face was contorted in pain, blood trickling through his tunic top.

'The three of you . . . must get away . . .' he gasped.

'No, Commander, you're coming with us,' Gurkan told him.

Awa was in no mood to leave Konjic. He was the one holding the crew together: without him there was no Rüzgar unit, even though it was now tragically depleted.

'Save yourselves,' Konjic croaked. 'Find the officers of the East Mediterranean Company on Chancery Lane in London. They will protect you. Get you home.'

'We're going to get out of this, Commander,' said Will. 'All of us.'

Konjic attempted a weak smile, then passed out.

Awa, Gurkan and Will exchanged glances with one another.

'We fight,' said Will.

'We fight,' echoed Awa and Gurkan.

'How many are out there?' asked Awa.

'I saw four bowmen on the gallery, plus the big fellow at the bar,' Will replied.

'There were two behind the bar and one who seemed like he was armed, standing beside the kitchen,' said Gurkan.

'Plus the blacksmith,' Awa added.

'Makes at least nine, perhaps a few more,' Will calculated.

The missiles stopped thumping around them. There was silence, broken by a beefy voice, saying: 'Did we get 'em all?'

'Dunno. Think so,' said another.

'Fire a couple more,' said Beefy.

'At what?'

'See if anything moves,' said Beefy.

'Only got a few bolts left.'

'Damn it, fire!' Beefy said irritably.

The Knights let fly with their remaining ammunition. One bolt struck the table, making it shudder and leaving a gash large enough to allow Awa to peer through the hole and get a better view of their attackers.

'Go on, lad, take a look,' said Beefy.

'Me?' said a new voice.

'Yeah, c'mon. You afraid of a few dead bodies? Want me to hold your hand?'

'I ain't afraid of nothing.'

The floorboards creaked as footsteps approached: more than one person.

Will pointed to the table, making a lifting movement. Konjic was bleeding heavily; he was slipping away; they needed to get him out of here fast. The footsteps drew closer. Awa peered through the hole, raising her hand, asking Will and Gurkan to wait. Closer came the Knights.

'*Now!*' she said.

The table was lifted clear by Will and Gurkan, who held it on either side and charged into the three Knights who were only steps away. Awa drew her weapon and cut through one, who had stumbled to the floor. He was rather young and she felt a moment's guilt at striking him down. The slain bodies of their beloved comrades, Kostas, Mikael and Ismail, reminded her not to feel remorse. It seemed the bowmen were out of ammunition, for they came rushing down the stairs. *Good.* But then the door to the inn burst open and four more Knights bundled in, brandishing lances. *Bad.*

'Back-to-back,' she commanded. They would go down fighting!

Will and Gurkan took their places behind her, the trio circling in a group. Their assailants were an angry mob.

'Who sent you?' asked Will.

Stukeley, the bodyguard who had sent shivers through Awa in Venice, drew a chunky broadsword. 'Shouldn't have followed us, *Turk*.'

'Turk!' Will exclaimed.

'A Tudor Turk,' said a distinguished voice from above. All heads turned to look at a finely-dressed gentleman, standing on the balcony, the Staff of Moses clutched in his right hand. Sir Reginald Rathbone!

'I rather thought Will was one of us, Stukeley,' Rathbone said to his bodyguard. 'Perhaps not. Dark times do bring out the darkest of deeds.'

Awa scanned about. The Knights were too many for them to fight, but all exits were blocked and they needed to get Konjic out. The Commander was slumped on the ground, presumed dead by their attackers.

'The Staff belongs to Sultan Murad III. Return it!' Gurkan ordered.

'This one *is* a Turk. What a curious little crew of strays.' Rathbone descended the stairs, the harlots giving him a wide berth. He smiled. 'To think that I, a humble servant of the Earl, hold the very Staff which parted the waters of the Red Sea.'

'I said, it doesn't belong to you,' Gurkan repeated, taking a step towards Rathbone, but Will raised his arm, keeping him back. 'We stay together,' whispered Will.

'Nor does it belong to you, *Turk*,' Rathbone quipped. He came and stood beside Stukeley, nodded at him, then the two of them made their way out.

'Kill them,' Stukeley growled as he and his master walked out with the Staff, the doors to the Stag closing behind them.

'Let's make it quick, I ain't had me supper,' said Beefy, as he marched forwards.

Was this it - death in a desolate country? Surely the Angel of Death was not going to take her soul in this uninviting land. Awa felt a *sakina* - a sort of stillness - come over her, just as she had when she last fought in the gladiatorial ring against the man and woman. Her warrior spirit awoke; her senses were amplified; she knew exactly when and where her opponents were going to strike.

Two Knights lunged at her, one with a sword, another with a mace. She leaped to one side, just as Gurkan behind her engaged two opponents and Will sprang into a pack of Knights. Awa's blade came down on the wrist of the one holding the mace, slicing it badly. Had her sword been sharper she would have taken his hand off. The mace-wielding Knight screamed in pain, falling to his knees. Awa placed her hand on the top of his head, steadying herself on it in order to kick the other Knight in the chest. He was a large fellow, and there wasn't enough power in her strike. He merely stepped back, raised his sword and brought it down on her. At the last second, Awa dived through his spread legs. Coming up behind him, she swiped her weapon down on his neck, causing him to hit the ground in a heap.

'Kill her!' someone screamed, and she saw a war hammer coming at her. She swerved and it missed her. Gurkan had taken one Knight out, as had Will, but they still had ten to fight. Awa ran up the staircase, then leaped from the balcony as the war-hammer-wielding Knight smashed through the balustrade. She landed on the bar in a crouched position, then dashed across it kicking glasses and bottles at the men around her, alcohol spewing out, covering the bar's surface and dripping onto the wooden floor. Awa then somersaulted off the bar, her raised sword slicing into the back of a Knight who had cornered Will.

'Thanks,' panted Will, twisting out of the way of another sword-thrust.

There was a roar from behind and she saw the hammer being swung at her again - and dodged - the spike shattering the table beside her. The lamp upon it fell to the ground, setting fire to the pool of alcohol that had trickled off the bar. Awa kicked out at the hammer-wielding Knight's knees; his legs momentarily buckled, allowing her to swing her blade at his head. Enraged and frustrated, he caught her arm, lifting her clear off the ground, and threw her across the room. Awa landed on an empty table, its lighted candle flying to the floor. She winced; her shoulder was sore, but she was still mobile.

Then someone grabbed her ankle, yanking her back.

'Witch!' cursed the Knight.

She was losing the fight. Seeing this, Will attacked him, making his grip come loose. Back on her feet, Awa put her blade through the Knight's chest.

'Get Konjic out, Will,' said Awa.

'You do it, I'll hold them off.'

Another Knight charged at them. Together they ducked and both put their swords through the man's abdomen. He died, screaming.

'I can't lift him,' Awa said breathlessly, her eyes never leaving their opponents. 'You need to do it.' She dashed off to defend Gurkan against the men who had surrounded him. She hacked high and low, her blade streaking from left to right, north to south, shredding anything before her. She hated what she was doing, but thank heavens she was good at it.

'Get together,' one of the Knights barked, as they congregated, only half of them remaining. The others were injured or dead.

Awa pushed on, with Gurkan by her side. He was a skilled swordsman and his lighter blade and swifter strokes kept the Knights on the back foot. Between the two of them they were holding their ground. She glimpsed behind her to observe Will carrying Konjic over his shoulder, out of the inn. She prayed there weren't any assailants waiting for him outside.

The fire which had flared up earlier was being put out by one of the harlots, when Awa observed the pool of alcohol on the floor under where the Knights stood. Ducking to her right, she grabbed a lamp, swivelled and threw it at the bar. It shattered and its flame ignited the alcohol, setting the whole bar area on fire as well as the bottles behind the bar, and the ground where the Knights were standing.

'Arghh!' they screamed, trapped.

'Time to go.' Awa pulled Gurkan away.

'We can't leave them,' said Gurkan, motioning towards Kostas, Mikael and Ismail.

'We must.' They had no choice but to abandon their fallen comrades, or else they were all going to end up dead. Outside,

Will had managed to lift Konjic onto a horse and was sitting behind their Commander, holding him tight.

'There are two other horses by the stable over there,' said Will, motioning to the side of the Stag. Awa sprinted into the stables, untied a mare, vaulted into the saddle and dug her heels in. The horse shot out of the shed.

'After them!' someone bellowed behind her.

Will galloped away down the Burgate. Awa crouched low in her saddle chasing him, with Gurkan on his beast behind.

'Witch!' the cry spread. 'Stop her - kill the witch!'

35

THE FARMHOUSE

WILL RODE HIS STEED HARD through the forest, away from Canterbury, away from the death and destruction of the Stag Inn and the loss of his friends. He gripped the slumped form of the Commander in front of him. If Konjic were to die, what was to become of him? He would be released from his bond to the Janissaries and could return to his mother. Yet that freedom wouldn't bring happiness if it was achieved at the price of Konjic's demise. Will had been just another galley slave, yet the Bosnian had trusted him, trained him, treated him with dignity and offered him a second life. Konjic had also instructed them in Aristotelian virtues - of wisdom, courage, justice and temperance. Will would be betraying every single one of these qualities if he ran out on him now.

Awa and Gurkan rode close behind. Will set the pace, but his horse soon tired, carrying a double load. They stopped for a brief rest as evening was closing in. There was no one pursuing them, that they could see or hear, but vigilance was needed if they were to avoid falling into another trap, such as the one set at the inn. By the manner in which Rathbone conducted himself, it was clear the Earl held sway in Canterbury. The employment of the Catholic Knights also indicated this.

Perhaps the Earl was going to deliver the Staff to the Pope? But then why wouldn't Rathbone have taken it from Venice to the Papacy, rather than bringing it to England first? Will was out of his depth, trying to understand the politics at play. He had to focus on what was happening to them this very minute. Their survival depended on it. Konjic would die unless they could find a place to nurse him and help him recuperate.

With Gurkan's assistance Will lifted the Commander off the horse and laid him on the ground. Awa passed them a canteen of water which she had found strapped to her saddle and they made him drink. Konjic was burning up with a fever. The bolt was protruding from his shoulder.

'Shall we pull it out?' said Gurkan.

'No!' Will and Awa cried simultaneously.

'There's a danger the head will separate from the shaft, leaving the metal head inside. The infection will likely kill him,' said Will.

Konjic groaned.

'It's all right, Commander, you're going to live,' said Awa, pouring some of the water from the canteen on to Konjic's forehead and rubbing it over his skin.

'We can't leave the bolt in there,' Gurkan said.

'No, we can't, but we'll need to open up the wound area first, and try to pull it free. If it's gone into bone, then it'll be tricky. We need some tools at the very least.' Will scratched his head, looking about.

'How do you know so much about arrow wounds?' Gurkan asked.

'We sometimes encountered them in the galleys during conflicts. The maimed were usually brought below deck, where they were treated and their wounds cauterised.'

'I have never carried out the procedure, but I did read about it in one of the medical journals in the library of Timbuktu,' said Awa. 'We require forceps to pull the bolt out, and then we need to cauterise the wound, and use a needle and thread to close the skin together.'

'We are in the English countryside - there are no towns we can go to, for fear of being spotted. Think, Will, where else?' Awa urged.

'A farmhouse! It might have a store for tools,' Will suggested.

'Take us to one,' said Gurkan.

'Right.' Will had no idea where the closest farm was going to be, nor whether it would have the necessary implements.

Konjic let out another moan, his hand going up to the bolt sticking out of his left shoulder.

'No, Commander, not yet,' Awa said, gently removing his hand. 'Hold on. We will take it out shortly. Will, Gurkan, scout around, but be back here within ten minutes.'

Will mounted his horse, as did Gurkan, the two of them trotting off in different directions. Will eventually came to a lane and followed it. The lack of light impeded his progress, along with the fear of losing the way back to Awa and the Commander. Gingerly he urged the horse into a slow canter – and that was when he spotted lamplight in the distance. On the next hill stood a farmhouse. Light shone from its interior, and its chimney spewed out smoke. There was a barn beside it.

'Perfect,' said Will, spinning his beast around and galloping back to Awa and the Commander. He had been gone for much longer than ten minutes and Gurkan was already there, having had no luck with his scouting expedition.

'I've found a farmhouse,' he said breathlessly. 'Let's get the Commander up on your horse, Gurkan. Mine is exhausted.'

At the farmhouse gate, they trotted through as silently as possible, keeping the horses off the shingle track to avoid making any noise. Will steered them towards the barn. Along the way, they passed two cows. A couple of goats were tied within a pen, lying on the ground, nestled into one another. Fortunately, no dogs barked, warning of their presence.

They reached the barn, bringing the horses in before hobbling them. Will fetched some hay for the beasts and a pail of water from a well. They all drank, apart from Konjic. Gurkan and Awa got the Commander settled on the ground as comfortably as possible. They raised his head slightly and set about trying to find the right utensils. Will lit a lamp and placed it close to the Commander. He then fetched another bucket of water and some cloth he'd found. Awa discovered a set of tongs and Gurkan started up a small fire in a pit. Konjic's breathing had slowed to dangerous levels and his face was a mask of agony. Sweat poured from his forehead.

Awa drew a dagger with a fine tip to it, wiped it down with a wet cloth and heated it over the fire. Will sliced open the tunic top Konjic was wearing, so they had a clear view of the wound. The bolt was lodged under the skin, only the shaft showing.

'It's deep,' Will said, dousing the area of the wound with water.

'Can you get it out?' Gurkan asked, his voice quivering.

'Yes, but it's going to be painful. And we don't have a needle and thread to close it up,' said Will.

'The only other way to seal the wound will be to burn the flesh around it, so it closes in on itself. Very nasty,' said Awa, washing her hands. 'Gurkan, try again to find a needle and thread. Go to the farmhouse if you have to.'

Silently he nodded, got up and was heading for the big barn door, when it opened. Will was immediately up on his feet, sword drawn. There was a gasp from the door.

'You ain't killed the poor fellow in our barn, 'ave yer?' It was a woman's voice.

'No,' said Will, replacing his sword in its scabbard and striding past Gurkan. 'Please, we mean no harm. This is our friend, he's been badly injured and we're trying to save his life.'

The woman stepped through the doorway, moving cautiously. She had mousy brown hair, tied back in a bun, and wore a long, patterned dress. She peeped over at Konjic, then stared at Awa for an awfully long time, as the Songhai woman went back to dabbing the Commander's head with a wet cloth. Finally, she took in Gurkan. They must have been an odd sight, in their foreign attire, in the middle of the English countryside, with a dying man on the ground.

'What do you need?' asked the woman.

'A needle and thread, if you please,' said Will.

The woman scrutinised Awa one more time. 'All right, I'll be back. Make sure your mate don't die on us.' She hoisted up her skirt, then hurried out of the barn.

'Help or trouble?' said Gurkan.

'Help, I hope,' said Will, as he returned to Awa's side, leaving Gurkan to stand guard.

Within a few minutes the woman had returned with her sewing kit and a man whose skin colour was as black as Awa's. When Awa saw him, her hand went to her mouth. The man also stopped in his tracks.

'My husband, John Moor,' the woman explained.

'Moor?' Will looked at the man carefully. 'Are you from Morocco?' he asked in Arabic.

The man froze. 'Who are you?' he replied in Arabic.

Will took a deep breath. He must try to reach out to this fellow, or they were going to be turned in once more. He decided to continue in Arabic. 'My name is Will Ryde. I grew up in Marrakesh, apprentice to Hakim Abdullah, famous quartermaster of the Bayt Ben Yousef. This is Gurkan from Konja in Turkey and this is Awa of the Songhai nation. We are visiting from Istanbul with our master Mehmet Konjic.' Will motioned to the Commander.

Konjic jerked in pain, whimpering.

215

'Talk later, dear, this gentleman needs our help,' said the woman.

John nodded. 'Let's take a look, Meg,' he said, approaching.

'Is the blade ready, Awa?' asked Will, as he wiped away the bloodstains around the wound.

'Yes. It's red hot, so be careful.'

Will took the blade, pointed the tip at the wound. He would need to open the wound up further, before using the tongs to pull the head of the bolt out.

'Wait!' said John. 'Have you done this before?'

'No, only seen it,' Will replied.

'Give it to me then. I was in the army, seen plenty of flesh wounds. The bolt looks like it's touching the shoulder-bone. Nasty. Let's hope it hasn't lodged itself in there, or else it will be a sow's supper getting it out.'

John Moor calmly leaned over the wound, swabbing away the blood, before he took a flat piece of wood and placed it between Konjic's teeth. 'That's to make sure he doesn't bite his tongue off,' he told Awa. He cracked his fingers, took the dagger and set to work, saying, 'Hold him down, because this is going to hurt.'

Will gripped the Commander's right arm, Meg his left; meanwhile Gurkan held down his legs, and Awa kept his head straight and pushed back against the ground.

When John Moor applied the blade to the wound, Commander Konjic did as expected.

He screamed.

36

THE MEⱭNÌNG OF HOME

THE COCK CROWED, HERALDING DAWN. The shaft and arrowhead had been removed by the nimble-fingered John Moor, who had cleaned up then stitched the Commander's wound shut. Konjic had thrashed about at first, but grew tired and fell asleep. His fever raged. Awa, Gurkan and Will took turns to cool him down with a wet rag. Thanks to his strong constitution, by sunrise his fever had abated and he sank into a settled sleep. John Moor returned at first light and said they should rest now, for although Konjic would likely wake in the afternoon with a very painful left side, he was going to live.

The dawn sky was a metallic grey and Awa knew there would be no sun today. She pondered the situation with John Moor. Perhaps the English should have called him *John the Moor*, as it was more apt. He spoke Arabic, but what faith did he profess to? There were Christians here, but also pagans, with their rituals.

Sitting on the ground in a circle away from the Commander, Awa, Will and Gurkan huddled close to one another. Decisions needed to be made, yet the gravity of those decisions filled Awa with trepidation, for whatever they decided would send her life in a new direction once more

'The Commander will pull through,' said Will, 'but he's going to be out of action for some time. Meanwhile, the Staff is on the move. We have to do something fast, before it disappears completely.'

'Konjic cannot return to Istanbul empty-handed. It will not bode well for him . . . or us,' Awa added.

'But we have no way of taking back the property of the Sultan,' said Gurkan.

Gurkan was right. They were poorly equipped, the senior members of the crew were dead, their Commander incapacitated ‑ and what's more, they had no idea where the Staff was being taken. Their foreign appearance didn't help either.

'You never told me you could speak Arabic,' Awa said to Will.

He grinned. 'It never came up in conversation.'

'Can you read it?'

'Of course.'

'So I won't need to translate my journal for you, Will Ryde.'

'What journal?' Gurkan enquired, looking from one to another.

'Awa is writing an account of her journey, like the great travellers of the past,' Will said.

'Am I mentioned?' said Gurkan.

Now it was Awa's turn to smile. 'I haven't come to that part yet.'

'Don't forget to describe my swordsmanship and athleticism, along with my handsome appearance and cultured personality. I'm sure your readers will want to know about the mighty warrior who saved you single-handedly from the scandalous inn.' Gurkan preened himself.

'I seem to recall being responsible for that myself,' Awa replied.

'Well yes, I suppose we all played our parts, large or small as they may be,' Gurkan conceded.

Awa stared at him incredulously, before he burst out laughing.

Clearing his throat, Will interjected, 'Come on - focus. We need to decide what happens next. Time is against us.'

'We have no local knowledge,' said Awa.

'But John Moor does,' said Will.

'Can we trust him?' Gurkan asked, serious again.

'He saved the Commander's life when he could have turned us in,' Will pointed out.

'He still might,' Gurkan responded.

'He does not seem like the sort who would betray a trust,' Awa said.

'He does not know what we're involved in though, does he?' Gurkan reminded her. 'Our task is to return the Staff of Moses from England to Turkey. His loyalties may be with these people.'

Will grimaced. Gurkan quickly backtracked, saying, 'Sorry, Will. What I mean is that in order to live here safely he needs to demonstrate that he is loyal to the English way of life, even though he may still have an affinity with his homeland.'

'The Earl of Rothminster is not acting on behalf of the Queen, is he?' said Will. 'Bringing the Staff to England does not serve the interest of the Crown. On the contrary, Murad will be furious.'

'The Commander wanted us to find the East Mediterranean Company. He said they would protect us, get us home,' Gurkan said.

'Home' meant different things to different people, Awa thought. What did it mean to Will Ryde?

The barn door opened and they all jumped up, drawing weapons.

'My, you lot are itching for a fight,' said Meg, walking in with a tray of steaming soup bowls. John behind her carried a platter with chunks of bread. 'We thought you might need some breakfast to keep your strength up.'

The food was delicious, and just what they needed. They ate heartily, after which John went back to the farmhouse to brew fennel seed tea for them. When he poured it from the kettle, the aniseed aroma was a comfort, as was the taste.

'Now, I hate to bring this up, but . . .' John exchanged a look with his wife before continuing. 'Now Meg and I, we live a clean life, not messing with anyone's business, nor causing harm to others. On this little farm which we built with our own hands, we keep ourselves to ourselves. If you're involved in trouble, we don't want that trouble finding us. Do you take my meaning?'

'We do, sir,' said Will.

'Which is why we need you to move on, as soon as your master is fit to travel,' said John.

'We aren't planning on staying. We have urgent business to attend to, which might mean we need to be on our way today,' Will explained.

Meg motioned to Konjic. 'He's in no fit state to travel, young man.'

'Can you keep him here for a while, let him recover?' Awa asked. 'We will come back as soon as we can.'

'What could be so important that you'd leave your master when he's in such a condition?' John wanted to know.

'It's for his safety,' Will replied. 'There's . . . Look, something was stolen which belongs to our master's master, who told him to find it and return with it - or else he must not return at all.'

'Return to where?' John asked.

Will exhaled. 'Istanbul.'

Meg clutched her husband's arm. 'The Turks! A bloodthirsty demonic land full of fire-breathing dragons, oh aye.'

'*What?*' Gurkan snapped.

Will held up his hand. 'I assure you,' he said gently, becoming used by now to defending the country, 'having lived in Istanbul, I can tell you it is no such thing. It is a jewel of place, like a city brought down to earth from heaven itself.'

'Well I never . . .' marvelled Meg, her voice trailing off.

Gurkan was nodding his head. Awa was yet to experience the city for herself, but she had heard plenty of stories from others. Konjic and his team were testament to the advanced, enlightened civilisation the Turks had developed.

'And what was stolen?' John wanted to know.

'It's an artefact belonging to the Palace. It has tremendous value and is . . . well, one of its kind. I'm very sorry but I can't say any more,' said Will.

John seemed to accept that explanation. 'One last question, if you please: who took it?'

'An English Earl,' Gurkan answered.

'Which one? There be loads of 'em,' Meg said forthrightly.

'Rothminster.' Will supplied the name.

'Oh, he's the fellow who lives over in Leeds Castle,' said John.

Will's shoulders slumped. 'That's the other end of the country!'

'I said Leeds Castle. I didn't say Leeds,' John replied, with a rare smile. 'Leeds Castle is in Maidstone, about half a day's ride away.'

It may have been close, but gaining entry to a castle was, in Awa's estimation, an enormous challenge. She had heard about moats and reinforcements. Siege-engines brought in to break fortifications. Their little band of three had no such resources. What's more, they were up against a formidable opponent, whose tentacles had reached into the palace of the most powerful man in the world.

'How long do you think our master Konjic will be out of action for?' Will asked.

'It'll be two days at least, before he's ready to be moved,' John replied.

'We could be there and back in that time,' mused Gurkan.

'Sorry to sound like a killjoy, but I hear the castle is impenetrable,' John added.

'We don't have a choice,' Will said simply.

Meg slipped an ivory hand into the palm of her husband's ebony one. Awa wondered if the couple had children and, if so, what colour they were.

'John,' she asked, 'why would a Moor settle in an uncivilised place like England?' Once she said the words, she realised the comment sounded disrespectful and felt embarrassed before the others.

'For love,' said John, entwining his fingers with those of his wife. 'It is true, this nation is not as advanced as where I or you come from, but after I met Meg, I made up my mind to stay.'

'It was not my intention to sound discourteous,' said Awa. 'Forgive me. If you allow me, I would like to ask how you came here. And are there other Africans in this country?'

'There are a few. In the ten years I've lived in England, I have met two others. They in turn have also met a few. How many there are in total I could not say, but there are a handful who go by such names as Blackman, Blacke, or Moor.

'I myself came to this country after my ship ran aground in the Mediterranean and I was picked up by a merchant vessel, sailing back to these shores. In the Moroccan army, I was a trainee surgeon. When I came here, there was no such work for the likes of me, so I took to sewing. I was already used to stitching up wounds, so now I stitched clothes for fine gentlemen and ladies. It's how I met my Meg, who was also a seamstress. The Lord of the Manor where she worked was a kindly old gent who had no offspring, so in his will he left his estate to some distant relatives and the people who worked for him. This farm and the small piece of land with it, was given to Meg. It's where we decided to settle down. We still earn part of our living through sewing.'

'Do you miss home?' Awa asked.

'Home? Home is the place where you find comfort,' John replied.

Awa gazed at John the Moor and his wife. Here was a lesson for them all. Two very different people, who had made their relationship work and who had created a heaven in this bleak landscape which they called home.

37

LEEDS CASTLE

BUZZARDS GLIDED OVER LEEDS CASTLE in the early evening dusk. It had taken them just half a day's journey, as John Moor predicted, for them to arrive at the Earl of Rothminster's imposing fortress. The land route into the castle was heavily guarded and the only other way in was across the water-filled moat.

Will, Awa and Gurkan surveyed the area from the neighbouring wood, watching the comings and goings of people to and from the castle. The drawbridge was lowered thrice a day, allowing carriages to exit and enter. Stukeley, Rathbone's bodyguard, marched out at one point, shouting orders at a cowering blacksmith, who hurried back inside the stronghold. Whether the Staff was within was anyone's guess, and the same applied to the whereabouts of the Earl and Rathbone: Will saw neither.

After two days of reconnaissance, the trio decided the time was right for their attempt to break in. They planned to scale the walls with a grappling hook and rope which they'd purchased. After that they'd improvise, depending on what they found inside. Commander Konjic would not be impressed, but these were forlorn times and desperate measures were required.

* * *

It was just after midnight. Keeping to the shadows, they stole silently out of the wood and across to the moat, on which they placed the raft they had constructed the day before and climbed aboard. They had agreed that the northern tower was the least accessible part of the complex, so it was the likely location of the Staff. Crouching low, with a canvas thrown over them, they paddled towards their destination as the crescent moon glinted overhead. The moat was enormous but eventually the raft bobbed to a gentle stop against the stone walls. Will pulled away the canvas.

'Keep us steady,' he whispered.

Gurkan gripped the wall with one hand and the corner of the raft with the other while Awa uncoiled the rope and handed Will the grappling hook to tie onto it. She then helped to steady the raft from the other side as Will stood up, righted himself, then began to swing the rope around, building up momentum before letting it fly upwards. Unfortunately, the first attempt failed. The hook missed the parapet and came plunging down. They ducked, and it splashed into the water, sending a ripple across the moat.

Gurkan threw the canvas over them and they lay flat, shielding themselves and the raft. Waiting. Minutes passed with no sound. Eventually, Will peered out from under the covering, craning his neck upwards towards the battlements. No one was there. He waited for a few more minutes, before retrieving the hook from the moat.

'Try again,' Awa breathed. 'Give it more width before you throw.'

Will nodded, doing as she instructed, before launching the hook. This time it sailed up and over, lodging on the battlements with a faint clang. He tested the rope. It held. He gave it a yank. It remained firm.

'I'll go first,' he said. 'If anything happens to me, just get out, head to London, find the East Mediterranean . . .'

'Yes, we know,' Awa interjected. 'But nothing *is* going to happen to you, Will.' She placed a hand on his arm. 'Now start climbing - before I decide to go first.'

He took a deep breath, checked his weapons, gripped the rope and hauled himself up the sheer surface, his knees bent, boots firmly on the wall, walking up at a near-vertical angle. It was hard work, far tougher than he had expected. By halfway up, his calves were aching, his shoulder muscles on fire. He almost stopped, but forced himself on, and didn't look down. The ascent continued, until he reached the top of the battlements, where he paused, manoeuvring himself into a position where he could peer over the edge. All clear. He then heaved himself up and rolled over the parapet. Without pausing to catch his breath, he leaned over and motioned for Awa to follow. Within a few minutes both Awa and Gurkan had joined him.

Gurkan puffed out his cheeks. 'Hard work.'

Bent double, they shimmied along the low battlements till they came to a doorway in the northern tower. It was unlocked. Opening it with a creak, they cautiously descended the spiral stone staircase in the pitch dark, feeling their way down the uneven steps, aided by the occasional shaft of moonlight entering the arrow slits in the walls. At the bottom, they set off down the corridor, the way ahead illuminated by cressets - burning torches set at intervals into the walls. Will was at the front. Rounding a corner, he held out a hand to stop them and put a warning finger to his lips.

'Heavily guarded. Outside a room. Let's work our way around from the other side.' They followed the corridor back, and after circling the entire tower, returned to the same room from the other side, only to find guards placed at a second entrance.

226

'This must be where they keep the treasures,' whispered Gurkan. 'How are we going to get in?'

'There might be a window,' said Awa.

Gurkan's eyes widened. 'What, you mean enter from the outside?'

'What choice do we have? I can do it,' said Awa.

'Likely be locked,' said Gurkan.

'Might not be,' Awa argued.

'Look, you two . . .' Will was saying, when they heard footsteps approaching. They dived into a recess, pushing themselves back against the wall, out of the glow of the cressets, holding their breath as Stukeley's ferocious form stomped past, heading for the guarded room. At least it confirmed their suspicions: something valuable must be inside. Was it the Staff of Moses? They slipped back down the corridor, picking up a lantern before ascending the spiral stairway once again and returning to the roof. Awa led the way towards the far side, where a window, if it existed, would show on the outer wall.

'Wait,' hissed Will. 'Look at these - skylights.' There were at least half a dozen, one built over every room. 'One of these must be over the vault room.' They fanned out, searching.

'Here,' whispered Awa. 'I think this is the one.' The glass had a layer of grime over it. She wiped it clear, then breathed excitedly, 'I can see it! They've placed it inside a glass cabinet, right below us.' Frustratingly, three iron bars were fixed into stone, above the leaded glass.

'We need to get these bars off,' said Will, gripping an iron bar with each hand and tugging on them as hard as he could. They barely moved. He tried again, his cheeks becoming hot with the exertion.

'My turn to try,' said Gurkan. He did his best but it was useless.

'Let me take a look,' said Awa, resting on her knees, the lamp placed beside the metal rods. Gurkan let out a *humph*, as if to say, *What chance do you have if we can't loosen it?* 'The rods are mortared into the stonework,' she noted, 'but this one in the middle . . . Both of you, pull this central rod together, see if you can loosen it. If we can get it out, I might be able to slip through.'

Will and Gurkan gripped the metal rod and pulled. Again, and again. 'Keep going,' Awa urged them. Eventually there was a grating sound, as the rod shifted, mortar crumbling. Little by little, the central rod loosened, till Awa was able to insert her dagger under the rod and lever it up. They repeated the manoeuvre on the other side and were able to lift one entire rod clear. The space was tight, but Will reckoned Awa was going to fit.

'Now for the glass,' said Will, applying Awa's dagger to the corner of the frame upon which the glass was fitted. He dug away at it till he reached the joint into which the pane of glass slotted. After scraping clear the opposite side as well, he was able to remove one pane of glass, then repeated the process with the other three, carefully handing each pane to Gurkan, who placed them at a safe distance.

'Lower me down with the rope,' said Awa.

They dropped a few feet of rope down. Awa then slid off the edge of the window, grasping the rope firmly as they lowered her into the darkened room. She signalled for them to stop when she was directly over the glass cabinet. There she saw the Staff they had been seeking: displayed lying on a pure white cloth. With luck, it would only be a matter of seconds before she retrieved it - and then they could escape to London., having taken it right under the noses of the Earl of Rothminster and Sir Reginald Rathbone.

Commander Konjic would be proud of them.

* * *

Awa was dangling right over the cabinet. Any further and she would be touching the top with the soles of her boots. The room was circular, with recesses built into the walls; some were occupied by pieces of elaborate armour in glass cabinets, others with coins shining inside glass boxes. As she twirled around on the rope, she caught sight of a cache of jewels glittering inside another locked cabinet.

She swung her body backwards and forwards until she could drop to the ground without crashing into the cabinet. Silent as a cat. Or so she thought. Barking ferociously, an enormous mastiff came charging at her. She stumbled back, her hand going for her weapon, but the beast was already upon her. Its jaws opened, then it abruptly stopped, as the chain tied to its collar pulled taut.

'Oh God!' said Awa, darting an anguished glance up at her friends' horrified faces.

The mastiff snapped away, growling and barking at her, but it was out of range. The guards, hearing the disturbance, had opened the door behind her. Scrambling up, Awa smashed the glass on the top of the cabinet with the hilt of her sword and snatched up the Staff. For the second time in her life she was holding the rod of the Prophet Moses.

'Stop!' someone shouted. Guards were pouring into the room - too many to fight.

Stukeley marched into the room. 'What the hell is going on here, eh?' he bellowed, then bared his teeth when he saw her clutching the Staff. 'You!'

Awa threw the Staff up, straight as an arrow, flying towards the skylight. Nimbly, Will caught it.

'No!' Stukeley yelled. 'Get 'em.' Two guards raced out of the room, with Stukeley behind them. The others remained, advancing towards Awa.

229

'Come on, Awa!' Gurkan shouted.

Awa bounded up onto the broken cabinet, grabbing the rope as Gurkan hauled her up. She might have got away, had a quick-thinking guard not thrown a knife, slicing it through. Awa plummeted back onto the shattered glass of the cabinet, hitting it hard, before falling off and landing on the stone floor.

Will watched in dismay as Awa plunged back into the room. *No.* She'd almost been free! He bent to squeeze through the space between the rods, when Gurkan stopped him.

'You need to get the Staff to the East Mediterranean Company in London. *Go*,' ordered Gurkan.

'You do it,' Will objected.

'You're English, you won't be noticed in London,' said Gurkan, shoving Will away. 'Now go!'

Will held the rope for him, before Gurkan leaped the final few feet, landing amongst the guards below, whipping his blade out as he did.

Will couldn't leave his friends. Not like this! He examined the Staff once more. So much tribulation this holy relic had caused - the death of his friends, the capture of others. Surely God would not want this. Then he remembered Konjic telling him about the perils of returning to Istanbul empty-handed. Will felt the turmoil inside him. Awa and Gurkan were certain to be captured. Likely to be tortured. Could he bear the guilt?

Only if he made their suffering count for something

'Damn it!' Will cursed. Then he turned and ran, ran for his life and for theirs.

38

SACRIFICE

AWA SPRANG TO HER FEET as Gurkan fell into a fighting stance beside her. At least she was not going to die alone in this desolate land, where the sun never shone. The mastiff howled, the eight soldiers circled, weapons drawn. She noticed the door was left open, then one of the soldiers slammed it shut. Silly. She shouldn't have eyed it.

'Let the dog loose!' cried one of the soldiers.

Another guard walked over to the beast, hand out. The dog stopped barking and licked the fingers of its trainer. The soldier crouched down beside the mastiff, rubbing its forehead, speaking into its ear. The man smiled through crooked yellow teeth at Awa and Gurkan, before reaching down and letting the beast loose. The hound bolted at her, jaws snapping, ready to kill.

Daggers drawn, Awa rammed both her blades through the head of the beast. Its jaws were inches from her face - she could smell the rank stink coming from its drooling saliva. Its legs gave way and it collapsed. Awa ripped the blades out. It was the first time she had killed an animal and she was sickened by the thought.

'My dog,' the trainer whined. 'My poor boy - the witch has killed him.' He charged at her, sword swinging. She ducked, twisting her body so her heel stuck out and tripped him, after which she brought her daggers down on him.

Gurkan was busy, fighting the soldiers. Awa went to help him. The strange stillness, the *sakina*, consumed her once more. Every movement seemed to be in slow motion, allowing her to predict the next attack and be able to counter-strike. She and Gurkan were holding their own - but for how long? Their only way out was through the door, which was presently closed. She had to manoeuvre them in its direction.

One of the soldiers tripped over the mastiff's body. Awa swung around and kicked another guard in the face, sending him sliding across a pool of the dog's blood and slamming into the wall. Awa reached for the door handle and pulled it open - but sensing a weapon was close, instinctively side-stepped, as a sword thrust whistled past her ear and through the open doorway. She elbowed her attacker in the stomach, making him drop his weapon.

'Gurkan!' Awa shouted. The Konyan rolled under a strike and threw himself through the open door, out into the corridor. Breathing hard, Awa pulled it shut and locked it. Fortunately, the soldiers in their haste had left the huge iron key in the lock. The guards pounded on it from the other side. The door, shook, but held securely.

'Come on, let's get out of here,' panted Gurkan, dusting himself off.

They sprinted around the circular corridor, heading for the roof. Then: 'Wait,' said Awa. 'I forgot - Will has already taken the raft. We'll have to get out through the main entrance.'

'Oh no!' Gurkan moaned.

They bounded back down the spiral stairway, nearly tumbling in their haste. The steps were oddly designed, some higher than others, and Awa hesitated a number of times, making Gurkan bump into her. To their dismay, they heard footsteps coming the other way. Two soldiers were clambering noisily up towards them. Being above them, Awa and Gurkan had the advantage. She was able to bring her sword around in the constricted space to strike down the first, as Gurkan dealt with the second.

Climbing over their bodies, they stole through the exit and under an ancient archway to reach a larger courtyard, where they saw a stable block. They crept over to it, pushing open the wooden doors without a sound. A brown mare neighed at Awa and she patted her on the nose. She buckled a saddle onto the mare's back, as Gurkan readied another horse for himself. Holding their mounts by the reins, they left the stables and made their way towards the postern gate, dreading discovery at every step.

Unfortunately, the horses' hooves clattered on the stone. Awa felt anxiety rising in the pit of her stomach. This was too easy, for ahead of them she could see that the drawbridge had been lowered, connecting the castle to the land. Beyond that was the countryside. If fate wished it, they would be free in moments.

As they reached the postern, however, there was a sound of metal sliding through stone, as an iron portcullis crashed down in front of them, blocking their way out with its vicious spikes. She spun around, and at the other end of the small courtyard, another portcullis thundered down, trapping them inside. Her mare panicked, rearing up on her back legs. Awa tried to bring the horse under control.

'Take aim,' someone shouted. Behind murder-holes set into the walls of the small courtyard, Awa could see at least a dozen arrows pointed at her and Gurkan. There was nowhere to hide, they were going to be shredded. She let the horse go and it trotted across to the portcullis. Was this how she was going to die? They had been so close to escaping. Gurkan reached out and held her hand. She squeezed it.

233

'Wait!' The voice boomed through the archway. It was Stukeley, Rathbone's henchman. Beside him stood his master, resplendent in a crimson doublet.

'My goodness, these young Janissaries are awfully resourceful, don't you find, Stukeley?' drawled Rathbone.

The bodyguard shrugged his huge shoulders.

'I have to commend your master, Commander Konjic,' Rathbone went on, addressing Awa and Gurkan. 'My sources do speak highly of him. He seems to have connections in the most unexpected places - even in London. Incidentally, did Konjic make it out of the Stag alive?'

'Don't say anything,' Gurkan whispered, gripping her hand.

'Young Will seems to have turned Turk and run off with the Staff.' Rathbone chuckled gently. 'Annoying - but we'll find him. In the meantime, perhaps you can arrange a session in the dungeon, Stukeley - if you would be so kind?'

The henchman smiled.

39

INTERROGATION

DARKNESS CREPT IN AROUND HER. The dungeon contained other cells, and she heard the muffled cries of men and women. The earth below her feet was damp. She imagined the cell flooding in heavy rains. Avoiding the withered straw mattress, trying to ignore the all-pervasive stench of human waste, Awa chose to sit on the ground with her back to the bars. At least there she was closer to the light.

Time passed. Awa was not even sure if dawn had broken, but she performed her *Fajr* prayers. To keep despair at bay, she kept reminding herself that this world was a bridge, as Prophet Jesus had said, to be crossed to the everlasting abode of light and peace. The vision gave her comfort.

Earlier, Stukeley had dragged Gurkan off for interrogation. She feared for the Konyan, and for herself. Was she going to receive the same fate? What would they do to her, these warped men, with their hunger for domination? She recalled the conversation she had had with her friend Suha at the Battle of Tondibi. If only women sat on war councils, there would be less fighting and more reconciliation in the world.

A sound made her jump. The flames of the torches on the walls outside revealed two guards, dragging a man along, his feet barely touching the ground. To her horror, Awa realised it was Gurkan. The guards stopped outside her cell.

'Get back!' one of them barked.

The other unlocked the cell door, keeping a wary eye on Awa, who shuffled to the rear wall. They pushed Gurkan inside and he collapsed as they slammed the iron bars shut, turning the key.

'Witch!' spat the guard with the key, as he stomped away.

'Gurkan!' Awa lifted his head onto her lap, pushing back the hair from his forehead. 'What did they do to you?'

He winced, arching his back. His right eye was partially closed and the left had a bad cut over it. 'I tried to stay silent, but I couldn't hold out.' Gurkan raised up his left hand, to show that two of his nails were missing, his fingers bleeding. He burst out crying, tears streaming down his face. 'I'm so ashamed.'

'There, there,' said Awa, wiping his tears. 'It's all right.' She had never seen him in such a pitiful state. He was the gregarious one with the carefree spirit.

'Don't let them take you, Awa,' he mumbled feverishly. 'They have tools they use for torture, it's . . . horrific. Try and run, get away. Death is nobler.'

'No, don't say such a thing, Gurkan. God is watching over us.'

Gurkan nodded. Awa remained silent, comforting him, holding his undamaged right hand. It was shaking. Eventually he grew calmer, albeit still in considerable pain and torment.

'What did they want to know?' she asked.

'Everything. About the Janissaries, the Sultan, Commander Konjic, all of us.'

'What did you tell them?' But Awa knew the answer before he replied.

'Everything,' Gurkan said, his brow strained, bruised lips quivering. 'I tried to resist, but I was scared. I . . .'

'Don't blame yourself, my friend,' said Awa.

'But I must, Awa,' Gurkan responded, agitated. 'I betrayed everyone. I'm a coward.'

'You are no coward,' she said firmly. 'I have seen you fight: you are courageous, and a good person. Strength is about pulling yourself together, even after you've been shattered into a thousand pieces. Falling is merely the first movement we take before rising.'

Gurkan shook his head. 'Every time I lied, they somehow knew, and increased the pain. In the end, I had to be truthful. What good am I? I have failed my friends!'

'It's because you're a good person, and you don't lie that it was obvious when you were making things up.' She stroked his hair. 'Showing weakness in the face of cruelty does not make you a bad person, it makes you a human being.'

The young Konyan thought about her words, before his eyes lit up with anguish once more. 'Will. Most of all, they wanted to know about Will - where he was from, how he had ended up in the Janissaries, did he have any family. Rathbone asked so many questions, it drove me crazy, trying to answer.'

'What did you tell them?'

'Where he was from. His mother, where she lived. Will had spoken about her in conversations we had, described her in detail. I told them everything. They weren't satisfied.'

Awa knew that Will did not even know if his mother was still alive, let alone whether she was still living in the same place. He called it Smithfield Market, Awa recalled. Should there be a chance she was still there, then what Gurkan had disclosed would place the woman in danger.

Though their own situation was dire, Awa had been consoling herself with the knowledge that Will had escaped - with the Staff. He would complete the mission by going to the

East Mediterranean Company, then would collect Konjic from Meg and John's farm and return to Istanbul.

Now those hopes had collapsed. If Will was captured, the Staff taken . . . then all the sacrifices they had made were in vain.

Oh Gurkan, what have you done?

40

CHANCERY

WILL RODE THROUGH THE NIGHT, heading west along the trail towards London. Guilt tore at his heart, remembering the look on Awa's face: there was no anger in her almond-shaped eyes, only the sorrow of parting, knowing they would never see each other again. He knew so little about her, yet he would miss her for the rest of his life.

Will kicked himself for allowing Gurkan to jump down and fight alongside her, but he knew that Gurkan was right - as a Turk, he would stand no chance of making his way around London without attracting the wrong kind of notice. At least for Will there was the slim possibility of completing the mission before heading back to John Moor's to rendezvous with the Commander.

By the time he arrived in London, after a rest at an inn and a change of horses, the sun was rising behind him. He slowed his steed to a trot, for the streets and alleyways to the east of the city were already bustling and crowded. London was his natal home, Will thought, but to be honest, compared to Istanbul, this city was drab. Even the towers of St Paul's, visible from the east of the city, were a poor imitation of the architecture of his adopted city. London had not yet discovered its Sinan, the

Ottoman architect who built some 200 of the iconic structures of the city on the shores of the Bosporus. Still, Will didn't care. He was back, and no matter how pitiful it seemed compared to Istanbul, London was home.

He was itching to go straight to Smithfield's and begin the search for his mother, but with the Staff of Moses strapped to his back, he knew his first duty was to contact the East Mediterranean Company. Their offices were on Chancery Lane, and after asking for directions he soon found the winding street which connected Fleet Street to Holborn. First though, he stopped beside a stall to break his fast with a meal of ale, bread and coddled egg.

'Just got off the boat, son?' asked the stall-owner.

Will realised he was still dressed in his Ottoman attire.

'Or are you one of them actors playing at the Rose over in Southwark?'

'Actor?' Will was bemused. 'Sorry, I don't follow.' He had no idea what the Rose was, so decided to play it safe. 'Matter of fact, I just got off the boat,' he told the man. 'Been overseas with a trading expedition. Returning home thought I'd surprise my old mum, with the clothes and all.'

'God bless you, lad.'

Will sat down across the road from where the offices of the East Mediterranean Company were located at number 12. It was an ordinary-looking building, half-timbered, its wooden frames lined with wattle and smeared with daub. In fact, it was similar to all of the other dwellings along Chancery Lane. After eating, Will went to hobble his horse in a stable nearby, then returned to the same spot to keep watch. As the morning wore on, workers started to arrive and enter the premises around it. Will waited patiently. Eventually a middle-aged gentleman, dressed smartly in doublet, breeches and hose and carrying a ledger, stopped outside the offices

240

and removed a key from his pocket. Will dashed across the road.

'Good morning,' he said. 'Excuse me, sir.'

The gentleman turned to look at Will. 'Yes?'

'Are you with the East Mediterranean Company?'

'No. Those are the fellows upstairs. We're the bookkeepers on the ground floor.' The man seemed to take in Will's clothing for the first time. 'I see you've just arrived from Istanbul. Here to see them on business?'

'Yes. I work for the Balkan Trading Company.'

'Of course. I've heard the fellows mention the name. Been waiting long?'

'A while. Do you know when they'll be in?' Will asked.

'They normally arrive soon after me.' The man surveyed the street. 'Tell you what, I'll let you in and you can wait upstairs in their hall till they turn up.'

'Thank you, sir, I'd welcome it.' Will followed the bookkeeper through the main door.

'At the top of the stairs there is an open area, where you can wait till they show up. Just let them know Master Philpot let you in. Good day to you, young sir.'

'Thank you and good day.' As Will ascended the staircase, a great fatigue suddenly hit him. Perhaps there was a bench upstairs where he could take a quick nap. Unfortunately, the landing - wooden-floored, tiled at the edges and with a window overlooking the street, contained no furniture other than an uncomfortable-looking wooden chair. As he went to sit down, mindful of the Staff upon his back, Will noticed that the door into the office was slightly ajar. Had they forgotten to lock up the night before?

Knocking, then pushing the door open, Will closed it behind him and entered the dim interior. The shutters were closed and a pungent odour filled his nostrils. The hairs on the back of his neck rose: Will recognised the smell of death. Quickly, he crossed to the window and pushed the shutters open to let the morning light and fresh air stream in. Papers were strewn over the floor, he saw, files thrown from cupboards, wooden cabinets smashed. The East Mediterranean Company had been burgled. *And worse.*

He heard flies buzzing in the office. Following the sound, he came to a cupboard made of oak, tall as he was, with a lacquered finish and brass handles. As he reached out and his fingers curled around a handle, a fly landed on his hand. He brushed it off, only for two more to arrive. A distinct low-level buzzing was coming from the interior of the cupboard.

Will turned the handle.

Something large fell out. A body, two bodies, covered in flies. He jumped back, close to vomiting, and knocked over a chair. Then he stood, transfixed, gazing in shock at the bloodied bodies of the officers of the East Mediterranean Company. These poor men were to have been his saviours. The ones who were going to get him out of his predicament. They would know what to do, how to return Konjic safely back to Istanbul with the Staff. By handing the Staff over to them, Will would be absolved of his duty and could slip away, find his mother and live happily ever after in London with her, reunited at last.

Will stared at the faces of the dead men. They weren't going to do anything for him. He began to mutter a prayer so they could rest in peace.

'Is all well up there?' It was the voice of the man downstairs. 'You there, what was that crashing about? Not causing trouble are you, lad?' Philpot started to ascend the stairs.

Will scrambled up, glancing around him. The place was a wreck. There were two dead bodies. He could be implicated. He had to get out.

'Hello?' Philpot was approaching the outer area.

242

Will peered out of the windows. Below was a drop to a cobbled yard. There was an open cart with bales of hay piled up beneath, but it was a long way down. As Philpot pushed the door open, Will threw himself out of the window, dropping towards the cart.

As he landed, he heard Philpot scream.

41

DEATH BEGUILES HIM

'HE'S DYING!' AWA SCREAMED. 'HURRY!' She hammered away at the bars of their cell. There was only an echoing silence in the dungeon, other prisoners choosing to remain silent, listening to her. Eventually her banging and shrieking drew the attention of a guard, who opened the iron gate at the far end of the corridor leading out of the dungeon.

'What are you hollerin' about, witch?' the man growled.

'Gurkan is dying, he needs help,' Awa shouted.

'What do I care if he dies? Nothin' to do with me.'

'He has information Rathbone wants,' said Awa.

The guard hesitated. 'What information?'

'If he dies, Rathbone is going to be very upset.'

The guard yelled at another behind him, asking the man to join him.

'Look!' Awa wept. 'He's stopped breathing. His eyes have rolled up inside his head.'

'Did you put a spell on him, witch?' said the other, ginger-haired guard, and sniggered fearfully.

'He's my friend,' said Awa, racing over to crouch beside Gurkan, who lay motionless on the ground. She put her ear to his chest then glowered back up at the men. 'You torturers - you are responsible for this! Now are you going to do something or not?'

The guards shrugged. 'If Rathbone wants him alive . . .' said Ginger-head.

'Yes, he does!' said Awa.

'Bring him over then, closer to the bars, so we can get a look at him,' Ginger-head ordered.

Awa bent over Gurkan, looping her arms under his and pulling him across. She had her back against the iron bars when one of the guards reached out, curling his arm around her waist, yanking her so Awa's back hit the metal. He kissed her neck through the space in the iron railings. Her fingers became claws and she ached to attack him, but instead she let him continue kissing her, his filthy saliva on her neck.

'Oh yeah,' said Ginger-head, encouraging his companion. 'We haven't had one her colour before. We'll take him out for you, witch - for a trade.'

Awa knew precisely what they meant. Bracing herself, she said, 'I'll do anything,' breathing deeply.

'Come on, mate,' Ginger-head nagged the other guard. 'Get the bloody door open then.'

The guard slipped his hand away from Awa's waist and she turned to give him an inviting look.

'Oh yes,' said the guard, unlocking the door.

'Me first,' said Ginger-head, muscling past. He came through, leering at her. She shuffled back, towards the straw mattress. 'Don't get too comfortable, witch.' He removed his sword belt, throwing it on the ground, as he approached her.

'Leave some for me, Ginge,' said his companion, clinging hold of the bars outside.

'You wait your turn,' the man snarled. Awa stared into his eyes, a tempting smile spreading across her lips. He started towards her, untying his breeches, grinning with excitement.

Gurkan leaped up, grabbed Ginger-head's sword from the ground, before lunging forwards and driving it through the chest of the guard outside the cell.

'What?' Ginger-head spun around.

Awa was upon him, punching him in the windpipe, then elbowing him in the stomach, followed by a crippling kick in the groin. Gurkan threw Ginger-head's sword through the air, Awa grabbed the hilt and with the flat of her blade, smashed it against the jailor's head. The man was still.

Gurkan came over to her, gripping her elbow. 'It worked. I'm sorry you had to do these things.'

'What - play the seductress? Let's pray I won't need to do it again.'

Swiftly, they removed the keys from the slain guard, before shoving his body into the cell with Ginger-head and locking it behind them. They raced down the corridor to the dungeon's gate. Turning the handle, they peered out. There were lamps shining outside. Beyond the lamplight the entire place was plunged in darkness.

Gurkan led the way, stopping beside the recess where the guards sat and where their weapons were stored. They helped themselves to a weapon each before running up a flight of stairs to the ground floor. Reaching the top, Gurkan stared out.

'Clear.'

It was so good to feel the cold fresh air on their skin, after the reeking cage in an airless underground pit. Night engulfed them, a drizzle of rain coming down and making the stone courtyard glimmer. Slowly they edged themselves back towards the stables for another attempt to escape. They would need the beasts if they were to put distance between them and their captors. Leeds Castle was silent but for two guards perched on wooden stools close to the massive main gates. This time, the drawbridge connecting the castle to land was up. They would need to lower it.

'Wait,' whispered Awa, pointing to a room beside the stables. 'There is the Armoury.' She entered, light-footed as could be, Gurkan at her side. Awa tucked some daggers into her belt, before collecting a bow and a pouch full of arrows. She already had the jailor's sword: Gurkan had taken the other. They were both well-armed now. 'You get the horses. I'll take care of the guards.' Gurkan nodded.

Once outside the armoury, they split up, Gurkan entering the stables, Awa remaining hidden in the shadows, finding a clear line of sight. She notched the first arrow, pulling back her bowstring. The guards were about twenty feet away. It would be a clean shot. Then a horse neighed.

'What was that?' One of the soldiers stood up.

'Probably rats,' said the other. 'Horses don't like 'em around their hooves.'

This time there was another sound from the stables, the movement of shuffling hooves.

'Someone's in there,' said the first guard, drawing his weapon.

Awa fired, striking the man clean in the neck. The second guard shouted: 'Attack!' Awa notched her second arrow and fired, by which time the guard had rung a brass bell beside him.

Gurkan emerged from the stables with two horses. 'They don't like me, these beasts.'

Awa heard footsteps behind her. She whirled, firing off another arrow. It missed the soldier, who ducked for cover. 'Prisoners escaping!' he yelled.

Gurkan was already in his saddle and Awa leaped onto the other horse. Soldiers spilled out of the barbican, screaming orders at each other.

Awa dug her heels in, urging the mare forwards. The drawbridge was still up. No matter. Gurkan unsheathed his sword, and as they went through the small courtyard where previously they had been caught, he slashed the rope, which was wrapped around a bollard with the other end tied to a chain holding up the drawbridge. The rope broke and with an almighty crash, the drawbridge descended. Just as Awa and Gurkan shot through the outer gate, the portcullis which had previously blocked their way, thundered down.

Awa and Gurkan tucked themselves low on their mounts and rode as hard as they could, rode like the wind towards the west – and London.

42

NEAR THE HEART

WILL'S FALL WAS CUSHIONED BY the load of hay-bales. He was winded, but alive. He jumped off the cart then sprinted off down Chancery Lane as if his life depended on it. He might be in his home town, but he had no one to turn to. He ran, like a terrified rabbit, through the streets, turning heads, the Staff of Moses still strapped to his back, his weapons on his belt. The alarm would soon be raised – an armed killer, dressed as a Turk. He had to get out of these clothes, find a way to disappear, lie low. How on earth had Rathbone's men found out about the East Mediterranean Company's officers? The dead men were agents placed by the Grand Vizier in London, to pave the way for a future Embassy. It was a reconnaissance mission, which had now ended with more deaths - all because of a Staff.

Will scampered without direction, his only aim to get away from the crime scene. Before he realised it, however, he was heading for home, making his way towards Smithfield Market. Somehow he knew the route, even though he'd been a child of five when he was kidnapped. It must be a homing instinct: for when all else failed, it was home every person gravitated towards. He had longed for this moment - and now here he was, close to being reunited with his mother, Anne. The mother he had not seen for eleven years. Would she even recognise him? He pictured her face, her blue eyes, creamy cheeks and soft smile. He ran faster, then he skidded to a halt.

There was a tiny open-air market behind Cock Lane, mainly selling second-hand clothes. He purchased without haggling a set of garments to replace his own, disappeared into an alley, stripped off and donned his new garb. To finish off, he jammed an old felt hat on his head, pulling it down as far as possible to cover his face. Taking one last look at his Turkish clothes, he stuffed them under a pile of refuse. Perhaps he would adorn himself with such fine clothing again one day, but not this particular day. Right now, he needed to blend in with the crowds. He re-joined the throng, this time sauntering at a steady pace as he approached Smithfield Market.

Will Ryde was back in his skin: he was a Londoner again.

The market was in full swing, with meat and fish stalls on the outside as he entered, and fruit and vegetables behind them. As he walked further into the market, he found tradesmen selling small animals and beyond that, clothes and metalwork. He passed through them all, till he came to Charterhouse. Here he stopped and took in his surroundings. Memories came back to him. He knew this place. They had lived over there - on the northern side of Charterhouse.

Crossing the street, he recalled a yard with grazing cows. It was still there. In the mornings, the cows would be led over this section of the road and make their way out to fields in the east, before returning in the evening. His mother used to call it Cow-cross and they would have to be wary of animal dung as they traversed the road. The cattle weren't there at the moment. In the fenced-off area where they kept the cows at night, Will spotted a spindly old fellow sitting inside the yard. His face seemed familiar too, but Will was in too much of a hurry to stop and speak with him. There was only one person he desired to see at this moment.

He walked past Cow-cross, trying to recall where he should go next. It came to him. There used to be a well, with a brass bell over it. He turned right and found it. A stout woman was pulling up a bucket of water. Will strolled past her then veered right to enter a narrow lane where open sewage-channels ran down the middle. The smell reminded him of a moment from his childhood. It was the day he and his mother had returned from the heath at Hampstead, where the air was fresh, and he had realised for the very first time that his own home was in a place that stank.

The memory still hurt.

When he reached the end of the lane, he instinctively turned left. This was it - his house was here. The fourth dwelling on the left-hand side. He came to a stop outside his home. It was tiny. The doorframe was lower than his full height. There was a small window, which had appeared so high when he was a little boy. Now it came up to his chest. It didn't matter, his mother was inside. Will knocked on the door.

No reply. He tried again. Still nothing.

'Hello!' said Will.

Silence.

'Oi, what's your game?' demanded a woman's voice from a house behind him. The dwelling was so close to his own, that if he reached out, he would be able to touch her walls.

'I'm looking for Anne Ryde.'

'And you are?'

He wasn't prepared to divulge his identity to someone he didn't even know. 'A relative, from the east.'

'God's light, she's getting a lot of family turning up today.'

'What do you mean?' Will asked.

The neighbour's stare was sharp, lips pursed as though she was weighing up whether to tell him anything else. 'Two fellas turned up earlier, asking about her. I'm thinking to myself, they must have found her down at Smithfield 'cause otherwise she'd be at home this time of the day, sewing.'

Two fellows! Who else was looking for his mother? Nausea rose from the pit of his stomach. 'What did they look like?'

'One was the biggest bloke I ever set my eyes on. Like a giant, he was.' The woman grimaced. 'He had a nasty scar over his right eye too, as if an eagle had attacked him. Right rude he was an' all, when he spoke to me. Treated me like his ruddy servant. The other one was a bit scrawny, reminded me of a mouse. If you ask me, they were trouble. I didn't give nothing away - didn't like the look of 'em, see.'

Stukeley. Will felt his head spin, his legs wobble. Had they found his mother! What were they going to do to her? Damn it. He should have come straight here, rather than going to Chancery Lane. He would have reached her before Rathbone's men. How did they know? Then he recalled the conversation he'd had with Rathbone when crossing the Adriatic. Foolishly, Will had trusted the man, had chatted on, told him where he was from, where his mother lived.

'You all right?' crowed the woman. 'Looks like the blood's been drained from yer face.'

'How long ago were they here?' Will asked, his voice quivering.

'Couldn't 'ave bin more than two hours since.'

'Thank you.' Will turned back to his house. The door was locked. He reached down, lifted up a brick under which was a clutch of pebbles. Rummaging through them he found the key. His mother still kept it in the same place.

''Ere, how'd you know Anne keeps her key there?'

Will ignored the neighbour. He turned the lock and entered. The room was dimly lit, with a small hearth against the far wall. To one side was a bed with an old rug at its foot.

On the bed lay a set of garments and in a wicker basket was a bunch of needles and threads. There were two chairs against the opposite wall, with a tiny table in between. Thank God his mother wasn't here. Will's legs gave way and he sank down on one of the chairs. He had dreaded finding her as he had found the two corpses at number 12, Chancery Lane.

He looked around. So this poky room was it - his home. A room he could cross in four strides. It struck him how poor he was. He had travelled so far, experienced so much, to return to this. *No.* He had journeyed here to find his mother - and whether she lived in a house the size of a shoe box or a palace, he belonged with her.

And now he would find her - before anyone else did. Placing the key back amongst the pebbles, Will strode off in the direction of Smithfield Market.

43

SMITHFIELD

A DELUGE OF RAIN ENGULFED Smithfield. It was as though a flood was being sent from above to calm the anger boiling within him. He stalked up and down past the market stalls, scanning all faces, eavesdropping on conversations. While the Londoners took shelter under canvas, he marched on, aware of the strange looks he was receiving. He didn't care. Let them know, Will Ryde had returned. Gradually his rage did cool, and his training took over. He was a Janissary, Will reminded himself, and he would use the skills he had learned to hunt down those who were seeking his mother.

The rain eased off and buyers returned to the stalls, the banter and barter starting anew. It was then Will noticed a woman sitting sewing between two stalls that sold fabric. Her head was down, she had a scarf covering her hair, her fingers moved with great dexterity. Will hastened towards her. They hadn't found her! She was safe all along, tucked away in this place, oblivious to the danger posed by Stukeley. His heart beating fast, he was almost there . . . then the woman looked up and Will stopped dead. She was a seamstress, but a younger woman, not his mother.

Seeing his stricken look, the woman asked: 'Are you well, master?' He saw that her top middle teeth protruded rabbit-like over her bottom lip.

Will shook himself out of his daydream. 'Yes,' he said dully.

She went back to her sewing, but he didn't move. She eyed him once more. 'You lost something?'

He had, but how could he explain it? 'I'm looking for someone, thought it was you.'

The seamstress began to adjust her hair. 'Might be.' She smiled.

'No, I don't mean like that.' Will blushed. 'I'm looking for Anne Ryde, she's also a seamstress.'

The woman nodded. 'I know who she is. Look, I can stitch anything she can, just as well. She's getting a bit old; her hands don't work so quickly any more.'

Old. His mother? Will still imagined Anne as a young woman. He couldn't for a moment picture what an older version might look like. 'Have you seen her?'

'No, love, not since the morning. Oi, Pete, you seen Anne about?' she called out to the stallholder standing on the other side of the path. He was a corpulent fellow, selling loaves of bread.

Pete slapped at a fly, trying to think. 'Oh yeah, that's right - I did see her 'bout an hour ago. She was headed over to St Paul's. Got a customer down in Godliman Street or something, I dunno.'

Will thanked them both and made to head off to Cheapside and St Paul's, when he noticed two men, dressed rather smartly in black and dark blue, standing near the edge of Smithfield. They looked out of place. Were they watching him? He made eye-contact with one, who hastily turned away. Two other men, dressed in similar attire, were pretending to converse at the far end of the market close to the cow-crossing. He *was* being followed! Were they the Earl's men, or more rogues sent by Rathbone?

The thought of that ogre Stukeley manhandling his mother twisted like a knife in his guts. What type of homecoming was this, when the son endangered the parent?

He reached St Paul's Cross and found the area around the cathedral busy with worshippers, clergy, hawkers and beggars. There was very little room to move close to the building itself, so Will skirted around the edges, trying to remain inconspicuous. Having been around St Paul's Cross a number of times and not seen his mother, or the more easily noticeable Stukeley, Will decided to find a place to wait. Picking up an old wooden crate, he placed it beside an outer wall and sat down. *Think*, he told himself. What other resources were at his disposal? Who else did he know in this city? No one. Without Awa and Gurkan, he was working alone.

A young lad came to a stop before him. 'Master?' the lad said.

'Yes,' Will replied, sitting up.

'You Master Will Ryde of the Jan - Janiss something?' the boy said, stumbling over the words he had memorised.

Will braced himself for whatever was coming next. 'Yes, I am he.'

'Got a message for you.' The boy handed him a sealed piece of paper.

Will broke the wax seal and unfolded the paper. It read: *Tonight. Nine. Pike's Head, London Bridge. If you want to see her alive bring the Staff. No tricks.*

The messenger was about to depart. 'Wait. Who sent you?'

'Dunno, didn't give his name. Warned me I'd better say the right words or else.'

'What did he look like?'

'Biggest fella I ever seen, nasty scar down his right eye.' The boy swallowed and looked around nervously.

Stukeley.

'When did he give you this message?'

'Just now.'

What! Will jumped to his feet, knocking over the box. 'Where?' But the boy had run off. 'Hey, come back!' Will gave chase, but it was no good. The lad had vanished in the throng.

Will ran towards where the boy had glanced around fearfully. He reached the pavement, stared off to the right - and was just in time to see a carriage shoot off towards the river. In the back seat, he could make out the large form of Stukeley. Sitting between him and another fellow was a fair-haired woman.

Was it his mother? If so, at least she was alive. He would finally get to see her, even if for a moment. He felt the Staff on his back. His mission was to return it to the Topkapi Palace, but his mother's life was more important to him than this piece of wood. Yet by failing to bring the Staff back to Istanbul, Konjic's life would be under threat. His head was spinning.

Pocketing the letter, Will headed back to St Paul's. He needed to go in and pray for God's guidance.

44

PIKE'S HEAD

SEVERED HEADS DIPPED IN TAR, then boiled to preserve them, were impaled on pikes on London Bridge. The striking stone bridge, stretched out across the Thames, was crammed with buildings, some seven storeys high: houses, eateries, workshops, catering to all needs, habits and dispositions. It was, in effect, a bridge-town within a city. Even at this late hour, the bridge was teeming with Londoners, though most appeared to be up to no good.

Will made his way onto the bridge, the road narrowing, laden with carts kept outside tall narrow edifices, some of which hung off the edge of the bridge, balancing on supporting struts. Rats scampered by, oblivious to the people on the bridge, as much as the Londoners were unmindful of the rodents. Cooking pots warmed on hearths placed on the street. Clothes billowed overhead, hanging from lines thrown between buildings on either side of the bridge, so that when Will gazed up, they materialised like a cobweb. Passage was tediously slow, as some walked on the left, others on the right.

'Pike's Head?' Will asked a crabby fellow with a bushy beard. He waved Will along, gesturing to the right side of the bridge.

It was just before nine in the evening, the allotted time in the note. He was alone, he had brought the Staff of Moses, strapped to his back, and he eagerly anticipated seeing his mother. Will reached the Pike's Head and was about to enter, when he belatedly spotted two men dressed in black and blue, about ten yards behind him: the same ones who had been following him earlier in the day. He squinted through the window of the inn. Sir Reginald Rathbone was seated at a small circular table, a glass of wine in front of him. He was dressed in a grey cloak. Only his fine supple boots distinguished his status.

Some instinct told the man that he was being watched. Rathbone looked up, caught sight of Will and smiled.

Will pushed open the door and entered, pausing to check to his right and left. As expected, a number of tough-looking men were seated at tables. They were loaded with weapons and pretending not to notice him. Rathbone came with muscle. Was he expecting a struggle? Will knew he wasn't going to leave safely with his mother by trying to fight his way out; he was completely outnumbered. He needed to use his brain instead.

Rathbone gestured for him to join his table. Will strode over and sat on the rickety wooden chair opposite.

'Wine?' Rathbone asked.

'I don't drink,' said Will.

'Haven't adopted the ways of the Mahomet, have we?' Rathbone asked in an unctuous tone.

'Where's my mother?'

'All in good time, Will Ryde.' Rathbone sipped from his glass, then made a face. 'I wouldn't recommend the vintage in this place.'

Will glanced about and felt a dozen pairs of eyes on him. None of the men were drinking. Their glasses were empty. He had walked into the wolf's lair without any support.

'Life is tough - tougher if you're a dim-wit like these brutes.' Rathbone gestured to the heavies he had assembled. 'Yet you,

Will, have proven yourself to be quite a resourceful fellow. I admire your tenacity and foolhardy courage. They have served you well. Perhaps you're just lucky and maybe your good fortune is about to run out. Who knows? Either way, I have a proposal to make to you.' Rathbone stared at him, his eyes piercing.

'Work for me,' said Rathbone. 'I need a man in Istanbul, an informant, in the Palace.'

'You want me to be a spy?'

'You already are! Employed by Konjic as a Janissary, what do you think that makes you, a scholar? Hah. You are naïve. Look, let's put all this behind us. You can say the Staff was taken forcibly from you, we send you back to Istanbul, you resume your duties, and every now and then, I'll be in touch.'

'What about my mother?'

'We'll take good care of Mistress Ryde. I'll even find her a cottage in the countryside, with some land and livestock, enough for her to live off. She'll never need to struggle on pennies as a seamstress again. Whenever you come back to England, you can visit her.'

The offer was tempting. His mother would get a new life. 'Why do you want the Staff?' Will asked, genuinely curious.

'The Earl of Rothminster is an ambitious man. He has a point to prove to his backers in England and on the Continent. The theft of the Staff symbolises the reach of his power. Besides, as a religious artefact, it's always a nice trophy to have, should we need to bargain with it in the future.'

'Who are his backers?'

Rathbone chuckled. 'Enough questions, Will Ryde. You are in no position to demand any more information from me. Now: are you with us?'

Will bit his lip. Wiped his sweaty palms on his thighs. Life was made of moments like this. 'I want to see my mother first.'

'Very well.' Rathbone waved to a fellow who had been standing next to the bar. The man disappeared and returned with Stukeley, who was gripping a woman by the arm. She had a black hood over her head.

Will's eyes widened as he stood up. Rathbone nodded and Stukeley removed the hood.

'Mother!'

For a moment she blinked, then her eyes searched his features, seeing in them the dear little boy who had been stolen from her on that terrible day. 'Will?' she said in wonder, her voice a whisper. 'My Will. Is it really you?'

'Yes!'

Stukeley let go of her arm. Will rushed to his mother and embraced her, holding her as tight as possible. Tears poured down his cheeks. He had longed for this moment for eleven perilous years and now here he was. Mother and son, reunited.

'Will, dear, who are these people?' Anne asked, holding both his hands.

'All will be well, Mother, I just need to give them something.' Will removed the Staff, which was wrapped, handing it to Rathbone, who received it gleefully and strapped it across his own back.

'What is it going to be, Will?' said Rathbone.

'The deal was the Staff for my mother.'

'Are you refusing my offer?'

Will hesitated. He didn't like Rathbone's tone. Stukeley loomed before him and Rathbone's men circled him.

'Yes, I refuse to work for you.'

'You are the outcome of your decisions,' said Rathbone. Turning to Stukeley, he said: 'Kill them both.'

261

45

NEARLY

STEEL GLITTERED IN THE LAMPLIGHT. Rathbone's men drew their weapons, as the fiend himself departed. He stopped to glance back at Will, as if to say something - then decided against it. He vanished out of the back of the inn, two of his guards following.

'Let my mother go!' Will demanded. 'She doesn't have anything to do with this.'

'No!' Stukeley growled.

Will drew his weapon and retreated, his mother beside him.

'Will . . .' She clung to his arm. 'I don't want to lose you.'

Men crowded around them from the side and rear, blocking the exit. *Crash!* The glass frontage of the Pike's Head shattered as an object came flying through. No, not an object - it was a person. The assailant went straight for Stukeley's throat, daggers drawn. Stukeley grabbed the attacker in mid-air, before they could plunge their weapon into his neck. Will gawked up and beneath the hood he saw:

'Awa!'

Stukeley threw her into the pack of men, but as he did so, someone else burst through the door, slicing the back of Stukeley's leg with a razor-sharp scimitar. Gurkan! Stukeley stumbled and fell, bleeding heavily. In the next moment, the Pike's Head was full of men dressed in black and blue, like those who had been following Will earlier in the day. They seemed to be fighting Rathbone's men. Will didn't have time to puzzle over it, as knives were being pulled, punches thrown, noses broken. Tables were smashed, chairs were used as weapons, glasses shattered and brandished, lethal.

It was a mêlée and there in the centre was the enormous Stukeley, who had got up once more. He was snarling at Will. Awa stood to Will's right and Gurkan on his left.

'Nice to have you back,' said Will.

'Let's fell this oak,' Gurkan quipped.

'Why not,' Awa said, advancing with her daggers.

Stukeley sprang at Will, broadsword coming down with all of his brute strength. Will sidestepped and the weapon broke the floorboards below him and was stuck there. Will advanced: the giant caught his arm in an iron grip. Gurkan attacked from behind: the giant dodged out of the way. Awa stabbed her daggers into his back and then yanked them downwards, tearing at the flesh.

Stukeley groaned in pain. Will then hit him in the face with the hilt of his weapon and Gurkan sank his blade into the Goliath's chest. Even then, Stukeley only dropped to his knees. It required another sword strike in the neck to finish him off. Gurkan happily obliged.

The brawl around them was still in full flow. Bones cracked, sinews split, blood dripped.

'Mother!' Will ran over to her, holding her tight. 'We need to get you to safety.' He swivelled as a sword came in his direction. Gurkan pushed the assailant back into the crowd and one of the black- and blue-liveried men dealt with him.

'Rathbone - I need to stop him. Awa, please look after my mother,' Will instructed her, before racing off.

Awa turned to Gurkan. 'Since you are still recuperating, please take care of Mistress Ryde,' she told him, then shot off after Will.

Will charged out of the back of the Pike's Head. Word had spread about the fight and a crowd had gathered around the front of the inn, so the way to the north of the river was blocked. He had no choice but to leave the bridge on the Southwark side. The many passers-by made the going slow. He jumped up a couple of times, but couldn't see Rathbone. Where had the man gone? It was then Will noticed a staircase on the outside of a building, leading to a roof on which more tarred heads on spikes were displayed. Someone was moving towards the heads. Rathbone!

Will barrelled headlong, taking the wooden stairs three at a time. He spotted Awa close behind him. She must have left Gurkan with his mother. He was pleased she was there, as she was the most skilled warrior of the three of them. He ran onto the roof. They were roughly in the middle of the bridge. Behind him he could see the tower of St Paul's and the city of London. Ahead was the district of Southwark. All of the roofs along the bridge were of differing heights. Rathbone had vanished from view, jumping onto a lower roof. Will rushed across, avoiding the grisly heads. There was space between the buildings and he leaped, landing safely. It reminded him of the crazy pursuit across the roofs of the Grand Bazaar. And Will didn't even like heights!

When he approached the next rooftop, he stopped dead. Rathbone's sword was drawn and he was duelling with another person. Commander Konjic! How could this be?

Awa caught up with Will and they both stared down at the clash between the two men.

'What were you thinking, Rathbone, stealing the Staff from the most powerful man in the world?' said Konjic.

'The Turk is decadent; the Ottomans have passed their peak,' Rathbone sneered.

'Perhaps your hatred of the Turk is due to your lack of understanding him,' said Konjic, as he blocked another attack. Rathbone's two guards, weapons drawn, stood within striking distance, ready to move in.

'The West is rising,' said Rathbone, springing another attack on Konjic. It was obvious to Rathbone that his opponent was nursing a wound; he was protecting his left side and his movements were restricted. Rathbone took advantage; it was an uneven fight.

'Come on,' said Awa, springing down to the rooftop below.

They drew the attention of the two guards, who came for them. Will tripped, colliding with Awa. They righted themselves - saw their opponents about to strike them. Will blocked the blow from Awa's enemy and she did the same from his. In his frustration, Will's adversary overreached himself. Will fell to one knee and was able to come under his foe's sword strike and drive his own weapon into the stomach of his enemy, causing the man to double over, before Will finished him off.

He rose to see Awa dispensing with her opponent. Konjic meanwhile was losing the duel with Rathbone. Only seconds later, as Will watched in horror, their Commander lay sprawled on the ground, having lost his weapon. Rathbone was about to deliver the killer blow.

'Commander!' Will shouted.

Konjic peered over, as did Rathbone.

'Blast!' Rathbone rumbled, leaving Konjic and racing to the side of the bridge as though he were about to leap off. Instead he removed the Staff of Moses from his back and prepared to throw it like a javelin. *What was he doing?*

'No!' Will started forward.

Rathbone threw, but so did Awa. The dagger left her fingers moments before the Staff left Rathbone's, and her steel struck him in the wrist, causing him to drop the Staff so it landed safely on the ground. His momentum, however, had carried him forward, to the edge of the rooftop. He momentarily regained his balance, before his costly boots slipped on the wet surface, sending him toppling down into the river.

'*Arghh!*' Rathbone screamed as he plummeted down into the Thames.

Will and Awa raced across to Konjic. 'Commander!' Will cried, helping Konjic back to his feet.

'The Staff,' gasped Konjic. Awa ran across to pick it up, holding it firmly, before handing it to Konjic. They inspected the river, but couldn't see Rathbone. There were ripples in the water, but no sign of the man.

As they waited to see whether Rathbone was going to emerge, Will noticed a boat about twenty yards away from the bridge. It was a small wherry, with a couple of men rowing. On it stood a man dressed in black, a hood over his head, watching them. Whoever he was, Rathbone had been trying to get the Staff to him. The figure examined them impassively, arms behind his back, statuesque in his posture. The boat did not stop to look for Rathbone. It moved away, down the Thames, heading east out of London and on to the sea.

46

AN INVITATION

A BRASS FALCON PLACED ON a steel globe and attached to the top of a wooden pole, caught her attention. Beside it was a depiction of a pyramid, also made from brass. The gardens of Nonsuch Palace were exquisite, full of sculptures and ornaments. Awa was a desert dweller, used to arid heat, and sporadic oases. Here, she thought, even the grass seemed luxurious, as though each blade was cut from the finest silk. It had rained nearly every day for the past month since the incident on London Bridge, when they had retrieved the Staff of Moses. There were an inordinate set of bureaucratic hurdles to overcome and Konjic said they must all remain in England until everything was cleared with the authorities.

Awa eyed Gurkan approaching. He was regally dressed in a fine woollen kaftan, embossed with red and yellow patterns. 'Ready for an audience with the Queen?' he quipped.

Awa herself wore a rich silk tunic and matching pantaloons under a floor-length coat made of the richest materials. Her Ottoman waistcoat was lined with fur, for which she was very grateful in this cold weather. 'I think so,' she smiled, and they walked side by side, out of the garden.

Gurkan still had a sparkle in his eyes, but after their ordeal at Leeds Castle, much of his confidence had been dented. Awa hoped he would eventually recover and get back to his normal, cheerful self. 'How are you coping?' she asked.

'Nights are difficult. I wake up in terror, remembering the torture.'

'It will pass with time.'

'I hope so,' said Gurkan.

'I was once locked in a tiny metal container in the desert for nearly three days without food and water. I was close to death.' Awa wanted to share this with him, thinking it might help. 'Weeks later, I would jolt awake and cry out, thinking I was still confined. Only now is the memory fading in my dreams.'

'I didn't know. I'm sorry they did that to you. Was it Odo and Ja?'

To hear their names still sent a shudder through her. It made her want to glance over her shoulder, ensure they weren't sneaking up on her, terrified they were going to snare her once more. *I should have finished Odo off when I had the chance*, she thought.

'Yes.' Her voice was so faint, he could barely hear it.

Will sat upon a stone bench in the grounds of Nonsuch Palace. He held his mother's hands, his head resting on her shoulder. It felt so good to be with her. In the past month he had spent every available moment with her. They had years to catch up on. Anne wanted to know everything that had happened to her dear little boy in the time away, and Will obliged, though he missed out some parts - such as the suffering he had endured in the galleys. Anne listened patiently, hearing about the architecture and buildings of Marrakesh and Istanbul, other times biting her lip, when learning how Will was torn from his kindly master, Hakim Abdullah, and sent to the galleys. On and on Will recounted his adventures . . . Eventually, he realised that he had barely asked his mother what she had done after he left. It was her turn to talk.

He learned about her frantic search for him, which had continued for years; she clung onto hope, but about a year ago, she had resigned herself to never seeing him again. However, Anne refused to move from Smithfield. If Will ever returned, this was the place he would come back to. So, she stayed in her humble dwelling, as close as she could to the market where she plied her trade.

She kissed him on the head. 'My little love. My boy Will.'

Will sat up straight and looked into her eyes. 'Mother. I love you so much.'

Anne hugged him. 'And I you.' She let him go, but still held his hands. 'You remind me so much of your father. He would have been proud of you.'

It was difficult for Will to show love to someone he couldn't remember. His father had died in mysterious circumstances when Will was two.

'Have you decided?' asked Anne.

Will nodded. 'I'm not going to leave you again.'

'Commander Konjic is an honourable man. You and your friends are fortunate to have such a decent human being as your leader. He saved you from the bonds of slavery. My son, you owe him your allegiance.'

'But . . .' Will felt tears welling up in his eyes

'It will be all right,' his mother promised gently. 'I'll be fine. You can visit.' She stood up. Straightened her dress and held out her hands for Will. He took them and rose up. She kissed him on the forehead. 'Come, son, we'd best meet up with the others. Can't keep royalty waiting, can we now!'

They walked in silence, arriving at the broad terrace situated at the rear of the palace. Tables and chairs were spread across the stone surface. Many of the guests due for an audience with the Queen waited in this area. Awa, Gurkan and Konjic were already present.

Awa watched Will and his mother approach. Konjic had given Will an advance, so he could buy fabric for Mistress Ryde to stitch into a fine dress to be worn on this royal occasion. Will's mother was quite striking in her outfit. Her golden locks of hair came down around her neck. Anne seemed like a kind-natured woman, and Awa liked her. She had visited Anne's home in Smithfield and was shocked when she saw the poverty and destitution amongst the Londoners. There was wealth in this nation, but it did not benefit the common people.

Will had been withdrawn over the past few weeks. Awa could see the choices he needed to make tearing him up inside. Was he coming back, or was he going to request Konjic for a release?

She took a quick look over at Konjic. The Commander appeared distracted, staring about, waiting for someone. Among the other guests congregated on the terrace, a fellow with a well-groomed beard kept peeking in their direction. He seemed quite taken with her and Gurkan. When Awa made eye-contact with him, however, he turned away, pretending he hadn't been studying them.

'To think I'm going to meet the Queen. Never would I have dreamed of such a thing,' Anne was saying.

Just then, an old man approached Konjic. The Commander bowed and exchanged pleasantries with him. They conversed for a few minutes before Konjic presented him to the group.

'This is Lord Burghley, High Treasurer to Her Majesty, Queen Elizabeth.'

None of them was certain how to greet the Lord, so they bowed and curtsied.

'Oh, don't worry,' said Burghley. 'Save all that for Her Majesty.'

'Lord Burghley has been an advocate for an alliance with the Sultan for many years. Our officers at the East Mediterranean Company were in contact with him. When I arrived in London, I went straight to see him,' Konjic told them.

'Terrible business, what happened to your men,' Burghley said gruffly.

'Lord Burghley, may I introduce Mistress Anne Ryde and her son Will, who is one of our finest young Janissaries. This is Gurkan, a dashing swordsman and Janissary from the city of Konya. And finally, Awa, the most skilled female warrior I have ever met.'

'Delighted,' said Burghley.

Konjic nodded. 'Will, the men in black and blue livery are part of a spy network established by the late Francis Walsingham, a close acquaintance of Lord Burghley's. The spies detected the arrival of Awa and Gurkan and brought them to me.'

Of course, Awa and the others had already heard this before, but not in the presence of Lord Burghley, and Konjic was using this as an opportunity to formally present their group to the Lord.

'If you ever find yourself in a tight spot, come and find me,' Burghley advised.

A footman emerged onto the terrace to invite the guests inside and to usher them through into a decorative hall, with dozens of ornate glass mirrors running along the wall. Gold leaf trimmed the glistening crystal chandeliers. The hall connected to an inner chamber, of equal size, before they were shown into the Throne Room, in a narrow file. Once inside, the guests were led to pre-assigned positions.

Awa gazed around, taking in the luxurious décor. Thick velvet drapes hung heavy on the side; gold and silver trimmings were fixed to all furnishings; the tiling on the floor shone black, blue, red and yellow. The Queen was already seated on her throne. Face as white as porcelain, chin held high, regarding all before her with a regal gaze. She was much older and frailer than Awa had imagined. Was this the same woman who only a few years ago had defeated the Spanish Armada?

Once all the guests were in position, standing some ten yards removed from Her Majesty, the first invitee was requested to present himself. It was the curious bearded fellow from the terrace. He was announced as a playwright.

'Your Majesty,' he declared in a dramatic pose. 'With your continued support and the blessings of Almighty God, I would like to announce that I have completed the next instalment of my play *Henry VI*. As such, I humbly request that I and my fellow actors be permitted to perform the drama for Her Majesty.' The playwright handed what Awa assumed was an invitation to the Chamberlain, who presented it to the Queen.

Her Majesty seemed pleased at having received the invitation and when she smiled, Awa got a good look at her black rotted teeth. Awa had seen such teeth in Timbuktu. Those who consumed too many sugary dishes and failed to perform the daily oral cleansing with a miswak twig ended up with teeth like that.

Having listened to the Queen's reply, the Chamberlain announced: 'Her Majesty accepts your invitation, Master Shakespeare. We will make the necessary arrangements.'

The playwright bowed low, then came back to stand with the other guests. Awa caught him observing their curious unit once more. Were she and her companions inspiring him in the development of his future characters? Awa frowned at the thought of an audience watching the depiction of a true person on stage. It was quite undignified, in her estimation.

The Chamberlain motioned to Lord Burghley and Commander Konjic. The two of them stepped forward, to stand a few feet from the Queen. Elizabeth began to speak.

'Travellers from the East, know that I, Queen of England, desire to send greetings of peace to the Honourable Sultan Murad, Lord of the East, presider over Ottoman lands, monarch to people of all faiths. It makes me rejoice, knowing that God hath sent such a wise and compassionate ruler to reign over the land of the Turks, with whom we desire good will and friendship. I send with you words of hope, praying for your safe return. As Queen of this realm I bequeath you two gifts from the people of this fair nation: a carriage of the finest craftsmanship, and an organ, which I know will delight the Sultan with its melodious resonances.'

Awa had absolutely no idea what an organ was. The Queen turned to her Chamberlain, who nodded to Konjic.

The Commander stood tall and said: 'On behalf of Sultan Murad, ruler of the Ottoman Empire, Majesty of the East, law-giver to all those who reside in his realm, I gratefully acknowledge Her Majesty's gifts, and shall with the Will of God return to Istanbul, to present these offerings of friendship to His Majesty. May Elizabeth, Queen of England have a long and blessed life and may her kingdom forever be protected from tribulation.'

Konjic and Burghley stepped away once more, but as they did so, the Chamberlain handed a wrapped object to Konjic. It was the Staff of Moses. The Commander had said their mission was secret. Lord Burghley, it seemed, had been able to ensure that the necessary discretion had been maintained.

The next person to approach the Queen's presence was the Earl of Essex, who was presented with some papers to take to King Henry IV of France. He was followed by some other earls, until the Chamberlain announced: 'The Earl of Rothminster.'

Awa stiffened when she heard the name, as did Gurkan, Will and Konjic. She had been kept prisoner in his castle; Sir Reginald Rathbone was his man. They watched the Earl approach. He was a man in his early thirties, with jet-black hair, slightly wavy, a well-proportioned beard. He was quite handsome. The Earl strode forward, his cloak swishing behind him as he bowed before waiting for the Chamberlain to approach.

'Her Majesty,' said the Chamberlain, 'instructs the Earl of Rothminster, with a royal charter, to explore the lands of the East, beyond those of the Turk, to seek out new trade routes and to go forth in the name of England.'

The Earl received the papers. When he turned, his eyes locked with those of Konjic and he smiled. He was a beautiful man, yet his soul, as Awa knew, was ugly. Rothminster returned to his position and the ceremony continued with a few more announcements before drawing to an end, when they were ushered back into the Outer Presence Chamber. Lord Burghley said his farewells and returned to the Queen's side.

When they were all back together, Gurkan spoke first. 'How can he get away with it?'

'He denied all involvement. He claimed Rathbone was acting on his own. As Rathbone is missing, he cannot be questioned,' Konjic replied.

'But we were kept prisoner in Leeds Castle, *his* castle!' said Gurkan, flexing the fingers in his left hand, which had only just begun to heal.

'The Earl has dozens of properties around the country. Leeds Castle is just one of them. Once again, he denied all knowledge. Since the matter did not affect the English Crown directly, Lord Burghley was not able to move against the Earl, despite Rothminster almost destroying all hope of an Ottoman-English alliance,' Konjic said bitterly.

'Why give him a royal charter to explore in the East?' Awa asked.

'If you have a political opponent, sometimes it is better to send them off to distant lands, where they can cause you less trouble than at home,' Konjic replied.

'Only to bring misery to those he meets in the East,' Awa huffed.

Konjic tried to smile. He gripped the Staff in his right hand, slightly leaning on it. His injury was healing well. John Moor, who had operated on him and thereby saved his life, and his wife Meg, who had nursed him and cared for them all, had been rewarded despite their protests and would be his friends for the rest of his days.

'Commander Konjic, I believe.' It was the clear crisp voice of the Earl of Rothminster.

'My Lord,' Konjic acknowledged him.

The Earl pursed his lips. 'You have a motley-looking crew, Konjic.'

'It is an effective team.'

The Earl narrowed his eyes.

'We have not had the pleasure of meeting before, my Lord,' said Konjic.

'No, we have not,' Rothminster replied.

'Though it seems by your very presence that we know each other well,' Konjic went on.

'Indeed.'

'I must congratulate you on your charter,' said Konjic.

The Earl scanned the piece of paper. 'I believe I may be seeing more of you and your servants, Konjic.'

'Perhaps.'

Rothminster surveyed Konjic with a penetrating gaze. 'You strike me as a good man, Commander, but where the good are put in charge of the wicked, empires will be destroyed. It is when the wicked are given oversight of the good, does empire become strong.'

'I would beg to differ with your kind of politics,' said Konjic.

Rothminster took a step closer to him. 'My type of politics leads to a clash of religions, a clash of cultures and a clash of races. Your type of politics unifies under an imperial cause. In the end I will win, because dividing and conquering is far easier than unifying the hearts of men.'

The Earl turned to leave, then briefly admired the Staff held by Konjic. 'Impressive thing,' he murmured, before spinning away, cloak flapping behind him, out into the gardens of Nonsuch Palace.

47

DUTY

S NOW COVERED THE LANDSCAPE OF Istanbul. It was now two months since Awa had returned from England. The winter was proving a perilous one for all the residents of the city, but more so for one who had never seen snow before. She wore a heavy coat of fur and a hooded robe, but somehow the chill still crept in. Songhai like Awa belonged to the sun, and the sooner she returned to it, the better.

'Our friends are dead, but their memories remain. With care we can preserve them,' said Gurkan, standing beside her, observing the Staff of Moses with a solemn expression. 'Was it worth it? The death of so many?'

Like her he was well-wrapped up, but had less trouble adapting to the wintry conditions. Two guards patrolled at either end of the narrow corridor where the religious artefacts were kept in the Topkapi Palace. Further guards were also stationed in a hidden location, should anyone try to steal these objects once more. The Rüzgar unit of the Janissaries, under Konjic, had been given responsibility for safeguarding the objects. Captain Kadri had assigned some of his best personnel to the task. Awa and Gurkan had already done their own shift of standing guard; today was their day off, yet somehow, they were still drawn back to this spot.

'The Staff means everything. It means nothing,' said Awa.

Gurkan shook his head, confused by her statement.

'It is a symbol of God's power, so it means everything to those who are custodians. It is a piece of ordinary wood, which can be broken, so it means nothing.'

'You've been reading al-Ghazali, haven't you?'

Awa smiled.

In the distance, they heard the first faint sounds of the organ playing its inaugural concert for Sultan Murad III. Thomas Dallam, the organist sent along with the organ by Queen Elizabeth, had spent nearly two months rebuilding the instrument after it was damaged in the sea crossing. Finally, he was ready and tonight was the first performance. Awa and Gurkan walked out of the hall where the religious artefacts were housed to a terrace overlooking the courtyard. The organ music was clearer now they were outside. It was a haunting sort of sound, which made Awa think about tall spires and buildings full of gloomy recesses and dark spaces.

'Will would have enjoyed it,' said Gurkan, motioning towards where the music played.

'He's enjoying time with his mother.'

'It'll soon pass. Konjic gave him three months before resuming his duties.'

The Commander was a changed man since returning from their travels, more solemn and thoughtful than before. The loss of young companions had placed a heavy burden on him. Konjic agreed he would let Will return every two years to England to see his mother. Awa doubted any other Janissary commander would have been so accommodating.

Awa felt a closeness, almost a kinship with her unit, yet she knew it was never going to replace her true family. Nor did she want it to. She had sent letters to her father. No replies came back. When stories reached Istanbul of what the Moroccans had done to the Songhai nation, there was a mixture of responses: some could not believe al-Mansur had attacked his fellow believers; others blamed King Askia for having been naïve and not arming his people with the modern weapons of warfare. A small minority felt there had been a missed opportunity and said the Sultan should have sent an army and taken the riches for himself before the Moroccans arrived.

They descended into the stone courtyard. The organist was in full swing, notes rising to a crescendo.

The great iron door at the entrance of the Topkapi Palace swung open. Awa turned to see who was arriving at this time. A solitary figure walked through, the light behind him, illuminating his presence. His hood was up, shielding him from the elements. He paused, swung his gaze about and marched straight towards Awa and Gurkan. The stranger reached them and lowered his hood.

Will!

'Awa. Gurkan. It is good to see you!' Will gripped them both by the arms.

'My God, what are you doing here, Will?' asked Gurkan.

'Where is Konjic?'

'At the performance,' said Gurkan.

'Performance?' Will echoed.

'Thomas Dallam, the organist - he's playing tonight,' explained Gurkan.

'Oh no! I'm too late!' Will started to run in the direction of the music.

Awa and Gurkan followed behind. 'What is it, Will?' Awa called. 'What's going on?'

'Assassins have been sent to slay the Sultan. I was told they will strike on the night the Englishman first plays the organ.'

'That means now!' Gurkan blurted out.

'Yes, now,' said Will.

Awa, Gurkan and Will unsheathed their swords, striding towards the music as the haunting melody was carried away with the falling snow, out over the sleeping city of Istanbul.

AUTHOR'S NOTE

S tories are out there, waiting to be picked from the Tree of Imagination. And so, I like to think that the story you have just read merely required a curious scribe to pluck it.

How the story ripened was a sequence of what appeared at the time to be a series of unconnected events. The first occurred when I myself gazed upon the Staff of Moses, housed in the Topkapi Palace, whilst on a family holiday to Turkey in 2014. I wondered how on earth this holy relic had ended up here. What had brought the Staff, from when Moses wielded it before Pharaoh, all the way to Istanbul?

The second event occurred the following year when, after a leisurely cycling tour of the grounds of Hampton Court Palace, I read that King Henry VIII was fond of striding around dressed as an Ottoman Sultan. People will always copy those who are powerful: even Kings imitate other monarchs.

Thirdly and finally, I came across a wonderful book called *This Orient Isle: Elizabethan England and the Islamic World* by Jerry Brotton. It explained the close ties between England - a Protestant Christian nation - and the Ottoman Turks, a Sunni Muslim empire. Upon delving deeper, I realised there were many indicators of Ottoman and Moroccan influence on the English court, in dress, jewellery, food and literature. What, I asked myself, would a quest story look like, with a multi-cultural cast of characters, set within the backdrop of sixteenth-century geo-political skulduggery?

Hopefully, something like *A Tudor Turk*.

*   *   *

Ultimately this is a work of fiction, but I have used a number of real historical events and characters to anchor the story. The fateful Battle of Tondibi, which led to the collapse of the Songhai nation, did take place in 1591, as did the opening of the new Rialto Bridge in Venice. Antonio da Ponte was the architect and Vincenzo Scamozzi his better-known professional rival.

Shakespeare gets a cameo at the end of the novel, but it's unlikely he would have been invited to Nonsuch Palace to attend such a ceremony. Thomas Dallam was indeed an organist sent by Elizabeth I to the court of Sultan Murad III, but this didn't happen until 1599. For the purposes of the narrative I've moved it to 1591. The Janissaries did have a tempestuous relationship with the Ottoman court, but the creation of the Rüzgar unit is purely imagined. The currency of the Ottoman Empire was the akçe. However, as the dinar will be more familiar to modern readers I have referred to this instead.

Though John the Moor is to the best of my knowledge fictional, there were individuals like him in Tudor England. A fine book by Miranda Kaufmann called *Black Tudors: The Untold Story* describes the lives of some of these men and women of African origin living in England during the period.

I have taken the liberty of assigning the ownership of Leeds Castle in Maidstone to the dastardly (and fictitious) Earl of Rothminster. It has such an amazing moat I felt compelled to put it in the story!

Ultimately the 1590s were a period of tremendous cultural exchange through trade and war. Unfortunately, it was too often the latter. I passionately believe that our differences are there so we get to know one another – marvel at our collective tales, our legends, poetry, language, technology, food and art. In so doing, we draw empathetically closer through the prism of compassion. Reason itself will guide us.

'Show love to your brother and to your sister, for we are all travellers passing through this mortal realm.'

Rehan Khan
www.rehankhan.com
twitter.com/rehankhanauthor

ACKNOWLEDGEMENTS

Life is full of risks, but the biggest one is doing nothing at all. My own limited experience in the world has demonstrated this. Acting positively will always create a healthy momentum in life and I must thank both my parents for inculcating this belief in me.

This novel would not have happened without the support of Bill Samuel who, having read my two self-published novels, introduced me to my kind-hearted publisher Rosemarie Hudson of HopeRoad. When Rosemarie and I toyed around with the idea of my writing historical fiction, I remember coming away from our meeting at Foyles bookshop in Charing Cross Road in London with a list of ten ideas. The novel you've just read being one of these.

There are many others who thoroughly deserve a mention. Isobel Abulhoul, Director of the Emirates Airline Festival of Literature, and her marvellous team, deserve a big thank you for creating a literary haven for book-lovers and allowing budding writers such as myself to soak in the atmosphere of one of the world's premier festivals.

Thanks once more to Lorna Fergusson, for being the first reader of the novel. Having worked with her on my *Tasburai* series, obtaining her advice particularly on the Tudor period was priceless. A big note of appreciation to Ellen Krajewski, whose insight allowed me to calibrate the narrative to the target readership. Joan Deitch, my editor, has been an absolute delight to work with. Her affectionate treatment of the text and the characters has only amplified the tale. Thanks also to James Nunn for producing a wonderful cover, and to all the other tireless workers who have made a contribution to this story.

Finally, I would like to recognise my two adorable and witty teenagers, Yusuf and Imaan. And of course, I give thanks to my enchanting wife and closest friend, Faiza - you always bring out the best in me and may you continue to do so.